Cayenne Heat

a novel based on real events

James Haydock

authorHOUSE®

AuthorHouse™
1663 Liberty Drive
Bloomington, IN 47403
www.authorhouse.com
Phone: 833-262-8899

Published by AuthorHouse 04/05/2022

ISBN: 978-1-6655-5572-2 (sc)
ISBN: 978-1-6655-5573-9 (e)

Also by James Haydock

Portraits in Charcoal: George Gissing's Women

Stormbirds

Victorian Sages

On a Darkling Plain: Victorian Poetry and Thought

Beacon's River

Against the Grain

Mose in Bondage

Searching in Shadow: Victorian Prose and Thought

A Tinker in Blue Anchor

The Woman Question and George Gissing

Of Time and Tide: the Windhover Saga

But Not Without Hope

I, Jonathan Blue

The Inward Journey: Original Short Stories

*"Be still my heart. I am a soldier.
I have seen worse things than this."*
                    -- Homer

Contents

Chapter One
Growing Up Parisian

My name is Arthur Maurice Bonheur. I was born in Paris in the early years of the twentieth century. I had an uncle who went by the name Arthur, and so my parents chose to call me Maurice. My father was the chief conductor on the Paris-Orleans Express, a position he won after working many years on a train he dearly loved. As I recall, depending on the memories of childhood, he was tall, handsome, and proud in his elegant chief's uniform. My grandma, who was never generous in any of her remarks about her kin, said in that gaudy uniform he strutted like a lustful rooster. Maybe so, but why not? He liked it when people on the train looked at him with warm approval. They knew he was there to help them should anything go wrong, and they liked him. He was a good man, a good father and husband, and a very loyal railroad man. Late in life he married a bank clerk who joked among friends that her husband was really her father. They laughed at that, made merry at his expense, but he said he didn't mind. I think maybe he did. A year after marriage I became their first-born and only child.

I am not able to say whether my mama was a good woman or not. I like to think she was, but I do know from what my papa told me that she left us when I was little. When I was not more than three years old, my dear mother abandoned us and left the country for Russia. She had read in one of her women's magazines that *"a gentleman of quality recently widowed and residing in Russia"* was looking for a nanny to care for his five children. She would have her own rooms and be on call whenever needed. Her room and board, said the advertisement, would cost her nothing. Her salary paid monthly would be "equitable." Chances are she interpreted that word to mean generous. She applied for the job and negotiated its terms without consulting her husband.

She became a nanny in the house of a rich and powerful politician, caring for his children rather than her own. She sent my papa a couple of letters to say all was well with her and life was good, but we never heard from her again. The long silence made us wonder whether living as a servant in Russia was better than living as a wife and mother in France. I can't say whether she liked her job, or whether her life in a big house was a happy one. I know only that my good papa, in spite of his demanding job, struggled to keep me with him after she left. I was a toddler and needing care around the clock. Eventually he had to turn me over to my grandparents who agreed to raise me. It was necessary to do that or lose his beloved job on the train.

My grandparents, Leon and Elsa, owned a small restaurant located near the station, and so Papa was able to see his little boy on a regular basis though without the bonding that usually comes with living in the same house. Until I was twelve I was a good boy living a good life even though at times I was in trouble with Grandma and often felt like an orphan. I went to a good school and learned some English, history, math, and other things. I liked learning new things every day, liked the way the new stuff fell into a pattern, and I was beginning to think I might become a teacher. Then at twelve a disastrous event occurred in my life that left me feeling afraid, empty, and lonely. Both of my grandparents died. My grandma died at seventy-one while taking a nap one rainy afternoon. Five days later Grandpa at seventy-six died in his sleep.

All the people who knew the couple said the old man loved his wife so much that when she died he couldn't live without her. They said the threads of life that had bound them together for half a century grew old and fragile and snapped. They said when that happened the old man no longer had the will to live. Well, I won't go out on a limb and disagree with that romantic stuff, and yet I know from living with the old couple they didn't seem to be close. Days would go by with no conversation whatever between them. Anyway, for a time I had no adult in my life, no guardian to guide me or tell me what to do, and I roamed Parisian streets as a waif. A few months later my Uncle Christophe of Lyon moved to Paris and became the manager of a nightclub known as *Le Chat Orange*, or *the Orange Cat*.

The club was located at 89 Rue Pigalle in Monmartre,

a famous urban district where struggling artists and would-be literary figures lived for a season in cheap lofts and apartments. Some who found fame in later years were Henri Matisse, Salvador Dali, Pablo Picasso, Gertrude Stein, Cole Porter, Scott Fitzgerald, Ernest Hemingway, and T. S. Eliot. Monmartre was also notable in an earlier time — *La Belle Époque* they called it — for Toulouse-Lautrec, several impressionist painters, and *Maxim's,* a restaurant in business even today. The *Moulin Rouge* or *Red Mill,* the cabaret where many of these people gathered, was only three blocks away from the *Orange Cat.*

Uncle Christophe generously allowed me to live with him in his tiny apartment above the restaurant and club, but only if I did my part to help him earn a good living. During the late afternoon after a few hours at school and well into each evening, I worked as an errand boy. I was only thirteen at the time but alert and observant. Well-heeled ladies and gentlemen of leisure and wealth patronized the *Orange Cat.* Women of the demimonde, wearing elaborate gowns and made up to look much younger, also frequented the place. The men ranged in age from young lads on a bender to lecherous old gentlemen whose vitality amazed me. In white ties and cummerbunds, they were agile and aggressive.

Montmartre was the center of Parisian merry making, the place to visit noisy, bawdy, unrestrained "Paris by night." In clubs called *La Lune Rousse* and *Le Désert Sec* by the French and *The Red Moon* and *Dry*

Desert by English celebrants, Django Reinhardt wowed audiences with his jazz guitar. In most of the clubs couples drank their fill and danced riotously until dawn. Surprisingly, most of the drunks remained in line, and the police seldom raided the clubs. On the Boulevard de Clichy were gaudy sex shops for deviant tastes. Pigalle was a vulgar neighborhood, so earthy in fact that visiting American soldiers began to call it "Pig Alley." In one section of Rue Pigalle were orange circles on the sidewalk. When a gentleman stood in one of those circles, it told the lady at the window above that she had a customer willing to pay well for her perfumed presence in private.

The *Orange Cat* in similar vein put on naughty shows that drew wealthy playboys and women with money from all over Europe and America. They came to be titillated by the wild spins and kicks of the can-can girls, the raucous music, and the *pied en air* said to be revealing and considered illegal. They came in long and short skirts to see black stockings contrasting with white thighs and frilly underwear. A florid woman calling herself "the Queen of Paris" visited the nightclub with her coterie of young girls every night. A middle-eastern Prince once gave me a tip of 100 francs to deliver a message to one of her girls. He didn't know the girl belonged to the Queen, and the indiscretion got him banned from the club. I couldn't be blamed, of course, and was soon earning more money in a week or few days than my papa was earning on his train in a month.

I had never seen so much wealth, so many people spending vast sums of money as if convinced their last day on earth was just around the corner. I can describe it only as wild, careless, lavish spending in the passionate pursuit of pleasure. All the people I had ever known, all my close and distant relatives, worked hard for a few francs and spent them frugally. They struggled to obtain their money and often went without necessities to save it. But at thirteen, though truly not a part of it, I lived at night in a different world. While the rich people played, I worked into the wee hours of every morning. The regimen perhaps hurt my health, and yet I earned plenty. In hindsight I know I hovered on the outskirts merely to serve. Yet I also know I seized my share of the wealth any time the opportunity presented itself.

It was not a very good world for a boy to live in but exciting and gratifying. People didn't work even one hour a day and yet had loads of cash money to spend. They slept all day and partied all night and spent lavishly on anything that caught their fancy. They believed legal tender in Paris could buy anything, and they denied themselves nothing. They were indefatigable pleasure seekers clothed in silks and satins and the finest broadcloth. They dined on rich cuisine: caviar, *pâté de foie gras*, and truffles. To please jaded palates and release inhibition for dalliance, they consumed foods that gave them gout and heart attacks, and every evening they drank rivers of champagne. At thirteen, viewing that scene with naive admiration, I concocted dreams of living that way. However, bad luck, or whatever one may call it, had other plans for me.

I liked what I was doing, but working during most of every night didn't make for an alert student each day. I wanted to learn but was often sleepy. In most of my classes the teachers droned on and on and put me to sleep. Then when they saw me slumped over my desk and paying no attention to what they were saying, they felt insulted and angry, and smote my back with a heavy ruler. More than once I was put on detention with a dire warning that if it happened again I would be expelled. It did happen again and again, but very little was done about it. Just about every teacher tried to shame me, telling me I was bright and capable but wasting my life and hurting my health. With each reprimand I solemnly promised to do better.

I'm sorry to say I didn't do better. Work interfered with school and I wrongly believed my work at night was more important. So I began to consider dropping out of school. I felt I wasn't learning anything I didn't know already. Also I was making more money in my early teens than any of my teachers, and that didn't sit well with them. I talked it over with my uncle, and when I turned fifteen he agreed I could leave school and work full time. Though in later years I regretted not going further in school to become a professional, the decision to be on my own doing a job I really liked made me happy. At night I felt alive. And yet it wasn't the kind of work I can write about with pride. I was a messenger boy delivering messages of lustful longing from rich old men to nubile young women. Sometimes I helped to arrange a tryst between a gentleman of wealth and a lady of the demimonde. They called me their *entre-deux* or *go-between* and rewarded me well. My uncle ignored the raw behavior that oozed from every pore of the *Orange Cat*. He justified what was going on by saying it was happening in every nightclub in Paris. If he meant Monmartre, I had to say he was right.

A special class of people chose to live in Monmartre, struggling artists mainly who allowed raunchy behavior because of their own liberal way of thinking. My papa by contrast was a staunch conservative, believing in the old-fashioned values of a past time. He became very angry when he learned that his only son had dropped out of school and was doing borderline work at night. He wanted his son to get a good education and perhaps train to become a railway employee. His dream was to turn his job over to me when time came for him to retire. He quarreled bitterly with Uncle Christophe, and they never spoke again.

The Orange Cat was called a nightclub by most people, but it was open during daytime as well. Some people came in the afternoon and remained until midnight. Others trooped into the establishment after dining and remained until closing time at three in the morning. A few came in for coffee and pastry at seven every morning. Those patrons consuming Colombian coffee and rich pastries often discussed the races. A fair number were in the habit of placing bets on the horses. I carried their money in a leather pouch to the bookmakers, and when a horse won I got a piece of the take. One fateful day I was told that because the group had inside information, they would be placing a large stake on a horse the experts were calling a sure loser. The horse would pay twenty to one if it won. So a modest bet of 500 francs could net an astounding 10,000 francs if the dark horse came in a winner. Even though some were saying it would be a miracle, those in the know were convinced the miracle would happen.

I was only the errand boy and had no opinion whatever. Wealthy men could afford to take a big risk. Unlike me, they wouldn't miss 500 francs at all when the horse came in a loser. My thoughts were neutral concerning the matter, and I paid little attention to it until a friend who is no longer a friend began to talk.

"Oh, they're throwing their money away!" he cried. "Don't be a fool, Maurice. You have a chance to be rich! Put the money in your pocket. Take it all. It's better they lose it to you than to the bookmaker!"

He seemed to know what he was talking about. The horse was a known loser, and I got to thinking that maybe he was right. I counted the money and the total came to 8,000 francs. I figured I could live quite well on that for a long time. So after thinking about it, greed got the best of me and I pocketed the cash. I didn't go near the track that day or to the bookmaker who would have taken it as misguided bets on a loser. I went to the house of the friend who told me to keep the money. Giggling and triumphant, I spread the money on a table in his room. I told him that when I was certain it all belonged to me I would buy him a gourmet dinner. We laughed and chatted and counted the money. For a brief time I felt as rich as any person who frequented the *Orange Cat.*

But as a cruel fate would have it, or perhaps the bettors really did have inside knowledge, the dark horse won. I didn't return to the club that night. I couldn't face my uncle and admit that I had not placed the bets of his patrons but had kept the money for myself. I knew he would become furious, call me a thief, and kick me out of his place. I walked the wet streets of Paris all night in a cold drizzle, trying to think of what to do next. No workable solution of any kind came to mind. Near dawn when I thought he would be sound asleep, I sneaked into the *Orange Cat* through the rear entrance. In the dimly lit hallway I bumped into my uncle. He had always been an early riser and wanted to know why I was up so early. When with some hesitation I tried to explain what I had done, he glared at me with intense anger. He was sputtering saliva when he slapped my face so hard I saw shards of light flying in all directions.

Then he rolled up a fat newspaper and smacked me over the head several times as though punishing a naughty dog. In a stupor I handed him his patrons' money in its original pouch. He grabbed it cursing and hissing vengeance. I ran from his blows to encounter my dear papa on the sidewalk. I explained what I had done and begged his forgiveness. Instantly I saw he was not in a forgiving mood, was becoming angry.

"Get away from me!" he screamed. "Get out of my sight, you dirty cur, you dirty little thief! You dropped out of school to become a thief? Your grandmother always said you had thievery in your blood. Get out of my sight and never come near me again!"

He was causing a scene. Pedestrians on the pavement, though in a hurry, paused to be amused by what was going on. He had called me a mongrel cur, and I felt his language was on the mark. I felt exactly like a beaten puppy. I scurried away from the snickering crowd as fast as I could. Before turning the corner I looked over my shoulder to see my father walking stiffly toward the station. I was certain he would be seething with anger for hours. I lost him that day. We never spoke to each other again, and I saw him only from a distance. What is more, on that same day I lost my job and all the trust my uncle had placed in me. In a fury he demanded I gather up my belongings and leave his place of business immediately. He would find an honest boy to do my job even if he had to pay the boy more than he ever gave me.

So with no home and no job, I was forced to endure several brutal months on the streets of Paris living from hand to mouth. Then one day out of desperation, driven by hunger and no place to sleep, I joined the army at seventeen and went off to fight a war. It was another terrible experience for one so young. It became the job of a boy to kill German men, or be killed. I was too green and too soft to kill, and yet my country demanded I do it or die. More than once I thought death would be better than living to kill. I thought I might let a German sniper shoot me down, hitting me in the back of the head so I would feel no pain, but the will to live even in bad times was stronger than expected.

In an ambush that became a skirmish I was wounded by a bullet in the left shoulder and sent to a hospital. While convalescing I met a slender and shapely young nurse with a pretty face, blonde hair, and abundant warmth. I fell in love with her and she with me. We decided to marry as soon as I was well again and out of the army. But of course I had to be settled in a good job before that could happen. So at twenty-one I was again walking the streets of Paris, not in search of food but looking for a job. I looked day after day for at least a month and found nothing. At the end of each day I went to the hospital to walk Gabrielle home. My clothes were becoming shabby and the soles of my shoes thin as paper, but she assured me I would soon find a good job with good pay. I needed only to keep trying and be patient. She was a good soul and really loved me but too optimistic,

Weeks glided by and left me with no job and no money. The little I had saved as a soldier was gone, and my pride wouldn't allow Gabrielle to support me. In time I took a job as a dishwasher, but the owner of the restaurant wouldn't pay more than eight francs a day plus room and board. I labored in a steamy kitchen many hours each day for ten days. Then entering the owner's office just before closing one evening, I found a wallet stuffed with cash. Without a moment's thought I grabbed it and thrust it in my pocket. I should have hesitated to know I was committing a serious crime, but I didn't. A common thief, I had broken the law and would surely be punished. Old Benedetti would bring in the police. They would find me and arrest me. The court would call it a petty theft, but a stern old judge would deliver a stiff sentence. I could go to prison.

Young and foolish, I quickly put those thoughts out of mind and went shopping. I bought a new suit, two expensive shirts, new shoes of fine leather, and a spiffy cravat. Dressed to the hilt and cocky in my new duds, I went to see Gabrielle. She looked me over and laughed gleefully, admiring my looks in new clothes. She said I was every bit as handsome well dressed as when I was a soldier in uniform. She wanted me to have dinner with her parents and set a date for our marriage. I made excuses about marriage because I knew they wouldn't accept a thief as a son-in-law. My uncle had called me a thief and my father had called me a thief, and my grandma had scolded me for thievery

As a child when I raided her cookie jar, she said she wouldn't allow a sneaky little thief to live in her house. With this last indiscretion I knew that my genes, or whatever sets the pattern of one's behavior, had conspired to make me a thief for life. With that thought in mind I couldn't face my girl's parents. Until I knew myself better, until I cultivated a few layers of self-respect, I wouldn't be able to face the future as a married man with responsibilities. So like a rabbit I ran. Saying not a word to Gabrielle, the one person in all the world who mattered most to me, I left Paris for an undisclosed location.

Chapter Two
Sentenced to Hard Labor

When I was growing up and in the habit of purloining cookies from a jar in the kitchen, my grandma quoted a Spanish proverb when scolding me. In English it went something like this, "Once a thief, always a thief." Then she would solemnly add, "You didn't become a thief, little boy, because you steal. You steal because you are already a thief. I want you to get it through your thick skull. I won't have a thief living in my house! Even though you're my grandchild, I won't have it!"

"I'm sorry, Grandma," I would meekly reply. "I won't steal nothing ever again. I promise with my hand on your Bible, no more stealing."

But of course I stuffed my pockets with the tasty cookies when I thought I could get away with it. Invariably, however, Grandma was there to catch and punish me. Years later in a peculiar twist of fate or show of irony, as I served my sentence in prison, I found it necessary to steal. I had to steal to survive.

As I grew older I believed thievery was in my blood. I stole when I was a child, I stole when I was a teenage messenger, and I stole from my employer Benedetti as a young man. So perhaps there was truth in the old proverb from Grandma's mouth. Acting on impulse, I had seized the restaurant's payroll and quickly gone into hiding. The police were surely looking for me, and I felt I could be arrested at any time. But as soon as I got to a town some distance from Paris, I applied for a job as a servant to a wealthy woman who lived on a large estate in the country. She was a good and gracious employer. No one on her staff was overworked, and we had time off to enjoy life. The authorities wouldn't have reached me there, and I could have saved enough money to marry Gabrielle. But I viewed myself as a menial, and that brought discontent.

I had been in the service of Madame Bordeaux only a month when I saw on her dressing table a carved ivory case containing her pearls. Near the box was a packet of money brought to the estate to pay the servants the following day. Again the thievery in my genes or just plain greed — even now I don't know which — nullified rational behavior. Without hesitation I stuffed the money and pearls in my pocket. Quickly I changed from livery to street clothes and hopped on a train for Paris. I spent the night in a cheap hotel. The next morning, as I was going in search of Gabrielle, two policemen began walking beside me. When I turned to speak to them, they clapped handcuffs on me and announced I was under arrest. Madame Bordeaux had concluded I was the only person who could have taken her valuables, and she lost no time reporting the theft. In jail awaiting trial, I wrote a letter to her begging her forgiveness and assuring her that her stolen property would be returned. I didn't get a reply. Later I learned she hated thieves and justifiably felt angry and betrayed. I wasn't feeling good either.

After two weeks of jail time not altogether marked by discomfort, I was hustled into a paddy wagon and carted off to a town thirty miles from Paris to answer a charge of theft. My crime, for which I was sent to the worst prison on earth, was stealing money and jewelry from my employer. It didn't matter that every single sou and every pearl was returned to her. I had committed a crime and had to pay for it. I had to be punished, and that was that. In less than a week I found myself in a courtroom with a hard-faced judge clad in a black robe. Perched on a high platform, he looked down on me over the top of horn-rimmed glasses. He had a full docket of cases and was all business. Within minutes he pronounced my sentence. I got no trial.

"It's a matter of crime and punishment," he intoned. "You stole from Madame Bordeaux, known in these parts as a kind and generous employer. That was a big mistake, sir. You committed a serious crime and a silly one at that. Now you must pay for your crime. I sentence you, Arthur Maurice Bonheur, to six years' hard labor in French Guiana."

I couldn't deny my guilt, but in body and soul I knew the sentence was too severe. Benedetti, for reasons I never understood, had not even charged me. But for a crime that hurt nobody, a theft with all the stolen goods returned, I got a deadly prison sentence. Angry and despondent, I broke loose from my captors and ran. They quickly apprehended me and frog marched me back to the courtroom. Two rawboned policemen stood close beside me, each gripping an elbow. They wouldn't allow me to sit. The judge scowled at me for a full two minutes without speaking a word. Then shaking his head and muttering, he pounded his gavel with ear-splitting satisfaction and gave me eight years' hard labor.

I would serve my time not in France, but at Devil's Island in South America near the equator. It was the prison called Bagne de Cayenne by the French and located in French Guiana. I knew the climate of the place to be unspeakably hot and the prison intolerably cruel. Reports of abuse were often in the newspapers. Magazine articles condemned the prison. Slaves built the odious prison colony in 1852. Victims of forced labor, hundreds died before the construction was done. By the time the institution opened to receive its first prisoners, it had already gained a questionable reputation. It became widely known before the end of the century as high on the list of the worst prisons in the world. For a minor crime that hurt nobody I would be going there to spend eight long years. In the early months of the first year, I promised myself, I would escape.

Within a few days I was taken by rail to the Atlantic coast. There in what the police called "a holding tank,"

I would have to wait weeks or even months for the convict ship to arrive. The car in which they placed me had several compartments. Each was just large enough for a crude bench for me to lie on in the fetal position.. When another prisoner was placed in the cell opposite mine, the two guards demanded silence. As they began to play a game of chess at the end of the car, I started a whispered conversation with the newcomer. Anatole Durand, as he called himself, was in his middle fifties and was sentenced to ten years' hard labor in French Guiana for violating an old woman.

Although he had spent several years in an African prison for a similar offense, he insisted he was innocent. He said he entered the woman's house when drunk looking for a place to sleep. She began to scream, and he tried to shut her up by cupping his hand over her mouth. They fell to the floor with him falling on top of her, and she was injured. He fled as she screamed rape, and a gendarme arrested him the next morning. He wasn't physical with her in any way, he claimed with great energy, but the authorities believed her side of the story and found him guilty. I tried to sympathize with the man. I tried to believe his story but doubted it was true. Later I heard it was rare for a rapist to admit guilt. In spite of what had happened, in spite of being convicted, Durand had convinced himself he was innocent.

The cell car stopped the next day in another town, and three more convicts became my companions. To my eye they looked very young, and I was amazed to learn that all three were going to French Guiana. Julien, Claude, and Lucas were farm boys who drank too much at a village tavern one evening in summer and got into trouble. On the way home they passed a tavern that had closed for the night. Drunken and merry and singing a bawdy song, they instantly decided they wanted more to drink. So crying, "Open the door, open! The night is young!" they banged on the stiff oaken door. Getting no answer, they broke a window, crawled inside, and helped themselves to bottles behind the counter.

The owner upstairs heard the ruckus, came running from the loft in his nightshirt, and confronted them with a broomstick. He was a feisty little man but no match for strong, rangy, drunken teenagers. In minutes he suffered well-placed blows to the head and belly and fell groaning to the floor. The three boys ran with bottles of booze and a few francs they found in the till. The next day they were arrested on charges of breaking and entering, heinous criminal assault, and theft. Each was sentenced to five years in French Guiana. Within thirteen months, as I was to learn later, the harsh environment there took the lives of all three. Julien was sixteen, Claude and Lucas seventeen.

The prison car ended its journey at a seaport on the Bay of Biscay. There we left the stuffy car that was beginning to stink and went to a spacious cell in a government building. Three guards stood by to keep order but paid little attention to us. As far as I could tell, they were sharing on the sly a baked ham and a bottle of rum. It was good to have enough space to walk a few steps before turning, and good to be able to lie down full length. We were together now, no longer separated and not required to remain silent. Destined to be in the same boat, the grisly convict ship bound for the tropics, we decided to support each other as friends. I had been told that when facing danger the group is forever stronger than any man alone, and very soon I believed it. Yet I found myself practicing the caution of one who can't trust anyone entirely. It was the lesson life had already taught me.

Anatole, a seasoned convict, was more talkative than the rest of us. In colorful language he told sensational stories of his prison experience. Though he directed his remarks primarily to the three youngest among us just to see their reaction, his stories made me think about my own condition and what lay ahead. I had been convicted of a crime and was doomed to pay for it. In those years after World War I, France was a squeamish and skittish nation trying to put down confusion and chaos. Hating disorder, the legal system was rife with anxiety, and the courts were quick to send men across the seas when they didn't deserve it. I was just one of thousands unfairly sentenced because of the times. Whether deserving it or not, I would have to spend eight years of my youth in a brutal prison among rough and desperate men away from any woman. Rejected by society and filled with hate, those with brawn and muscle and no moral code whatever were known to prey upon the weak. I was tolerably well built and good looking, but weighed only 138 pounds. That made me a perfect target. I couldn't be weak. I had to be strong enough and wily enough to fend off degenerates. I resolved to be alert and cautious at all times.

Lying full length on the concrete floor of our cell and breathing the stench of dirty feet when sleep wouldn't come, I thought of what lay ahead. I loved a fine young woman and wanted to marry her. I wanted to live with her for the rest of my life and raise a family in a comfortable house I would buy. I wanted to work hard to support our family, and I wanted her to love me as much as I loved her. Because she was doing good work as a nurse, I wanted to go back to school and study for a profession too. That way, like her, I could make a contribution to the community in which we lived. I wanted to improve the world we lived in, make it easy and pleasant for her and me, and I wanted her to be proud of me. I wanted to be a respectable citizen of worth proud of myself. With more education I could perhaps obtain a job in the same hospital where she worked, or maybe become a teacher. My dream was to find a good job that would allow for advancement. We would never have to worry about money.

The dream didn't jibe with reality. To marry her as soon as possible, I committed a crime against an employer who had treated me well. It was a foolish crime of youth and passion driven by tainted genes.

"Once a thief," my grandma had said, "always a thief." Even today I regret that it happened. But I have never regretted loving that serene and beautiful girl. Thoughts of her lived in my mind and heart every single day; her image sustained me. To return from exile and prove myself worthy of her gave me hope and strength. I would escape from that tropical prison as soon as I could. Somehow I would find a way to stroll with Gabrielle on the boulevards of Paris. I would dine al fresco with her at a sidewalk café and luxuriate in her laughter, her smiling face, and the way she held her fork. I would go to French Guiana, but not for long. I wouldn't let the state steal from me the best years of my life.

When morning came we were shackled and marched by gendarmes through the town to a small prison on its outskirts. Never in my life had I been an object of any person's curiosity, and so I was surprised to see people looking at me as though I belonged in a zoo. We were told to keep our eyes glued to the pavement and not glance at the crowd even once on pain of harsh punishment. Of course several men couldn't resist looking at the pretty girls and were later flogged. After marching at least a mile under a blazing sun, we entered the prison to stand in a large courtyard. Guards ordered us to undress for a thorough body search. I had never stood naked before other men, and to say I felt uneasy would be an understatement. The guards were trained to look for anything a man might conceal in a body cavity, and they probed without mercy. Afterwards we got ten-minute showers, striped prison uniforms, and very short haircuts. Then to bleak cells we went to wait many days for transfer to the convict ship.

After a week or so we were vaccinated against tropical diseases. Each of us got three inoculations and a temporary prison number for the ship. As we waited for departure, we spent our time untwisting old tarry rope to make oakum for caulking deck seams on ships. It was a job that brutalized thumbs and fingers in minutes, causing blisters and black hands. The pain was excruciating the first few days, but later fingers and thumbs grew numb. We worked in dead silence in a heavy stench of tar, turpentine, and unwashed bodies. They say the Chinese invented water torture, a single drop falling every five seconds on the forehead. I will say the French invented silence. Any man among us who mumbled a few words got nine lashes across his back. Any man who complained of sore hands or an aching back got lashes.

Even though the big ship sailed for French Guiana early in the year, not a person in my group was on it. We were stuck in that stinking little prison, that so-called holding tank, for several months enduring daily abuse. Hard and nasty work took up most of our time. When confined to our cells, we were not allowed to lie down. The bed folded against the wall, and there it remained until one hour before lights out. To sit and slump against the wall was also forbidden, and so when not working at useless labor we walked in continuous movement. When the bed was lowered on command, we were so exhausted from work and walking we fell immediately upon it and slept like the dead.

The tiny cells had chamber pots for use during the night. Rules called for emptying the pots every morning, but that seldom happened. When the stench became unbearable, one poor wretch was ordered to empty all the pots. The job was so nauseous that many of the men ordered to do it vomited and couldn't eat breakfast afterwards. By the time we were ready to ship out, because we were made to suffer before our prison sentences began, most of us were bitter and determined to flee later. Every man among us wanted to escape from French Guiana as soon as he got there, myself included.

When the authorities heard the ship would soon be in port, more than three hundred convicts were selected as the ship's cargo. We were the chosen ones, separated from the other prisoners and not required to work. Officials gave us more food, better food, and even old magazines to read. Later I learned treating us better was intended to prepare us for the rigors of the voyage. A few days before we left, army doctors gave us a cursory physical examination and pronounced us fit. Only a few of the three hundred were declared unfit. One was the healthy stepson of a millionaire factory owner with ties to politicians. Another was a young man dying of clogged arteries to the brain. Still another had a viral condition thought to be contagious. A dozen or more were dead before the voyage ended, and fifty or more were sick.

Those last days of waiting were wretched, especially for those with loved ones who came to see us off. I remember two little girls clinging to their father and crying hysterically as they tried to move him out of the marching line. A guard ordered them back, threatening to hit them with his baton. The mother clung to the man's neck until ripped away by the angry guard who spat upon the poor woman and swatted her buttocks. I suffered no trauma that day because no one came to see me off. Many among us were seeing wives and children for the last time. Some older men were certain they would never return. A sentence of ten years for men in their mid fifties was a death sentence, and they knew it.

I desperately wanted Gabrielle to see me off, and I wanted to tell her to wait for me no longer than two years. If I had not returned by then, I wanted her to choose another man. I was going away for eight long years but firmly believed I could escape and return within two. Even though she wouldn't be able to leave her hospital duties to say farewell, I wanted her to know I would be coming back into her life. I kept telling myself it was *not* wishful thinking. I would see her again. I was lonely for her. In a dense crowd I was lonely. It was painful to see my fellow convicts saying goodbye to friends and relatives, for I had none. Thoughts of a quick escape consoled me. I didn't know that even after serving his sentence, a man wouldn't be allowed to leave the penal colony. France had passed a law that required convicts to remain as free men in French Guiana for a time equal to their original sentence. Almost to a man that amounted to servitude in a vile place for life.

In the first week of September the day came for departure. The old convict ship stood quite visibly off shore, her hull a tall black wall as formidable as any prison wall. Her stacks were belching black smoke that drifted skyward. She was there to take on a cargo of miserable men who would be near death before her voyage ended. In the courtyard we saw for the first time young guards from French Guiana, all muscular and swarthy, about a dozen in number. They were dressed differently from the guards we had known on French soil. They wore blue uniforms of a military cut and looked like soldiers or policemen. Circling their waists were wide leather belts with holsters containing pistols. Those of higher rank carried flexible batons weighted with lead to be used when necessary. All of them walked with a quick military step resembling a cocky, self-assured strut. Not a one was older than thirty.

The chief guard, fit and handsome in his crisp blue uniform and wearing stripes of rank on his sleeves, demanded we stand at attention to be counted. When four convicts turned up missing, a prison official immediately led the chief guard to a small enclosure where four men lay huddled on burlap bags. Three of them had lost a leg. The fourth man was white as a sheet and sweating profusely. Though too weak to stand or walk, he was included in the count. All of us were now the property of the Penal Administration of French Guiana.

Grimly we shouldered the big canvas bags containing all we owned and marched through the town to the waterfront. Again people turned out to gawk at us as if we were circus gorillas on parade. Some mindless creatures sprawled on the curbside hooted insults and abuse, but we couldn't respond. Guards, prodding us with nightsticks, cautioned us to maintain strict silence and keep our faces locked forward. On pain of punishment we couldn't even glance at those trying to get our attention. The convict ship, bobbing at anchor in a calm sea, waited for her cargo.

Chapter Three
Crossing the Atlantic

Some of the people who came to see us off were laughing and hooting as though attending a festive event. Barking dogs nipped at our heels and mean little boys threw mud balls at our legs and feet. We were told to ignore it all, and we did it to avoid punishment.. Half a mile from shore, gently riding the waves, was the old ship that would take us to a place known to be a French possession in another world. The old vessel stood so high in the water a man half blind couldn't miss her. Except for her stacks she looked like a prison there in the water, and of course she was. Throbbing engines spewed black smoke from her stacks. On her decks were mariners preparing to sail. Her name was displayed in large white letters near the stern. Someone had named her, perhaps with tongue in cheek, *Dame Coquine.* In English, *Saucy Lady.*

A barge of vast size was ready to take us to the *Saucy Lady.* Expertly it came to the side of the ship just under the gangplank that was quickly lowered. On board we dropped our sea bags through a hatch. Below in a dim and tight compartment, sailors stored them by number. In single file we marched down a narrow stairway to be shoved into a huge cage made of steel. It was large enough to hold sixty men, and the guards counted each of us as we entered. Other cages held an equal number, and within an hour the hold with its five steel cages was stuffed with human cargo. A smaller cage near the ship's boilers was reserved for troublemakers. Inside our cage the stink of sweaty, unwashed bodies had to be tolerated. By command all portholes were closed until the ship was well at sea. With little ventilation, the air in the hold was heavy and noisome. When I felt a vibration beneath my feet, I knew the vessel was moving. Knowing I might never see Gabrielle or French soil ever again, a cold desolation blocked all thoughts of the future.

I had thought the dark hold of any ship was always cool, even cold depending on the season, but that of the *Dame Coquine* was steamy, hot, and stinking. Away from the harbor on the Bay of Biscay the portholes were opened to make conditions more tolerable. I was able to breathe again and caught a glimpse of the shoreline quickly receding. A guard told us that every other day we would spend half an hour on deck. I looked forward to that, thinking it would be a respite from the stinking hold. Then I learned we were there to be washed with ocean water from a high-pressure hose while sailors below sloshed water in the grimy cells to ward off disease. Standing on deck in the early morning, just as the sun tipped the eastern horizon, we breathed deeply the salty air and felt invigorated. Yet for fifteen minutes, as the hoses were made ready, we were not allowed to talk and had to stand facing the sea.

Then came the order to strip in chilly air, stash our clothes on the quarterdeck, and stand in single file. Suddenly without notice blasts of cold water knocked us down but washed away grime, sweat, and body odor. Guards with rifles ready to fire watched us closely. In the past, insane prisoners had tried to disarm them. Some equally insane had thrown themselves overboard. Our washing down wasn't so dramatic, but when two or three men refused to stand after being knocked down, a guard with a whip lashed their backs. Water from the pressure hose made the deck clean, but the whip brought a trickle of blood. The rebels were forced to wipe away the blood with their shirts.

I was soon to discover just how bad the food was and just how little we got for each meal. The captain claimed half the men were seasick and eating very little. I could vouch for the seasickness, for sour puke was everywhere. That had nothing to do with the meager rations measured out to us from a large metal pot. The old scoundrel was buying less food to enrich his own pockets. A similar fraud occurred with the daily half liter of wine each of us was supposed to get during the voyage. Greedy guards charged vulnerable men with misconduct and seized their ration of wine for themselves, calling it retribution.

In time I learned that most of the guards had chosen to work under harsh conditions simply to line their pockets. Their pay was low, and they made up for it with acts of unlawful graft. Corrupt guards were taking advantage of the young and weak. Julien, Claude, and Lucas, the farm boys I met before coming aboard the ship, got very little wine. A Corsican guard named Giacamo managed almost every day to accuse all three with bogus infractions and seize their wine as punishment. We knew it was happening but could do nothing to stop it.

Even though discipline was strict in other places, it was lax in the cages. We were able to talk, play cards, read in poor light, smoke, and quarrel. Every now and then a fight would break out to cause a volley of foul language and violence, but quickly it was stifled. The captain, who called himself a born-again Christian, was ready to punish any man who used language he deemed improper. So every man had to watch his mouth. Invariably in the cages conversation turned to French Guiana: what we might find there and how soon we might escape. Some in my cage had maps of the region they had torn from an atlas after conviction. They spent hours poring over small print and memorizing names of towns and villages in Dutch Guiana and other places. It all seemed futile to me but gave hope to them.

I too was beginning to shape plans to escape as soon as I got there. I would go with a seasoned convict who knew the forest and the lay of the land. With him to help me, I believed a permanent escape would certainly be possible. I didn't know until I got there how difficult even a carefully planned escape would be, how the indifferent and unforgiving jungle would militate against it. I was naïve enough to think escaping from the notorious prison would be easy.

As the ship moved along, getting ever closer to the tropics, I endured each dreary day as best I could. I managed to get enough to eat and drink, and I kept the brutes away by flashing the knife I carried always on my person. I got enough sleep and began to make friends with one or two men I thought I could trust. Then of a sudden violence once more erupted in our cage. Two burly convicts began stabbing each other with daggers made of soupspoons sharpened on the concrete floor. Though the fight lasted fewer than ten minutes, blood oozed over their naked bodies and made a mess.

The man who seemed to be winning slipped in the muck and fell on his face; his opponent pounced to finish him. But before it could happen guards entered with weapons, batons, and a bullwhip. One very loud crack of the whip ended the fight. A prisoner with numerous puncture wounds was taken to the infirmary. The man who appeared to be the victor was sent to the hot cell with a burning whip mark across his back, a welt that later festered. There he remained until the voyage ended. When finally released, he was too weak to stand and yet had managed to stay alive. Two young men in our cage died of the heat. As many as six perished in another cage. No cause was ever given for their deaths.

When the old ship crossed the equator, the heat and humidity was worse than any I've ever known. Most of us wore only a damp towel around the waist and a smaller towel supplied by the ship's crew to cool our sweating heads. Some men passed out and lay as if dead on the dirty floor. If they were not up and walking after a few hours, they were taken to a holding room adjacent to the infirmary. Medical personnel looked them over and pronounced their condition either fake or genuine. Too often a condition labeled fake was genuine, and the man suffered.

When the water supply became contaminated, the ship's stewards poured rum into it to make it potable. Later it got so bad not even the thirstiest among us would drink it. Dehydration set in and many fell ill. Quickly the stewards replaced the rum with permanganate, a strong oxidizing agent. It turned the water purple. It left a metallic taste in the mouths of some and a painful burn in the belly of others. A few couldn't drink the medicated water at all. The result was severe dehydration. I was able to drink my portion but held my nose each time I drank.

Just about every day, as the ship moved into the tropics and the weather grew hotter, the steam engines stopped and the old vessel lay silent. That told us at once that a man had died to diminish the cargo in the hold. When a man died, his corpse was hastily and unceremoniously dropped overboard. We heard that on some occasions, especially when several corpses were brought on deck, the ship's chaplain spoke a few words printed on a small card. That was never confirmed, and I never saw the chaplain even once during the entire voyage. One could make an appointment to see him, or so we heard. But that, I believe, was more fiction than fact. Though some convicts along with the captain professed to be Christians, the ship had no religious services. The captain had a tight schedule to follow, and so the passage to French Guiana was all work and no play. Perhaps he spoke to his god alone.

One morning after almost three weeks at sea an officer on board called out, "Land ho!" I rushed to a porthole to see in the distance a blue landmass poking above the sea. Within two hours the ship was entering the mouth of a muddy river and moving gingerly against the current. Gawking at the sights and jostling one another for a longer and better look, we could see monkeys in the tall trees and gorgeous birds. Moving slowly along was the green and vibrant jungle. An elbow pushed me away as I realized I could be surrounded by that jungle for years. I would have to penetrate it somehow to escape.

I slumped to the dirty floor and leaning against the hull got away from the present by means of memory and imagination. Beneath my closed eyelids I saw with extraordinary clarity the days of my childhood and the years I spent as an errand boy in Paris. I felt the ambience of the cocktail lounge in the *Orange Cat* and heard the orchestra playing lively jazz above the murmur of happy voices. I breathed the exotic aroma of wealthy people having a good time. I was strolling the streets of Paris, absorbed in the glare of neon lights, when a heavy boot kicked my thigh.

"Get dressed, you, and make ready to land!" a guard ordered as the ship came to a crude dock and stood still.

Slowly with striped prison garb covering our bodies we climbed out of the stifling hold to find ourselves in blazing sunshine, blinking like water rats. A small city with gleaming white buildings and red rooftops lay before us. It called itself Bella Vista, *beautiful view* when translated, and it did have a beautiful view of the ocean, river, and jungle. Its streets were narrow and dusty but clean looking. People of several races sauntered along the walkways in the tropical heat to reach the waterfront. The entire population of Bella Vista, or so it seemed, had turned out to see our arrival; and they were making it a festive occasion. Officials in seersucker suits and wearing pith helmets to protect them from the sun and heat, some with their wives and children, were standing on the pier. Although the town's colonial appearance seemed pleasant enough as we stood on deck and gawked at the scene, many of us turned our heads to look at a small Dutch settlement on the other side of the river. There close at hand lay the promise of freedom.

Corsican guards herded us into a military line to be counted. As many as thirty who couldn't stand or walk lay in the shade to be taken to a hospital. The administrative head of the prison, a tall and swarthy gentleman in civilian clothes, stood on deck to observe the procedure. Down the gangplank we went in military fashion to the long pier. As we marched toward the city streets, a group of black women in gaudy but pleasing dresses waved handkerchiefs of welcome. One called out to us in accented French, "Soyez forts, messieurs!" Another called in native Spanish, "Se fuerte, caballeros!" *Be strong, young men!* We heard no English. Then marching toward a huge gate in a high wall, we began to see fellows like ourselves, convicts serving their time. They were brown as chestnuts and wore stripes, straw hats, and sandals.

"Anyone from Marseilles?" one of them asked, trotting beside us to receive an answer, "Marseilles? Anyone from my town?"

Because we were not allowed to speak, he got no answer. We filed through the gate into a spacious, sun-washed courtyard. At first the yard of red dirt seemed pleasant enough, but the sun was intolerable and the odor of unwashed bodies sweating in the heat assailed us. A mongrel dog so thin I could count its ribs ran from a corner of the old building to the gate. A rat larger than any seen in Paris scurried along the base of the wall to dive into a hole. Overhead birds of prey, possibly a bad omen, circled in a clear blue sky.

"Oh my god!" I heard a very young convict moan. "Am I to live in this god-forsaken dump until I die? Oh please, God! I want to go home! My mama misses me and my little sister misses me. My old papa lost his sight and needs me to guide him. I don't deserve to be here, dear God. Even the judge knows I'm innocent."

Robbed of hope and stunned by the ghastly reality that now confronted him, his narrow shoulders trembled and he sank to his knees in prayer. A guard with a heavy nightstick whacked him hard across the back. The blow threw him facedown to the ground. When he sat up, the red dirt covering his face, the guard hit him again.

"No squatting, you maggot!" the official representative of the prison shouted. "No sitting or kneeling in this place! No laying down! No taking it easy! You only stand or walk here!"

The young man's anguished cry of pain and despair went unheard by anyone who might have helped him. In less than a year, as I found out later, he would die of overwork and sunstroke. From the courtyard they moved us to an overcrowded barracks. Human beings value space, and when they don't have enough space they grow vicious. It was a lesson I quickly learned in Bella Vista. The penal administration, well versed in human behavior, had deliberately crammed the barracks with too many convicts. Violence inevitably broke out and men died. Savage behavior causing death kept the prison population in check. Too many wretched men doomed to live in decrepit buildings was the order of the day. It was prison policy, standard procedure.

Chapter Four

Inside a Monstrous Prison

The prison units at Bella Vista were called camps, particularly the ones in the jungle. We were told they would be ready to receive us after two days of orientation. Guards marched us into run-down structures they called barracks. Each building, designed to hold forty men, had fifty-five or more. So once again I was fated to live in close contact with convicts of every stripe. My group went into a building someone had christened *Nid d'oiseau* (Bird Nest). With heavy bars on all the windows, it couldn't be called a nest at all. It was a birdcage, and we were the jailbirds inside. Though laughter was rare, prison wit and humor were not. The few with a sense of humor made our bitter predicament easier to endure.

Some of the older convicts firmly believed it was humor that kept them alive. So with forced humor they made themselves obnoxious. The barracks were a forum for bawdy jokes and off-color stories, the more naughty the story the better. The person who could tell a good story with comical touches became a valued entertainer, earning popularity and respect. His story eased listeners away from a harsh reality when he told it well. Any time he told it poorly he was taunted without mercy. Some stories, particularly those told by older convicts with time under their belts, divulged information worth knowing.

A few hours after lockdown an older convict began a story based on what he had gone through in another prison. We listened quietly until a clanking on metal interrupted him. Several liberated convicts had come to the barred windows and were tapping on them. We went over to see what they wanted and heard them whispering. They had luxury items for sale — tobacco, bananas, and coffee.

"How can we pay for that stuff?" someone asked. "We don't have no money, and I'm sure you ain't here to give it to us."

"Your clothes, hotshot! They're like money! Them guards don't give a damn whether you have clothing or not. And you won't neither when you start working like beasts of burden under that hot sun. If anyone should ask, you can always say yer duds was stolen."

With some misgiving we did business with them. We had fewer clothes that evening but cigarettes to smoke and bananas to eat. Next morning several men who had not traded their clothes discovered most of them missing. The thieves who came in the night to steal our stuff on the ship were busy with the same scheme in the barracks. I learned that clothes were very necessary when a man was trying to escape but often a burden when working like oxen in the heat. Clothes were stolen and sold at a very high price to would-be escapists. In some camps nudity was common because clothing was scarce and the sun hot. In most, however, the convicts wore ragged shorts or loincloths with no shirts. Quickly the tropical sun turned them brown. Those with sensitive skin suffered blisters eased by tobacco juice when available.

The second day the warden assembled us in the courtyard and made a brief speech. Its aim was to allay any fear or anxiety we might have concerning prison life in Guiana. He wanted also to emphasize how impossible it would be to carry out even a meticulous escape. His size and bearing impressed me as he spoke.

"In this place," he said for all to hear, "you may go one way or the opposite way. Those of you who give us no trouble will serve your time free of suffering. The other way, trying to escape, is plainly foolish and not recommended. I know many of you dream of escape. But you should know before you try it that either the jungle or the sea would stop you dead in your tracks. In the jungle you'll die of hunger, heat exhaustion, snakebite, or betrayal by your comrade. On a flimsy raft the sharks will get you if heat, thirst, sun, and drowning don't take you first. I know many of you won't listen to me as I speak these words, but I'm here to tell you politely: don't try to go the second way."

It was a good speech and convincing but not convincing enough. In spite of what he was saying and even as he said it, I knew I would try to escape the first chance I got. It was simply a matter of waiting for the right time, and time was passing. Our names were placed in the registry and we were given identifying numbers. Mine was 51080. It burned into my brain an ugly fact. Since 1852 when the prison was first established by Napoleon the Third, more than fifty thousand men, who might have contributed substantially to French society, had come there to suffer and die. The farm boy Julien was given the number right after mine, and that placed us in the same barracks.

But as soon as I was able to talk to him I learned he was going to the barracks of a degenerate who wanted him as a lover. Julien went off quietly, convinced he was doing the right thing, and I never saw him again. A month later I heard he went to the hospital complaining of severe stomach pain. A week or so after that he was dead. The doctor in attendance never knew exactly what caused his death. The thug-lover sent his personal effects to his mother and asked her to send money for a tombstone. She gave the devil that killed her son several hundred francs. He spent them on rum and a mark who also died.

After three days of orientation and a cursory medical examination, I was marched to a labor camp in the jungle called *Lune Bleue* or Blue Moon. That meant separation from a man calling himself Gérard with whom I had planned to escape as soon as possible. He went under guard with five other convicts to install electrical lights in a village close to the Brazilian border. News of his death reached me later. He had drowned with another man when trying to escape by sea in a dugout canoe. A wave capsized the canoe, hardly more seaworthy than a heavy log, within sight of people on shore. His body washed up on the beach. The sharks feasted on his friend. Gérard's intense longing for escape made him careless, and his desperate escapade ended before it began. The incident placed in my mind an important fact to remember. I would have to be patient when planning my escape, and I would have to be very careful with details when executing it.

Men of every description and every social station worked side by side in the sweltering labor camps. The penal administration recognized no difference between old and young, weak and strong, day laborer and chief executive in civil life. Degenerates from vice dens worked side by side with elderly defrocked priests, shopkeepers, and schoolteachers. Petty thieves worked beside rapists and killers. Unlike the guards who prided themselves on rank, no convict was above another. Except for political prisoners, we were all on the same level, at the very bottom of the social ladder. We were dehumanized beasts of burden required to labor to exhaustion every day at the same task.

Men with clean fingernails and soft palms who had never held an axe in all their lives were put to work chopping down gigantic trees in tropical heat. For them and for me it was a deadly game, and yet the warden had said we would not experience undue suffering. Half the men sent to a jungle camp would find the labor beyond their strength and die prematurely. It was common knowledge that hundreds sent out to the colony died in their first year of overwork, abuse, or a dread disease. Dysentery, a nasty and painful malady, killed a man every day in just one horrendous jungle camp. I found it hard to believe until I learned the disease could be passed on from one man to another.

In the timber camp where I worked, the guards sounded a klaxon to jar us awake at five in the morning. At five-thirty in new and shifting daylight they marched us half naked into the jungle to labor all day with only half an hour's rest for a watery lunch. We labored every day in all weather. Often the rain was so heavy we had trouble seeing the trail. More often, a blazing sun blistered our skin and blurred our vision. Each convict had to produce a sizable stack of wood to be made into lumber. If he fell behind and didn't meet his quota, he received on coming from the forest only two slices of hard and stale bread for supper.

Each man had to cut down a tree, chop off its limbs, and drag the heavy trunk away from standing timber. Late each afternoon the guards checked to see that all the men had done their job. If a convict came up lacking, he went hungry. I was young and strong in those days, though not very big, and managed all right. But downing a tree with only an axe was a daunting task for the strongest among us. A bucksaw would have made the job efficient and easy. But no person in charge cared to make a convict's daily work easy. We had been sentenced to years of *hard labor*, and that's exactly what we got.

Any person with a warm heart, rare in French Guiana, might have wept to see wretched convicts trooping barefoot and naked into the jungle every morning. In our bellies to sustain us until noon was a cup of weak coffee and a piece of bread soaked in grease. Some mornings we had a tasteless mush or gruel with a thin slice of meat, but on most days we got two pieces of bread and a pint of coffee. On that we worked until a guard came with watery soup in a black pot. Flies swarmed around the pot and often fell into it as he put the lukewarm liquid into tin bowls. We ate it anyway, joking that flies added protein. Maybe twice a week the soup had bits of rancid meat that we greedily ate. Drenched in sweat and suffering from painful mosquito bites, we chopped trees so hard they blunted the heavy axes. Then returning weak and wet, we had no dry clothes to change into because we had bartered them away or had them stolen. For supper we got a glass of water, a piece of bread, and a few ounces of rice covered with a sugary brown liquid. Frenchmen love their bread, but good bread in a jungle camp was not to be had.

It was a miserable existence that was now beginning for us. We had no money even to buy a pinch of tobacco. We bartered away the bar of soap issued to us monthly and went dirty. We got a tepid shower once a week when it should have been every day, and we had to reckon with diseases that laid even the strongest among us low. We had come from a temperate climate and were not equipped to work under a tropical sun in a humid jungle where the heat was intolerable even in deep shade. We were bitten incessantly by mosquitoes bloated with human blood and by huge insects I had never seen before. Any man swatting a biting mosquito had to reckon with spurting blood.

When we were not slowly killing ourselves at hard labor under a blazing sun or downpour, we were dying of disease or badly treated by inhumane guards. I saw my companions falling sick and dying almost daily. I saw their corpses rotting in the mud half a day before removal. I saw my own swollen feet oozing blood after vampire bats had gnawed on them in the night. Also I ripped my skin to scratch away tiny insects that bored into my flesh. Every morning I woke up sick to my stomach and short of breath but wouldn't give up. To do so meant to die, and I wasn't ready to die. Somehow I found the strength to carry on. Soon, I promised myself, I would leave that horrid place and find a life.

Adding to the physical suffering in a hostile climate was the mental suffering that assailed us. I quickly learned that Bella Vista had no social order and no moral code. The town had churches that citizens attended, but they were off limits to convicts. If a prisoner or liberated convict got religion and wanted to attend a church, most likely he was turned away. The only moral guide among convicts, and for the town as well, was a crude *laissez-faire* philosophy, declaring that every man had to shift for himself. Reduced to an ugly struggle merely to exist, every man was in revolt against the system and governed entirely by self-interest. Each of us became an island in that vast prison system, never part of the main, and the isolation made us all intensely lonely.

We hungered for normal and friendly conversation, for harmless horseplay at times, and for camaraderie. But not able to trust each other in our jungle camp, we shut ourselves away in a world of our own to view each other with suspicion. With nothing to look forward to after work and too exhausted to hear or tell a good story, we suffered from boredom. Some men inevitably sank to the level of animals and tried to lose themselves in lustful longing. In all the jungle camps abominable behavior was rampant. Coarse and ugly older convicts sought younger partners for gratification of their lust. The guards turned a blind eye to it, especially when a bribe was available.

Most of the new convicts listened dutifully to the warden's speech but made up their minds to escape as soon as they could. More than a few left with a few lumps of bread stuffed in their pockets and a bottle of water slung around their necks. They believed with a passion that they would succeed while others had failed. Some tried to swim across the river to reach Dutch Guiana. In a current stronger than expected, they drowned. Others fled into the French jungle trying to reach Brazil. A few unfortunates got lost and wandered in the hostile jungle for days and weeks before perishing. Most returned beaten by natural forces and shaken by acute pain in all their joints. They suffered from contagious dysentery and from tropical malaria transmitted by mosquitoes larger and fiercer than any they'd ever seen. Many men were gravely ill on returning. They died in the ill-equipped hospital or while waiting to be admitted. One could count on the fingers of one hand the number who gained freedom for a few weeks or months only to be caught. Not one living soul managed to secure permanent freedom. It was an object lesson quickly taken to heart.

As the weeks passed I gathered other important lessons. Living on a level that swiftly became primitive, we began to go barefoot and nearly naked. Wooden sabots were issued to us but caused painful blisters on heels and toes. Leather shoes were available only to those with money. Anyone fortunate enough to have good leather shoes saw them quickly stolen. Clean underwear, clean fingernails, even a clean neck and face belonged to another place and time. Water in the barracks was mainly for drinking, and it often brought diarrhea. Any attire that made a man look presentable ceased to exist. Very few had the luxury of owning a toothbrush, and toothpaste of any kind was unknown. So in the midst of unwashed bodies one began to curse his sense of smell and hope it would diminish and disappear. The coarse food, often half spoiled and reeking with bacteria, quickly damaged taste buds as well as stomachs. Also we had no magazines, newspapers, or books to read. We couldn't receive a gift or package to remind us of home, and so the gulf between present and past grew larger and larger.

Snickering guards told us that any man determined to adapt and remain alive after six months, would exist as an ape even though his dear mama saw him as an angel. To accept the brutish existence thrust upon us would make our lives easier, they said, but not for long. Then slapping their thighs with glee, they hooted derision.

"Face it, losers! Even the fittest among you will die within a year or two. Life in this place, as you must know, is nasty, brutish, and short. So if you have a capsule filled with money or gems in your guts, let us know so we can be there to take it when you go."

And they laughed at their little joke, haw-hawed as if they had made a rare and funny and very clever jest. Three of the eight men I first got to know were already dead, and the other five would die in less than three years. I was one man in a cargo of 300. Within five to seven years nearly half of that number would no longer exist. I had never experienced such hardship in all my life, even as a waif on the streets of Paris. I lacked the physical strength of many who fled and died, and of some who didn't flee but died anyway. To survive, I had to put my trust in brain instead of brawn and take care.

I had to avoid conflict at all costs but would fight tooth and nail like a wild animal if forced to do so. I nourished a fierce determination to live, and that kept me alive. But living meant escaping and escaping meant climbing an icy mountain nude.

After three weeks of hard labor at Blue Moon, I was sent with nine other convicts to a camp called Hollow Reed. Somehow we had managed to endure the harsh conditions at Blue Moon without falling sick. So we were chosen for transfer because we appeared to be stronger than most of the other men. Hollow Reed was notorious as a deadly place. It was deeper in the jungle, and the convicts there were known to be violent and dangerous. Three of us in the original ten met death after a few weeks. A man we called Rocky caught malaria. Another man was killed by thugs in a fight, and the third died of venomous snakebite. I obeyed all the rules, kept my nose clean, and began to shape a plan involving escape. Every day I thought of a future where I could live not as a dirty beast of burden, but in freedom and leisure as a well-groomed man. As each day dragged on and on in that dangerous place, as the important *hope* that sustained me from the time I set foot on the red soil began to fade, I became more restive and desperate.

Chapter Five

My Stint at Hollow Reed

Under guard we tramped down a dusty street to the outskirts of Buena Vista. There we came upon a quaint little shop where a Chinaman sat relaxing in the shade. He wore baggy trousers and an Asian conical hat, commonly called a coolie hat. It provided good protection from the sun and rain. As we approached he stood up quickly, bowed, and welcomed us to his shop. Hanging on a string in the tropical sun were six golden, deep-fried chickens. Only the feathers and entrails had been removed. In the store was a strange assortment of everything one could imagine. The guard said if we had the money, we might buy something. Although only three of us had money, we crowded inside to stare at tobacco, fresh bread, canned meat, and bottles of rum.

Two skinny clerks watched with eagle eyes to be certain we didn't steal anything. Yet despite their vigilance, several men walked out with stolen goods in their armpits and pockets. That's when I realized rapists, child molesters, and murderers live by a moral code that allows them to commit any sort of crime with impunity. It didn't matter to them that the shop couldn't afford losses. I didn't buy anything because I had no money. I didn't steal anything either. Though branded a thief in France and sent to French Guiana as a convicted thief, I didn't steal a thing. The little store was struggling to stay in business.

Half a mile from the shop a narrow path entered the forest. From there until we reached the camp, the guards told us, we would be on our own. We stood amazed. Were they leaving us on the outskirts of town at the edge of the jungle to make our way inside unattended?

"Just follow the path," they told us. "The camp's only a dozen or so miles from here, and you can take your time getting there. But be there before the sun goes down. You don't want to be walking in the jungle after dark. It gets cold and damp; you won't be able to see four feet ahead of you. Also big cats go on the prowl as soon as darkness comes. Just keep following the path and you'll get there before dark."

Across the river within easy sight was Dutch Guiana. Should we bolt and swim across the river and hope to find freedom? Nah, a stupid idea. We quickly agreed it had to be some sort of trick to test us. If we ran for the river we could be shot. So we walked the path, trudging resolutely deeper and deeper into the hot and humid jungle, believing a wild beast might want us for supper, and expecting to find a guard around the next bend to escort us into camp. For a couple of hours we walked under a canopy that shut out the sun. High in the trees and flinging themselves close to us at times, agile monkeys screeched and chittered, chiding us for invading their territory. We found no guard waiting for us. We had to acknowledge we were strictly on our own.

That caused us to sit in a circle in a small clearing and discuss our situation. For all intents and purposes we were free men. Should we run to the river and try to make it into Dutch Guiana, or stay put? Seven men out of ten argued we would be inviting suicide by leaving the trail. Three declared dark of night would kill us, and night would be coming soon. So we walked doggedly along the trail, exulting in the thought of being free when knowing deep down we were not. The guards who left us to go it alone knew prisoners in the past had tried to run but found disaster. It was a little game they played — would this bunch run?

After three hours we came upon a camp the inmates called *Chien Galeux* or Mangy Dog. It was a name cynical inmates had given the place. The official name by the penal administration was *Chien Fidele* (Faithful Dog). Nearby were gaunt men in loincloths hacking away at underbrush. They wanted to speak to us, but their guard ordered us to keep moving. Later we met a group of men in loincloths coming toward us with axes slung over their shoulders. I heard friendly chatter. They seemed to be in a good mood after completing their day's work. One convict, however, a man suffering from insect bites and grotesquely skeletal, told us the incessant hard work was killing him. Then in a hollow voice he said we would have it better at Camp Hollow Reed. That surprised us.

"You won't be cutting down gigantic trees with dull axes there," he muttered. "That's what kills a man, that and the fever. I was a lawyer back home and never owned a rotten axe, never touched an axe. Here on the equator they make me chop trees hard as steel ten hours a day with a goddamn axe not sharp enough to cut a banana in half!"

"What crime did you commit to be sent here, counselor?" a cocky young man we called Julot asked with a wry smile "Were you unjustly sentenced like all the rest of us?"

Emaciated and exhausted but holding on to a sense of humor, the lawyer managed to chuckle softly before replying. "I got mixed up in a Ponzi scheme even more lucrative than the one old Charles Ponzi pulled off shortly after the big war. Made a lot of money, lived high on the hog, had my pick of sexy women and fast cars and fancy houses. Then a bitter old dowager complained I had stolen thousands of francs from her. I was hauled into court to face charges of fraud, theft, and elder abuse. Argued my own case and did a good job of it too, but regrettably I lost."

"And now you lose again, you dirty old crook!" Julot taunted as we walked on. "Too bad, you nasty old scoundrel! You just can't win, can you? I hope your victim, the little old lady, got her money back, but I doubt it. I'm sure she needed it more than you."

"Oh, another smartass!" the lawyer screamed. "They're everywhere! Cocky smartasses everywhere!

Well, I have some advice for you! Give up being a smartass, boy! You'll be in my condition soon enough!"

The skeletal man shook a bony fist behind Julot's back and managed to yell for all to hear: "In every bunch a stupid smartass! A smartass not able to see human suffering, a stupid smartass!" The man's suffering was genuine. He was in great pain and knew he would die soon.

As the day wore on we moved slowly and rested more often. We sat at the foot of gigantic trees, their roots serving as benches, and caught glimpses of monkeys scurrying from limb to limb above us. Brightly colored birds — parrots, toucans, macaws — were there too, singing birdsongs with downright joy, or so it seemed. In a place made deadly and terrible by men for men, the lower animals, as we call them, seemed to be living happy lives free of pain and restraint..

That thought was with me as we straggled into Hollow Reed near sunset. It was a sight I vividly remember. Forty acres of big and tall trees had been cut down and burned in the field. An army of hapless convicts had sacrificed themselves to remove stumps the size of a small truck. The backbreaking labor of countless months in searing heat eventually killed the workers, but in time a jungle camp was erected. Five decaying buildings with tin roofs sizzled in the dying sun. I tried to imagine how anybody could install a tin roof under the tropical sun. Did they do it at night? Or were roofers forced to work with metal so hot it burned them? Painting the buildings was a grievous job too, though not as bad as the roofing. The original yellow paint had faded to a baby-poop tan and was almost gone. The buildings needed painting again. I shuddered to think we might have to do it. A cursory glance at Camp Hollow Reed and its surroundings assured me that wretched men in the hundreds had lived and died there in utmost misery

After signing in with name and number, we entered the mess hall and ate supper. It was a cavernous room but noisy. Unlike the prison eatery in France where silence was the order of the day, at Hollow Reed we could talk while eating and even complain. Guards leaned against the wall with rifles loaded but paid little attention, allowing free activity within reason. The tasteless food was abominable, but after walking all day through the hostile jungle I was hungry enough to eat it. Half an hour later we were escorted to a barracks that smelled of urine and dead rats and was in dire need of a careful and thorough cleaning. Grime on the walls indicated it had not been cleaned in decades.

Arranged in a long row were bunks made of rough boards. Not a single bunk had springs or a mattress. Sleeping on hard boards was a standard procedure in most of the camps. When darkness came, I found an empty bunk near a window and lay down. While attempting to fall asleep I surveyed my surroundings. An oil lamp in the center of the long room threw shadows on the walls of dark figures moving about like phantoms. The keeper of the barracks, a rat-like little man with narrow shoulders, a prominent potbelly, bleary eyes, and a big nose, pranced in and turned off the lamp. Tired men grunted and slept.

Every barracks in the jungle compound had a keeper, a convict who looked after the building when its occupants were away at work. One of his duties was to keep the place clean, but he seldom did more than sweep the floor. He brought coffee to the inmates every morning, filled a barrel with river water that had to be strained and boiled before use, and remained in the building when all the others had left to see that no personal items were stolen. Between supper and bedtime he sold or traded tobacco, soap, sewing thread, needles, food items, shoes, and clothing. The job was profitable and much sought after. Above all, the keeper had to be trustworthy. When tempted to steal another man's property, he had to convince himself the theft wasn't worth it. He would lose his job, endure a flogging, and be assigned hard labor in stifling heat. The fear of severe punishment kept him honest. On this night our keeper called out, "All present! All thirty-six present!"

I wasn't able to sleep. I lay on the hard board staring into the gloom for hours. I tried to sleep on my left side, but the position hurt my hip. So I lay on my back staring at the ceiling. Near midnight a shadowy form rose up, moved toward the unlocked door, and quickly went outside. Moments later a slimmer shadow flitted outside. I thought the figures had gone out to use the latrine but remembered that facility was in the same building. When they didn't return I could sense something was up. The hours dragged on, and when first light began with a blast of the klaxon, I got the full details of what had happened. Two convicts were missing from my barracks and three from another. Five desperate men had escaped! I was young in those days. Mind and heart were warm with hope. To know men were trying to escape gave me even more hope. I promised myself I wouldn't suffer in that jungle camp for long. At the right time when factors were favorable, I too would escape.

I was curious about the job I'd be doing there in the middle of the jungle. I hoped it wouldn't be painting buildings in the blazing sun. The next day, to my everlasting relief, they told me I would be assigned to a workshop where straw hats were made. On arrival in Bella Vista I had seen inmates wearing wide-brimmed straw hats to protect their heads, ears, and faces from the tropical sun. Now I would be doing my part to manufacture them, and I rather liked the idea. I sat at a table with a pile of fiber from palm trees in front of me and was taught how to braid the fiber into a sturdy material that would be passed on to another convict to cut and shape into a rudimentary hat.

He in turn would pass along the near-finished hat to receive a hat band and chin strap. Another man would put the hat in a cellophane bag to rest in a large box. On a good day I began work early in the morning and finished with blistered fingers in early afternoon. The rest of the day was mine to employ as I saw fit. My co-workers went back to the barracks to rest, but I got into the habit of going into the jungle to walk along a narrow path. There alone, witness to sights and sounds new to me, I realized trying to escape with others was too risky. I reasoned it would be harder for authorities to track down one man than several. I would have to go alone. I would have to learn the jungle's secrets as fast as possible, and hope for the best.

I did go it alone for more weeks than I remember, but slowly I made friends with other convicts. I learned that one had to belong to a group to survive assault by crazed convicts intent on rape or robbery and not beyond murder. I was living with vicious, angry men who settled mild disagreements with a fist in the face and a kick in the groin. When a fight broke out, a couple of guards would take their time to break it up. They had been told by their superiors to act with caution. Rushing to break up a fight could mean a severe blow to the head or a knife in the gut. I heard from more than one person that the guards sometimes goaded violent men to fight. It was good entertainment for them.

"Stay away from the toilets at night," I was told. "Even if you have to piss in a can, just stay away from the toilets at night. Them brutes, the big ugly guys, will pound you. They will use you for their pleasure and squash you like a bug when they are done with you."

It was good advice to be taken seriously. At least once a week I heard screams coming from the toilets at the end of the building. When morning came, a guard would find a body or wounded man in a pool of blood on the cement floor. Two or three unlucky convicts would be ordered to clean up the mess. The body couldn't be taken away until examined by someone from the hospital. I followed the good advice offered me and managed to survive as a newcomer without becoming a victim. At all times I kept a low profile and remained close to my group.

At night it was inevitable I should think about the past and better days in my life. I thought of Gabrielle and the few happy days we spent together. I remembered eating with her on the sidewalks of Paris. Our favorite was a little bistro with a very thin waiter who seemed to hover over our table like a bird of prey with his little pad. He served us good wine at a good price. Then one day in the prison commissary a letter was handed to me. Protected by a lavender envelope, it was only one paragraph, and I read it carefully. Even today it sticks in memory. It was written in French in a feminine hand, and I could hear her voice as I read her words. They were a powerful reminder of dear Gabrielle and my wasted youth even when translated.

"My dearest Maurice," she began. *"When you were unjustly sentenced to spend many years in a prison called Devil's Island that is now being called hell on earth, I felt my life at twenty-two had ended. You were only twenty-three*

when you left for that tropical hell, and we both knew you might never return. You assured me, however, that while it was likely you would never see the soil of France again, you would escape as soon as possible and be with me in some other country. I took that to be almost a promise, but soon realized it was a dream, yours and mine. So wherever you go I will follow. Regardless how long you are there, please don't lose the hope that nourishes you and gives you strength. If we can't embrace once again after two years, you want me to live my life perhaps with another man. Well, my love, let me say this emphatically: as long as you live that will never happen. I shall wait for you because without you I am less than me. And I know you are well aware that you are less without me. Write, my dearest, and I shall respond. I love you so very much."

It was the only mail I ever got from Gabrielle. Even though for a time I sent letters almost daily, I believe she never received even one. Because she never heard from me, she probably went on with her life, married and had a family. As the years passed I often thought of her and the life we might have had together, but always I hoped she did exactly that. Prison officials surely opened my letters, decided they revealed too much of their operation, and threw them away. Rampant double-dealing and the attempt to hide it made that a certainty. The corruption ranged from top-ranking officials to the lowest guard and from the guards to savvy convicts. It was a way of life for just about everybody in a penal system France wanted to keep under wraps for fear of losing face on the world stage. Officials in France knew the prison called Devil's Island was as Gabrielle described it, an unforgiving *hell on earth*. They could have changed it, were they so inclined, but for multiple reasons they didn't.

Chapter Six
Advised Not to Try

As time crawled along at a snail's pace, I became more acquainted with the muggy jungle and learned to respect its terrible power. I believed it would be folly to blunder deeper into that strange and dangerous world trying to reach Brazil. Others before me had tried it only to get lost in the jungle and die. I would take the easier route and escape into Dutch Guiana. At the Hollow Reed camp I talked to prisoners who had made it to the Dutch colony and beyond, but had been caught and brought back. One man had spent several months there posing as a Dutchman. He had acquired the manners and language of Dutch people when living in Holland. Yet somehow he was exposed as a Frenchman by the way he held and smoked his cigarette! I found that story just a little hard to believe, and yet it could have happened.

From those who had escaped, only to be caught and returned, I learned important strategies I could use: how to travel in the uncharted jungle, how to identify a jungle path, how to detect signs of danger at a water hole, how to find edible food and untainted water, and whether to move by day or by night. Also in broad daylight how would I become invisible when approaching an Indian village or a civilized town? That requirement was important but the most difficult of all. Any time I asked about it, I got half a dozen different answers. I was told if my skin were darker, I might pass for a native, but even then my speech would give me away. When my comrades heard the details of my plan, to a person they advised me not to try it. Emphatically they declared any chance of succeeding was small indeed. I would be arrested, returned to prison, and thrown into solitary confinement. Three years would be added to my sentence. Perhaps I should have listened to them, but I didn't.

In time I gained the trust of a young Sicilian who was even more passionate to escape than I. Russo had been the butt of cruel jokes and homosexual proposals from older, vicious convicts. They were making his life miserable and he had to get away from them. He told me he would save himself from the animals surrounding him or die trying. So with some misgiving I took him on as my partner. Down by the creek in deep woods we began to build a raft of bamboo. We planned to flee within a week or ten days. In the meantime we gathered provisions: water in a wooden keg that would float if it fell overboard, bread tightly wrapped, rice in an air-tight container, sardines, beans, onions, canned ham, condensed milk, and a bottle filled with matches tightly corked. All these things we pilfered surreptitiously from the shops and the prison pantry. I was a thief again but feeling good about it. I knew I had to steal to go on living. Bolstered by the arrogance and optimism of youth, Russo was certain we would soon be free. Fleeing with a congenial companion, I decided, was better by far than trying to make it alone.

It was raining the day we planned to leave, torrential rain one finds only in the tropics. We thought we might postpone the adventure for a sunny day with better weather. But since rain came about every day, we decided to go anyway. After supper and when our work was done, we went to the creek and uncovered the raft. Quickly we pushed it into the water and let it drift with the current. A dark night made navigating down the creek difficult. After giving it a try and hitting rocks in shallow water, we paddled to the bank and found shelter under a fallen tree. Mosquitoes attacked us even in the rain, and within minutes our hands were bloody from swatting when bitten. The pesky insects made their way into our ears and up our noses. Maybe they wanted out of the rain.

Even when the rain subsided we couldn't make a fire to fend them off, for anyone pursuing us might see it. In a dry area beneath the tree we had no mud to smear on our bodies. Russo went looking for it. He put plenty on his face and neck, and brought some for me. We had no tobacco juice to ward off mosquitoes, and so we were thankful for the mud. Even so, we suffered painful bites through the night. It was our first night in the jungle close to the prison and not a good night. We lay among the roots of a massive tree and hoped no roaming night animal would make a meal of us. Near dawn from sheer exhaustion we fell asleep. Howler monkeys in the canopy above us — called baboons by the locals — jolted us awake. At last the sun filtered downward, and all was suddenly very different. In daylight the bugaboo jungle became tolerable. Nocturnal sounds that made us shiver became laughable.

After a meager breakfast of coffee and bread hard enough to crack a tooth, we pushed off again and drifted into the river's current. It began to take us away from the bank into the view of anyone who might be standing on shore. That caused alarm, and so we paddled furiously back to the bank and decided to move only in darkness. When it began to rain again, sheets of water reduced visibility almost to zero. Under cover of the heavy rain, we tried crossing the muddy river. That's when we found our paddles were too small to buck the current or steer the raft. We swirled toward the French shore and could do nothing about it. After what appeared to be hours of struggle, a favorable current caught us and carried us toward the Dutch settlement. By then the rain had passed on to another location and the sun was out. We paddled to shore and chose a little inlet for landing. Clutching our bundles, we crawled up the bank and let the raft drift. In no mood to celebrate our freedom, a faux freedom at best, in clammy clothing we gulped down tasteless food and tried to sleep. Our plan was to tramp through a dense jungle. We knew we couldn't do it in the dark. So with a couple hours' rest, three at most, we were up again and moving.

Our friends in camp had told us we might find a path that would take us through the jungle to a native village some twenty miles to the west. With no compass and not even the sun to guide us, we found no path and no direction whatever. To put it with painful directness, we got lost in a deadly maze and came abruptly into a clearing where a group of Indians were at work. They spotted us as soon as we stepped from the trees and came trotting toward us. All of them carried machetes for cutting bamboo and some had rifles. Russo grabbed my arm and tugged at it; he wanted to run. I persuaded him to stand as still as a statue.

"If we run," I said to him, "they will surely cut us to pieces. Don't move. Stand your ground and try not to show fear."

Up they came, close and menacing, gesticulating and jabbering. We understood not a word of their language, and they not a word of ours. They wore loincloths and white marks, perhaps symbols, on their faces. Chanting, they danced around us as though celebrating.

We tried to buy them off with a few coins and even our shoes. They took all the coins and shoes and anything else that caught their fancy. Jabbing us with their rifles and threatening with wild movements to hack us into little pieces, they marched us into the nearby town where the authorities lost no time throwing us in prison. Later I found out that officials in Cayenne paid the natives well for capturing runaways. They were chas*seurs d'hommes* (chasers of men) in a long-standing program supported by the French. We languished in the damp cell several days, eating almost nothing and drinking polluted water that brought severe diarrhea to Russo and a moderate case to me.

When officials sent us back across the river and dumped us on the riverbank at Bella Vista, we were weak and sick and barely able to walk. We lay in the shade breathing raggedly until prison guards came to pick us up. Literally they picked us up like rag dolls and making jokes at our expense, tossed us into a pickup truck. The good warden debated as to whether we should go to the prison infirmary for rest and recovery or to solitary confinement on bread and water. Supported by guards as we tried to walk, we went to solitary confinement.

Officials branded us guilty of a very serious infraction of prison rules. We had yielded to a crazy wish to escape, and for our trouble we got severe punishment without a hearing. I remembered the nice little speech the warden delivered when we first arrived. Had he forgotten his closing remarks about no punishment for any first attempt to escape? It was our first attempt, but trying to argue the point would have made for extra time in the hole. We were in the disciplinary section of the camp for two months, locked in separate cells on coarse food with not enough to sustain normal weight. The only exercise I got was pacing the tiny cell for hours each day. Insects crawled on my skin when I lay down.

Within a week I found myself rapidly losing weight and talking to myself. One day a big spider crawled into my cell. Half crazy, I tried to make friends with it. Contact with any kind of living creature, I reasoned with fevered mind, was better than no contact. When a morose guard finally came to release me, I was so disoriented I couldn't understand what he was saying. Only later did I learn he was upset and angry about a strong odor coming from my unwashed, emaciated body. I had fowled myself with excrement. I never saw Russo again. I asked about him but got a scoffing response and silence. Maybe confinement killed him, or maybe he killed himself. I never found out.

From the hole I was sent to one of the four blockhouses and cleaned with a pressure hose. Each house held forty convicts waiting to be tried for offenses ranging from stealing a porcelain cup from an administrator to rape or murder. Some were charged with theft as petty as stealing a toothbrush, others with refusing to work or insulting a guard. Most were there because they had tried to escape and were caught. One man was sent back from as far away as Cuba after being away for half a year. He spoke fluent Spanish. Another somehow made it through the jungle to Brazil but was brought in by a native tribe. He had gained their trust but stupidly stole a golden trinket he claimed he had found.

The men in the blockhouse asked what I had done to be there. They lost interest and walked away when I replied, *"failed to escape."* In the flickering light of a small lantern I lay down on a bare board, as did the others. I had one ankle in a shackle attached to an iron rod. Though smooth, the board was hard as concrete and the heat was stifling. The shackle rubbed my ankle raw, and a terrible odor assailed my nostrils. It came from a large bucket of human waste. The bucket was emptied once a day supposedly, but only when it was full. A host of insects seemed to like it. I slapped mosquitoes, sweated profusely, struggled to breathe, struggled to sleep on one side without pain, and slept not at all.

I soon discovered that life in the blockhouses went on day after day miserably and without change. We lay around nearly naked in tainted air and terrible heat, mumbling to ourselves or to each other. We paced the floor to get exercise but never got enough. Strong men soon became anemic. More than a few waited and suffered and died before their day of trial came. An old convict with a dread disease that had eaten away half his face pleaded in a voice that made one shudder: "Kill me, kill me, please! For God's sake, will somebody kill me? I got a knife! Take it! Slit my throat!" We heard that awful sound for hours night after night.

The old man was longing to die but couldn't do what he hoped another might do for him. Acts of kindness were not uncommon in the penal colony, but in that blockhouse the man got no sympathy from anybody. Every night an exasperated voice, dripping with contempt, would cry out in response to his pleading: "Take my knife, you evil old bastard, and do it yourself! Why do you think anyone here owes you a favor? Jab my knife deep in your gut, old man, and give us some peace!" Inevitably someone giggled or laughed.

Old half-face died shortly afterwards, and those who had mocked him missed him, spoke kindly of him, brought him up as a character in their stories. In time, suffering from dysentery and loose bowels, they would lose all desire to eat and waste away. Every stricken man needed medical attention but never got it. The administration viewed all of us as rebellious, troublesome, and expendable. We were placed last on the list for any kind of medicine or doctor. Fearing the slow starvation I saw all around me, I forced myself to eat whatever god-awful food I could get my hands on. I even choked down a handful of fat cockroaches known for their high protein and nut-like taste.

Even though our daily ration was miserably small, I managed to eat anything others turned down. I wrestled with the moral question of taking the food other inmates needed to stay alive. But I told myself that if I left it untouched, it would go back to corrupt guards. I ate to survive, to stave off the debilitating weakness that was killing so many of us. One enduring passion possessed and sustained me: *I would remain strong to escape a second time.* All my life I had been unlucky. Trying to escape again could bring terrible bad luck, but I had to take the chance. It was my destiny and I would not deny it.

Each day seemed to become longer and longer, dragging by in the stench and heat with no end in sight.

Our one distraction was the mail boat that came once a month. Some of us got letters from home. Others sobbed behind clenched fists on receiving nothing. I felt like crying too but didn't know how. Every so often a mail boat brought escapees back from neighboring countries, and for several days they were the center of attention. We gathered around them to hear their stories, and I learned from them. I was able to obtain from another inmate a little book with blank pages in which I jotted many notes. Eventually I received notice that because it was my first attempt to escape, the Tribunal would go easy on me. I was amused by that and wanted to laugh out loud, but any laughter I was capable of at that time burned in my throat.

When I thought I had served my time for trying to escape, I was sentenced to thirty-seven more days for *insubordination.* I'm not able to explain how that charge came about or how I managed to endure the extra time. I do remember feeling relieved when they sent me back to Camp Hollow Reed even though it too lacked the comforts of home. The place was dirty, damp, intensely hot, and very uncomfortable. Also my fellow inmates were not much better than those in the blockhouse. I had to be careful with my few belongings, my boots in particular. Thieves were on the prowl. When a man took a shower, he had to worry about his clothes and shoes being stolen. They could suddenly disappear in front of witnesses. Yet compared to what I had endured in that awful "disciplinary place," Camp Hollow Reed was like a posh summer resort on the Riviera. Notwithstanding, I made up my mind to escape as soon as possible. I was done with crossing the river to Dutch Guiana. I would gain my freedom this second time by sea.

Chapter Seven
Money Comes My Way

At Hollow Reed I went back to my old job and worked for a couple of weeks in the hat shop. Then as things seemed to be going well again, I found that a tropical insect had bored into the soles of my feet. I had to be taken to the infirmary on a stretcher because both of my feet were so painful and so badly swollen I couldn't stand or walk. The condition was new to me and scary. The pain was so intense I thought I might lose a foot or even both. In the camp were men hobbling about on one foot, yet still required to work. Deranged convicts in rags with every deformity imaginable shuffled about in that camp. Not a single one was excused from work of some kind. For a time it looked as though I might become one of them, but in the infirmary they killed the bugs in my feet to allow a full recovery. Even though I went back to the hat shop to resume my usual work, the chief guard decided to put me in a jungle clearing where men were trying to grow vegetables. My first day in that place was a disaster. Monstrous black ants attacked my body and left my flesh raw and bleeding. Also the sun beat down on my neck and shoulders with the force of red-hot hammers.

The next morning, suffering agonizing nerve pain

and feverish, I pleaded again for admission to the infirmary. The doctor rejected my request, saying I could soothe the damage to my skin with tobacco juice. When I replied I had no tobacco and no money to buy any, he gave me a small plug, told me to chew it to make it wet, then rub it on the sunburn and lesions left by the biting ants. He had nothing for the nerve pain. I followed his instructions and found some relief, but even as I suffered intense pain the guard sent me back to the clearing. I knew being there would produce more misery, and so for two weeks I tried to escape work by claiming sickness every morning after coffee.

Unknown to me an ugly guard of unsavory character was keeping a careful record of what I was doing to show to the warden's disciplinary committee. Ten days passed and I was summoned to stand before them to answer questions. With great care they reviewed every little detail of my recent conduct. They sat in comfortable chairs behind a table cooled by electric fans. I was required to stand in heat. With a contrived expression of sadness and dismay, I stood shifting my weight from foot to foot, waiting for something to happen. The pain I felt mattered not to them. They couldn't feel it.

The man in charge, the chairman, addressed me directly: "Number 51080, Arthur Maurice Bonheur. According to this report, you feigned sickness after drinking your coffee for a total of thirteen mornings. You made a pest of yourself at the infirmary when you asked for painkillers not available to convicts. You refused to work, and you responded with insolence when required to do so. Well now, Mr. Bonheur, please tell us what you might say in your defense?"

"He has nothing to say in his defense," interjected the guard who had recorded my infractions and made them known to these esteemed wielders of power. "All that you see in that little notebook is true and accurate. It's a record of that man's daily misbehavior."

"That may be so," retorted the chairman, "but I want to hear from the defendant himself. Let's hear his side of the story. Bonheur, did you really feign sickness thirteen mornings after having your coffee?"

"Well, sir, I don't know if I can answer that. I didn't keep a record of my behavior like my loyal guard did. I didn't have a pencil or paper."

I tried to explain I was sick and feverish because an army of black ants devoured me at the vegetable garden. My skin was ripped and torn and my nerves damaged. I suffered pain so intense I could barely walk, much less work in a jungle clearing. They laughed at those hyperbolical remarks and declared I was absolutely insincere in all I had said. They meted out punishment of ninety days in a solitary cell and made it clear I would get more of the same if I didn't settle down.

An hour later I lay in irons on cool but slimy concrete. It was better by far than nursing a gaggle of vegetables under a scorching sun and suffering from oversized ants and other insects. If I had to say one good thing about tropical French Guiana, I would tell the world it's a place favored by insects. They love it there and thrive. As for me, except for an occasional cockroach that I could eat when hungry, I hated the insects and the way they lived. I feared and respected the jungle but liked its colorful birds and the monkeys that skittered in the canopy. The insects on the jungle floor were another story.

Every morning, upon awakening in that putrid cell, a guard gave me a piece of bread and a glass of water instead of coffee. On the rim of the glass and on the bread were insects. It was hard having no coffee at first, but after a while I lost my craving for coffee in the morning. Moreover, I didn't mind having dry bread when it was clean. I was never a heavy eater, and as a Frenchman I had a congenital taste for good bread. Also I learned to live with the irons. Even though they left bloody sores filled with puss on my ankles, I was able to walk for exercise. I scratched off the days on the grimy wall with marks that looked like this: /. And I drew a line through every four marks to make a unit of five. So I knew exactly how long I had been confined when on the 55th day the guard on duty announced my sentence was complete.

"Get all your stuff together and get back to camp," he said in that loud, commanding voice all guards used. "You're a lucky sonobitch! You got ninety days but you're out much sooner."

"All my stuff? What stuff? I own nothing but the clothes on my back, and one can hardly call them clothes. My very dirty shirt is in tatters and my trousers in rags. I have no underwear, no socks, and no shoes."

"Well now, you piece of scum. Don't go crying like a baby to me. You know I don't give a tinker's damn about you and your stuff. Just behave like a man and move the hell outta this hole right now."

I refused to leave. I told the guard to shut his dirty mouth and go to hell. Taken aback with surprise, he demanded I pull myself together. He thought I was crazy, and so he paid little attention to what I was saying. Jabber from a crazy man was usually ignored. I wanted to goad the guy.

"You're right about it being sooner, *Asticot*! I still have thirty-five more days to serve in this rat hole, and I'm staying!"

"You calling me a maggot, you bag o' scum? Hey! You calling me a maggot? You'll be staying longer, but right now you're leaving!"

"If you drag me out of here expecting me to work, you got another thought coming!" I shouted. "I won't be going to work tomorrow, and it means you'll be hauling my ass back here. So save yourself the trouble, Ape Guy, and leave me alone."

"So it's Ape Guy now, huh? Hey! Looks like I evolved real fast from maggot to ape. Yep, it's likely you'll be coming right back tomorrow, but you're coming out today. So it's up to you, Bozo. Go without a beating from good ol' Gus or not go and take the beating."

I knew what Gus was capable of giving, and so I went. Since I had been away from the barracks for more than two months, not even one man seemed to know me. I thought I had made friends with two or three, but they were no longer my friends. I was a troublemaker and a glutton for punishment. To be seen with me meant trouble for them, and quickly I became a pariah. With nothing else to do, I lay down on a board and waited to go back to my cell. Not an hour went by before two men hustled me to the chief guard's office.

"Bonheur!" he demanded. "What in hell is going on with you? I'm hearing you refuse to go back to work. I want to know why."

"I refuse to work in that clearing, sir, because I hate vegetables, and I hate that blazing sun and black ants eating my flesh. In the cell I'm in the shade with cockroaches — no black ants and no tropical sun."

"You don't mind speaking your mind, that I'll say for you! If you had another job, would you simmer down and stay out of trouble and out of my hair? You won't be in the sun, and no insects will bother you."

"I think I would simmer down, sir. I guess I would."

"All right. I'll hold you to it. Tomorrow you'll go into the infirmary to work as an orderly. Behave yourself or it's back to the clearing."

"Thank you, sir. That job has to be better than digging in the dirt and smelling dying vegetables and fighting ants the size of my fist under the hot sun. I'm from a temperate climate, you know, and I can't tolerate a tropical sun and creatures like them ants."

"This prison is no paradise, Bonheur. We both know that. Now get with the new job and don't give me any more trouble."

It wasn't a glamorous job being an orderly. I had to sweep the floor, empty bedpans, help the sick take their medicine, help them with eating and drinking, walk with them for exercise, and bathe some who couldn't do it themselves. Whenever a patient got really sick and made a mess of his bed, I had to change it, holding my breath. Some were incontinent and woke up every morning with soaked mattresses and worse. To air the stinking mattress in the sun was an ornery job and a hard one. Just getting them in the sun and back again was hard enough for a little man like me. Also airing then wasn't a proper sanitary measure. I knew it and the administration knew it, but that had been standard procedure for decades. I really don't like sick people, never have. But being with them when they needed me was different. So except for cleaning the beds of sick people I didn't mind the job all that much. Some patients had good stories to tell. I like a good story.

One day while going for water I saw an orange tree in the backyard of the chief guard. It was loaded with fruit. The following day I filled my buckets with oranges instead of water and sold them to inmates. I made enough money with that one batch of oranges to buy myself a shirt. The next day I confiscated more ripe and juicy oranges and made enough to buy a pair of used trousers. On the third day as I was eagerly picking oranges high up in the tree, the chief guard himself surprised me.

"So, Bonheur!" he shouted. "Is this how you behave yourself? Is this how you repay your man for treating you kindly?" I could tell he was very annoyed with me but suppressing his anger.

"You must know I had no clothes, sir, until I found this tree. When the good doctor shows up, do you want him to find a half-naked orderly tending patients and casting aspersions on his dignified profession? I felt I had to find a way to get some clothes, and I saw this tree so full of ripe oranges just waiting for someone to pick them."

"You make a good point about no clothes, Maurice. No doctor wants to see you in a loincloth. I didn't know you had no clothing suitable for your job. But you will not be stealing any more of my oranges. I have some chestnut trees. You can have the chestnuts."

So I began to do business in chestnuts. I roasted them on a piece of metal and sold them in the barracks. As my capital increased I dealt in bread, tobacco, and small bottles of rum made in Guiana and supplied by a

Chinese gentleman. I bought the rum from him at prices lower than I demanded. Like others in the prison colony, I was making money as a businessman. As my business thrived for nearly three months, I almost forgot about wanting to escape.

The chief guard, as I recall that fellow now, was a generous fellow. Somehow he had managed to hang on to his humanity in a place where inhumanity ruled the day. But the poor man was plainly unlucky. He got mixed up in a scandal involving a bribe from a convict who wanted to escape. Prosecutors claimed he allowed the man to leave the camp, gave him an hour to get away, and then sent the dogs after him. Even though he had a competent lawyer to defend him, in a brief trial my chief guard was convicted and confined to a cell. Most of us thought he would surely get off with a light sentence. But one morning before the sentence was handed down, and before his wife could visit him with hot biscuits and ham, a guard found him dead in his cell. Because of rank and position, the poor fellow had been given a sheet for his bunk. Wet and twisted, the sheet made a fair noose. He tied it around bars in the high window and hanged himself. The incident caused lots of chatter in the barracks, even in the town. I didn't like to hear it. The man had done well by me.

In only three months doing business, I made and saved a handsome sum of money and was thinking of another escape. I learned early that one must have money when escaping. I heard as well the horror stories involving guards running down convicts and gutting them, hoping to find their money. Everyone knew the money was in their bowels after swallowing it, or in a special canister in their rectum. The stories were gruesome but believable, and I bought a cylindrical container to hold my money from a merchant in Bella Vista. Also I bought clothes to protect my body from the elements. I already had a pair of good leather boots for walking. My plan was to keep them in a canvas bag while at sea and use them as soon as I touched shore again. I began to sound out some convicts who had saved money from selling butterflies, and we began to plan the event. My second attempt to escape, this time with several men, would have to be more than a mere attempt; it would have to succeed.

I had been in the penal colony for more than a year and knew much more about the place and its surroundings than when I made my first attempt. I knew better the climate and the primeval forest, and I thought I knew something of that vast blue ocean just waiting for us. I would go not with one ignorant man, but with a savvy group of men seeking freedom at the risk of dying, and I would not fail. It didn't pay to escape and get caught and serve time and escape again and serve more time. I knew hapless convicts who had fallen into that dreary pattern, but Arthur Maurice Bonheur wasn't about to become its victim. Well, at least that was my thinking, and I couldn't blame myself for thinking that way. I was young and healthy again and fairly strong. Also I had a good supply of hope. I would overcome all obstacles and live free again.

Chapter Eight

The Blue Ocean Beckoned

It was Christmas in tropical French Guiana. The sun-baked town of Bella Vista was gladly celebrating the season. Citizens of the town decorated palm trees on the main street in a futile attempt to make them look like European Christmas trees. In the penal colony the guards were jovial and celebratory, but only a few convicts spoke of Christmas. They didn't want to know what it was like back home, and what the season meant to them when they were growing up. One group, and I was part of that group, was thinking of the holiday as the perfect time to escape. For days we had planned our departure, parsing every detail, overlooking nothing. We had spent time and money gathering equipment. We had taken risks to buy and steal the food we would need.

Just as darkness came on Christmas Eve, six desperate and driven men slipped into the blackness of the jungle and hurried to a native canoe hidden in bushes near a creek. Luck was with us when we found the canoe one evening on the beach and hid it away. We answered to these names: Bonheur, Bigelow, Georges, Lapin, Marcel, and Pierre. Our time on earth ranged from twenty years to fifty-seven, Georges being the oldest and Bigelow the youngest. We had decided the odds in our favor on this night were better than at any other time. It was a major holiday, and prison officials were already drinking prodigiously. Eager to celebrate the season, they were lax in their duties.

Our stolen canoe, made from the trunk of a rubber tree, carried a makeshift sail and supplies of coffee, rice, beans, condensed milk, dried beef, and bananas. In a large keg we had thirty gallons of clean water. We had managed to buy supplies at minimum cost from an old convict who had gained his freedom but often visited the camp. Some items we got from shops and the prison pantry. From the creek we reached the river and traveled down it several miles to enter the open Atlantic. This time I was not in a flimsy raft at the mercy of wind and current but in a sturdy canoe with strong men. Three men on either side with paddles made the craft well balanced and powerful. It also had a good sail and a man who knew how to work it. The ocean was eerily calm with swells that gave us no problem. The tide was withdrawing, and with it we went into the ocean without effort.

Away from the shore we hoisted our sail, but in calm air we had to douse it and paddle again. In dangerous water we knew nothing about and in the dark of night, we were as giddy as children on a playground. And like children at play we chatted friendly, excitable banter.

"In a few days we'll be seeing a lighthouse that marks the entrance to the Orinoco!" Marcel exclaimed. "Didn't

Columbus discover that river on one of his voyages to the new world?"

"Well, maybe," said old Georges who had been a schoolteacher. "I seem to recall he wrote about coming to the mouth of the river in 1498 on his third voyage. And about a hundred years later the Englishman Walter Raleigh sailed up the river looking for El Dorado."

"Damn right!" said the man we called Pierre. "And we'll be sailing up that river too but not looking for a city of gold. We'll be looking for something better, a big hunk of golden freedom that will last for the rest of our lives! I'm of the opinion we'll be free men within a week!"

"You don't believe you're a free man already?" I asked.

"Only for the moment, Maurice. I'm looking for permanent freedom, the kind the bourgeois class in France have always had. They were free before the Bastille fell that sultry day in July, and they had even more freedom after the Revolution."

"Are you giving us a history lesson, young man?" Georges asked with a sly wink in my direction. "Well, it does seem appropriate," he chuckled, "to reflect at this moment on liberty, fraternity, equality."

We were laughing when Pierre at the tiller spoke of a breeze from the southeast. The sail filled tight and we moved smoothly over building waves. Though taking on some water, the canoe was proving its worth. I was dead tired from all the preparation and planning and was thinking of sleep when I heard Marcel say, "Didn't I hear thunder? Listen! I think I hear thunder in the distance. That means a storm!"

"Oh, it couldn't be thunder," Lapin who had signed on as navigator replied. "You don't hear thunder, Marcel, and you don't have to worry about a storm. Thunder, I'm pretty sure, comes in cloudy weather. The night is balmy. We got a million stars up there."

"My god, Rabbit Man!" Marcel exclaimed, placing emphasis on the meaning of *Lapin*. "Are you stir-crazy? You been locked away so long you don't remember the sea and the weather it kicks up? You came to show us the way as navigator, but you don't seem to know much about navigation or the weather or conditions at sea. A storm could rush in and knock us in the water in minutes."

"I have to admit I wasn't entirely honest with you," Lapin gasped as Marcel glared at him. "You're right. I don't know much about boats or the sea. I was desperate to come but had no money. I'm sorry to tell you this, but I think I can pull my share of the weight. I'm sure gonna try."

Lapin's confession was startling as we heard it, but at the moment he was off the hook. We could see a storm approaching fast, and we had no time to consider his case. A good breeze was up and we were moving fast. Suddenly a rogue wave hit us broadside and almost capsized the canoe. Somehow it remained upright though swamped with water. Two men started bailing as fast as they could, using buckets brought along for bailing. The dugout with Pierre steering rode the waves well, slicing through them, or riding down into a trough at breakneck speed to sprint upward and over the next wave. But soon we discovered our food was a sodden mess and our sail ripped to shreds. Daybreak came with a loud thunderclap, and we could see the shoreline only a few miles away. We headed for it with a good breeze behind us.

Not a person said a word. We were thinking people on shore might surely see us and raise an alarm. An hour later the canoe was racing through the surf, all on board holding on tight. Two of us jumped into the water, as the waves began to draw back, and pulled our craft onto the beach. Pierre gashed his thigh struggling with the canoe and was barely able to walk. I ripped off a strip of cloth from the battered sail and wrapped it tight around his leg to lessen the pain and stop the bleeding. We had to wait for him to give the injured leg a rest. So we sprawled exhausted in sullen silence on the white sand. Half an hour later we heard Marcel tell Lapin quietly and patiently, almost as a father speaking to a wayward child, that he had forfeited his right to be a member of our group. The censure came as no surprise.

"You misrepresented yourself," said Marcel. "You lied to us, Rabbit Man. Five good men are in danger of losing their lives right now because you lied. I ought to kill you for putting us in peril. I'm sure you know you deserve it. I'll do it in a heartbeat if you refuse to walk. Now go!"

Without a word Lapin picked himself up from the sand and toddled toward the trees. In minutes he disappeared, dissolving like a ghost in the mysterious jungle. We had not selected Marcel as our leader, and we might have gone against his decision to punish the offender with exile. Instead we stood by and watched a man go quietly and obediently into solitude and death. Then without comment we turned attention to our own predicament. Most of the food we had taken so many risks to steal was gone, washed out of the canoe as we struggled with the storm that hit us with incredible force. Some bread remained but was sodden. We spread it out in little pieces to dry. Though salty we knew we could eat it, and we had some tins of condensed milk. Each of us got an equal share of the milk and bread before we sprawled on the sand and slept.

When morning came we decided we couldn't make it by sea. Not a man among us knew anything at all about how to maneuver a canoe in a wide ocean or how to keep a course. Moreover, even though the dugout suffered little damage in the wild surf, it had no sail. We agreed to rest a while longer and then set out through the jungle. We hoped we might find eventually a village or town. There we might buy provisions, find a seaworthy boat, and go onward to civilization and freedom. We trudged along the beach, but at times we couldn't follow the edge of the water and had to retreat into the forest.

On the beach swarms of biting flies had a feast on bare skin. In the humid jungle we fought mosquitoes that squirted blood when swatted. Other insects I had never seen pestered us. And the jungle air was so humid we could hardly breathe. All day we plodded in water and mud, prying leeches from our feet and legs. As night came we tried to build a fire in drizzling rain that became a downpour. When swarms of huge mosquitoes attacked us after the rain, we smeared gobs of black mud over every inch of exposed skin. It helped a little but smelled like human waste. The odor of the stuff made sleeping difficult.

Daylight came on fast as it always does in the tropics, and we set out again, struggling through jungle undergrowth and reaching the sea near noon. I climbed as high as I could in a flexible mangrove tree to get a view of what lay ahead. I saw nothing promising. We were trudging along a peninsula that jutted many miles eastward into the sea. We had to cross the dry land to get back on track. That meant trudging through mud, stagnant water, and tangled mangrove roots to reach firm ground. When finally we made it to a clearing dry enough for sleeping, we built a fire to keep the insects at bay. Though the night was warm, we slept as close to the fire as we dared. When morning came we had suffered fewer bites but were sweating, disoriented, and hungry.

After a long discussion in which we found ourselves quarreling, every man but me decided to give up the grand adventure and go back to French Guiana. I thought it was a foolish decision and insisted on continuing another day or two to see what lay ahead. I argued they had signed on with me for better or for worse, and better times were bound to come soon. With stubborn resignation they emphasized in rebuttal the hard reality confronting us. Nature and the elements, bad luck, and even our own bodies were going against us. We had very little food and a bleak prospect of finding more. Quite simply, the time had come to call it quits. Returning to captivity was a bitter pill to swallow. On that we all agreed, but what choice did we have? No man among us wanted to die of thirst or starvation. Contrary to popular belief, the jungle does not give up its edible or potable riches easily.

Dazed and disoriented, we moved in what we believed was the opposite direction. We expected to get back to the place we had left in three days at most. Perhaps we could hide in plain sight among the Dutch long enough to regain our strength and plan something new. Just as we were moving out, Lapin emerged from the jungle and stood at the edge of the clearing. All the time we were struggling to move through uncharted and hostile jungle, he was observing and following. We could tell he was sick, starving, and feverish but offered no help. He had to pay for putting our lives in danger. We left him there in the jungle to die. I suffered pangs of conscience later.

The way back was even more difficult than the way forward. Our stamina was ebbing away, our physical strength nearly gone. Equally important, every ray of hope we had nourished for so long was almost gone. We could no longer dream of attaining freedom and a good life. Our thinking centered on survival long enough to be imprisoned again with more painful years added to our sentences. Any dream we might have had was shattered by the simple drive to survive. My attempts to encourage were met with grumbling and complaining. After half a day of wading through waist-deep mangrove marshes, we found high and dry ground on which to rest. Our stomachs were empty at suppertime, but exhaustion quickly brought fitful sleep. When morning came, we began to slash a trail with two machetes.

All day we pushed against lush, rubbery, and resistant vegetation, taking turns at swinging the machetes and resting every three hours or so. When darkness came, we spent the night with bellies filled only with water from a creek. The next day, no longer thirsty but with no food to sustain us, we plodded again through jungle growth. Gigantic trees that soared to immense height gave us shade but nothing else. At noon we found a nest of grub worms and beetles in a rotten log and ate them voraciously. The worms were tasteless but gave us a morsel of food and some moisture. Later that day, Georges caught a big gorgeous bird and wrung its neck. In minutes he was plucking it while Pierre built a fire.

Marcel fashioned a bowl of bamboo, filled it with precious water from our one jug, and got it to boil just as the bamboo caught fire. With his shoe he swatted out the embers, and we boiled the bird after gutting it. Each of us ate a small portion of real meat and felt better. Near sunset we came upon a small stream of fresh water and caught a turtle. Marcel broke its shell, dug out its sweet flesh, and cooked it over hot embers. We ate it with great satisfaction, each of us blessed with a rare portion of sweet and tasty meat. Our bellies growled after eating. No longer did we think of starving before reaching the river.

The next day we saw prints of human feet on a trail and followed them. We stumbled onward, happy to be on a trail, and came upon an Indian village near the river. With due caution we crept into the village to find only women and children who ran away as we approached. A slender old woman sat cross-legged in front of a hut and stared at us without flinching. We must have been an awful sight to her eyes, for we had suffered terribly. I pointed to a couple of sun-dried fish that were hanging nearby, and with a crooked smile on her leathery face she gave them to me. Then she brought from inside her hut a large bunch of ripe bananas and a jug of water. We ate the fruit like ravenous animals and found more in empty huts. To our surprise and delight we found in one hut a large tub of turtle eggs. Instead of having a shell as with most eggs, the turtle eggs were larger and covered with skin. I jabbed one with a stick, and thick yellow liquid oozed out.

"That's the yolk you're looking at," Georges, the ex-schoolteacher, explained. "Let the white of the egg run free and then suck out the yolk. It's high in food value, has lots of protein! The white of the egg has even more protein but isn't as tasty."

We followed his advice and ate the eggs, punching a hole in each and draining the white. Then we sucked out the rich yolk in the same way I remembered sucking a Spanish orange as a boy. Each of us had his fill of turtle yolk, and we left some eggs for the rightful owner. After going for days without food, our bellies were more than full. No longer racked by hunger, we lay in the shade to aid digestion. Some of us were dozing when the men of the village returned. They were not pleased to see us. Trying to pacify the men, I gave them a few coins.

With grunts of dissatisfaction on seeing us in their village, they took the money, ambled away, and left us alone. Then unknown to us they decided to alert the authorities. Two men ran four miles to the white settlement and brought back five strong Dutch soldiers who took us by surprise. They were armed and we were not, and so we didn't resist. After all the suffering we had endured and after finding nutritious food, it was no time to die. The soldiers tied our hands behind our backs, and took us to the station in a long and narrow pirogue. We had reached the river. They imprisoned us in a stockade with a dirt floor.

Although we had breathed free air briefly, once more we were prisoners to be punished with solitary confinement on bread and water. The Dutch authorities, speaking English as well as French, didn't abuse us but didn't coddle us either. We found an old tarpaulin to sleep on. In the middle of the night Pierre had to get up to relieve himself. The rest of us slept on the tarpaulin-covered ground as though it were a fine mattress all night. Dutch guards rousted us from sleep very early in the morning, gave us breakfast, and required us to wait to be processed. Near the noon hour in Bella Vista we were hustled through the town and into a blockhouse. My second attempt to escape the hell of French Guiana had failed with even worse results than the first. I was too miserable, too sick in body and mind, even to think about a third.

Chapter Nine

"Too Weak to Stand, Hospital!"

In the blockhouse I had plenty of time to think. My comrades believed Lapin, our incompetent navigator, had wrecked our escape. Whether he deserved it or not, he became our chosen scapegoat. Yet the group had never become during those few terrible days a cohesive, functioning unit. I had believed I would find strength in numbers, but I was wrong. I fled the prison with five other men, thinking I would need their help, but alone I might have done better. When things turned sour and the forces of nature turned against us, we sacrificed a man for nothing more than dishonesty spawned by desperation. We blamed him for all that went wrong when really he had no more to do with it than any other man. It was a moral question I wrestled with for a long time; we should have blamed ourselves. We failed miserably trying for a grand escape that would be permanent. Defeated by sea and jungle, five wretched men returned sullenly to captivity. The prison authorities never found out what happened to Lapin. We believed the unforgiving jungle showed him no mercy. It beat him down after a few days. He may have lived a week. The jungle executed Lapin after we condemned him.

Big and muscular Marcel had torn a foot on sharp vegetation, and the wound had become infected. A competent doctor could have solved his problem, but he refused to see a doctor. Strong and proud of robust health, he thought the wound would heal itself. Seeing that he was able only to hobble, an old acquaintance began to bully him. Bad blood existed between the two because Marcel at one time had beaten the man in a fight. It was a public fight set up by corrupt and greedy guards. To lose with many betting on him to win was humiliating for Fabio. So now he was badgering Marcel at every turn and making him miserable.

"Get this, you stinking weasel! I won't take this from you!" Marcel warned with tightened jaw. "You'll see little man!" Fabio, who was really big and beefy, laughed with a loud cackle and slammed his fist toward his enemy's face. The blow had the power to knock a man out, but a well-placed elbow deflected it.

When night came Marcel slipped his good ankle from the shackle, found Fabio in his bunk, and plunged a knife into his heart. A brief investigation quickly targeted him as the instigator. However, before the man could be charged with murder, gangrene ravaged the infected foot, turning it from red to black as the tissue decomposed. He went to the hospital where maggots were applied to save the foot. Three days later, just as a surgeon was about to amputate to save his life, Marcel died suffering intense pain. He was a leader, that man, and I felt a sense of loss. Yet had he lived for a trial, he would have gone to the guillotine.

After a day or two I found the lack of fresh air in the blockhouse unendurable. Pacing the floor in the stultifying stench of urine and sweating bodies, I began to feel I should have gone off with Lapin to die in the jungle. It would have been a better fate than returning defeated to squalor and captivity. Neither the sea nor the jungle had been kind to us. And why? Because both lack human emotion. Insensate elemental forms of nature, they lacked any human feeling whatever. They were unaware of our presence. It didn't matter to them whether we lived or died. Total indifference was the hallmark of their existence.

Though perhaps conscious of their own existence, sea and jungle were unconscious of ours. Even though we believed both offered the promise of freedom, they really offered us nothing. They were simply there. Struggling against them, we had a measure of hope and could dream of living as respectable human beings. In the blockhouse we had no such dream and very little hope, but plenty of danger. Marcel had warned us that a group of vicious and greedy convicts wanted to rob us of the money we didn't spend during our brief escape. They knew we had not reached a civilized post where we might have spent it, and they waited to strike. However, when they found out we were not bleating sheep ready to be shorn, they left us alone.

A motley crew of discontents I found in the

blockhouse, men of all ages and from all walks of life. Professional men of high rank in civilian life existed side by side with petty thieves and street rats. Because most of the men worked under a blazing sun almost naked, no sign of rank was visible. All the men were roasted to a dark brown. Some of the older convicts were burnt to black and looked more African than European. Every person had watery, bloodshot eyes harmed by the intense light and heat of the tropics. Some were nearly blind but granted no favors.

Those belonging to a gang, or family as they called it, wore red and green tattoos on their faces and bodies. The tattoos, often grotesque but intended to convey meaning, affirmed allegiance to the gang. Though supposedly placed in irons every night, gang members often gathered in the shadows looking for a weakling (a solitary man) to assault. If he opened his mouth to complain, they killed him. Assaults could and did happen even in the daytime. I was told guilty killers received minimum punishment. I never knew why.

As time passed the stench and heat in that terrible place became more endurable. Even though I slept with one eye open I slowly began to relax and fall into boredom. Then one day we were told an execution was about to take place. In the courtyard outside our barred windows the executioner himself would feel the blade of the guillotine. His name was Culette, and he had been the official killer of men for several years. I heard his story repeated several times before the day he was scheduled to die. He owned a small boat and for an exorbitant fee he took convicts trying to escape across the river to the Dutch side.

That indiscretion would not have brought him the death penalty, but as the authorities began to find bodies on the riverbank, Culette was charged with murder. He had taken men across the river all right but had killed them and gutted them, looking for money in their bowels. He knew no convict would try to escape without money and would often swallow it to keep it well hidden while seeking freedom. He was not above murdering another human being for a few francs. Shaken by the grisly discovery, hardened officials who thought they had seen the full spectrum of human depravity, quickly sentenced Culette to die.

On the day of the execution the rain flooded the streets. It rained often, but sun stole the rain. When I speak of rain, I mean a tropical downpour unlike any ever seen in the temperate climates. It began as little more than a steady drizzle, but within minutes the skies opened to pour down a cataract. The weather delayed the big show for an hour or more. We stood at a barred window to get a view of what was going on a few feet from us. When the rain passed on, the warden and a couple of guards sidled up to the hideous machine and stood at attention beside it. Culette was brought from his cell and ordered to stand at attention until commanded to kneel. A group of townspeople, some with their children, came to witness the event.

The current killer of men dropped the blade with a loud bang to test it. Women shrieked and children squealed, taking the false alarm for the real thing. Minutes later came deadly silence as the crowd stared.

In the arms of the guillotine I heard Culette cry, "Do it neatly, *mon enfant*, and hurry! I'm not here to have fun!" He was known to be a braggart even in the most serious situations. His attitude reflected in his behavior was interpreted by some as that of a man who loved life even as he took life. Other people thought his boldness a façade to hide the real man. His old mother stood by muttering he had been a good boy.

The executioner nodded in response to Culette's request, and the heavy blade fell. In seconds the man's head lay in the bloody basket there to catch it. On its face was a sardonic half smile. The procedure lasted only a few minutes. Except for his mama, not a soul staring at that awful scene felt any remorse for the dead man. Yet many admired his bravery. He had killed countless men officially and unofficially, and he deserved what he got. Three days later with the same machine officials executed a young Chinaman who also took the procedure in stride. His offense, as I heard days later, was "taking liberties with a white woman." According to prison gossip, the sex was consensual and the man didn't deserve what he got. He was only twenty-two.

Time. We were serving *time*. Weeks and months went by one after another at a snail's pace. Many weeks in the blockhouse had left me ashen and anemic. I found myself not able to eat and got in the habit of drinking coffee only instead of eating. My teeth were going bad. Meat and even bread I could hardly chew. Slight of build and weighing only 138 pounds when in the best of health, I rapidly became thinner. Observing my condition, a doctor gave me some medicine that soothed my troubled stomach, but left a bitter aftertaste and caused constipation. In time I couldn't drink coffee or even water because of the repulsive taste.

I began to think I was dying. Again I went to the doctor who gave me quinine as a tonic. I think he believed I had malaria. I knew quinine couldn't cure my condition, and so I feared I'd be dead within a week. The next day, barely able to walk, I trundled off again to the doctor. He looked me over, clicked his tongue, and said I should be given milk and plenty of it. A guard lifted me from the examining table and put me on my feet. I tried to stand and walk, but in a dark whirl of flashing points of light I fainted. On his clipboard, the doctor quickly scribbled, (as the guard told me later): "Too weak to stand, Hospital."

I languished in the hospital, a unit apart from the prison infirmary and very different from the hospital on Isle Royale, more than a month. I vividly remember how inadequate it was, how unclean and smelling of death. Its dark corridors and many rooms reminded me of the haunted houses I had seen in the movies as a boy in France. Its staff of convicts was lazy, uncaring, and untrained. Most of them while on duty did little more than stroll up and down the hallways. Only one doctor was present during most of the week, assisted by another who came on weekends. The doctors seemed to be honest men trying to relieve pain and disease, but even the best were overwhelmed by the enormity of it all. The men who lay in those dirty sick beds on urine-soaked mattresses covered by grimy sheets suffered a litany of diseases: fever, diarrhea, anemia, malaria, dysentery, tuberculosis, hookworms, pernicious neuralgia and more.

Most of them were beyond medical help. Medication that might have saved some of them was not available. A chronic shortage of medicine, particularly drugs that could be stolen and sold, was a fact of life. When a patient left dead or alive, another on a long waiting list quickly took his place. Each patient in a dirty bed had a pot for bodily waste. When added to all the others the stench every morning was beyond description. The patients who could eat sat in the midst of fowl odors to consume a few ounces of bread soaked in milk or porridge. Those who were about to die drank a few ounces of orange juice with the help of an orderly.

In the wards several men died each day. The cause of death could be traced to any number of diseases even though the death report in most cases was rendered in two words: *pernicious anemia.* It was double talk to gloss over the fact that convicts not more than twenty-five were dying before their time of painful diseases that had a cure. Hookworms in the intestines could have been eradicated by a caring staff but were allowed to waste away healthy bodies.

One case I remember well as though it happened yesterday. A blond young man with heavy blue eyes lay sweating and shivering under a frayed and dirty sheet in the stinky bed next to me. He tried to smoke a cigarette but was too weak to hold it and too shattered even to light it. He dropped the cigarette and slumped backward, his mouth wide open and his eyes in a fixed stare. A fellow convict pretended to check his pulse, quickly pronounced him dead, and stole his shoes. Another took his personal items, and a third stole everything else he owned. I didn't even know his name.

The attendant, an inmate convicted of sodomy, on seeing the man dead and the victim of thieves, became noticeably angry and created a scene. He cursed all of us near the patient and begged a guard to punish those who had dared molest the dying man. Looting corpses was his time-honored privilege. It was a "special right" that came with his job. It made the position a precious commodity to be sought after by hundreds of convicts but gained by few. Every man who had the job kept it as long as he could. He gave it up only when he fell into trouble or died.

"That poor guy was too young to die," growled a spectral patient struggling to sit upright in his bed. "It's a damn shame I say."

"Maybe it's better he died young," said another. "He won't have to suffer any longer. I curse my condition for not dying with him."

"He told me only yesterday he'd have his freedom in a few days."

"Did you believe that? Not a soul in this god-forsaken dump will ever go away free except in a body bag! He got his freedom all right. It just came a bit sooner than any of us expected!"

Macabre prison humor was alive and well in the most unexpected of places. It often focused on death and dying, for that was on everyone's mind. The next day a very sick patient occupied the young man's bed. He would slip into a coma and die of a fever in five days. In brief remarks between us I got his name. It was Ray. I never knew his last name. The urine-soaked mattress would be aired in the sun for one hour on the day of his death to accommodate yet another patient to die the next day. And so it went year after year smoothly like a well-oiled machine.

When the prison cemetery could no longer hold another corpse, a new one was built. I heard bizarre stories about many corpses stacked in a single grave, a mass grave. Judging from what I had seen of the prison system in the town of Bella Vista, I was inclined to believe what I heard. Convicts felling enormous trees and hauling away massive stumps died simply of sheer exhaustion. They were buried in the same cemetery they had given their lives to build. I wasn't glad to hear that only through death could unfortunate men escape the savage toil that was thrust upon them. It saddened me to hear it.

Chapter Ten

The Charnel House

Near the end of my stay in the hospital, I was to be tried for my second attempt to escape. I would not be the only one on trial. Those who went with me would be there too. The number on trial in a single day would be twenty or more. The president of the Tribunal would question me in his official capacity, and the prosecuting attorney would demand the maximum penalty. A guard with very little knowledge of the law or legal procedure would conduct my defense. No legal argument would come from him and no exculpatory evidence would be presented. All he could do was plead for tolerance, a virtue rare in French Guiana. Rapidly the procedure would be crowned by a harsh sentence, and the guilty party led away in shackles.

"This time they won't go easy on you, Bonheur," my guard confided. "Two attempts to escape in so little time ain't good, you know."

"I do know, Quito. But tell me. If you were in my shoes, wouldn't you do the same as I did?"

"I dunno. Really, man, I dunno. I guess some people love freedom better than others. I'm not sure where I stand. But good luck inside."

On the whole Quito had a good heart even though he could be a nasty opponent if you crossed him. I thanked him and went inside. I was looking at many months of solitary confinement, or three to five years on one of the "salvation" islands offshore. They were called *Îles du Salut* or Islands of Salvation because early in a former time residents on the mainland had taken refuge there to escape an epidemic of yellow fever. As it turned out, I was able to convince the Tribunal that my health was in decline because my medical records showed it. They gave me a lighter sentence than expected but stamped *INCORRIGIBLE* on my record.

Had he not died before the trial, Marcel might have gotten off lightly though I doubt it. It was his first time to escape, but "murderous revenge in cold blood" was a different matter. That demanded a death sentence. Old Georges, Pierre, and Bigelow got two years' solitary confinement, a death penalty for all of them. The old man was the first to go. Bigelow, though much younger was the second, and Pierre went later. Our man Lapin the liar, "Rabbit Man" as Marcel called him because his name was the word for rabbit, was tried and sentenced in absentia. The jungle had already given Lapin a harsh sentence, and so the judicial ruling was merely a formality. Six of us had made a run for freedom and dignity. We failed in the attempt and received suffering and harsh sentences. I was the only one to live long enough to plan another escape.

I learned with dismay that INCORRIGIBLE was not

a light sentence. It was, in fact, severe punishment. I was marked as rebellious, unbroken, a convict with an unquenchable thirst for liberty. I was a troublemaker, unwilling to bend to authority. So I had become a member of a notorious gang hated and harassed by prison guards and shunned by most in the prison population. Incorrigibles were prisoners who had tried to escape more than once and would never give up trying. With each escape the prison guards were held responsible, punished with a loss of pay, and required to recapture the escapees. It was extra work at no pay and dangerous work. The guards viewed all Incorrigibles as their nemesis, and they went out of their way to make the lives of desperate men seeking freedom at all cost as miserable as possible.

For a month we were confined on Isle Royale but were later sent to one of two merciless camps on the mainland, Camp Charnéle and Camp Godeberta. The former was often called the Charnel House and the latter with medieval history behind it was sometimes called the Lady. I was sent to Camp Charnéle, the worst camp in all of French Guiana. It was located deep in a swampy jungle where malaria and dysentery raged. Hapless men labored many hours each day cutting down trees in mud and water. All were fair game for mosquitoes, leeches, snakes, and rot. Any man not working at the standard pace got a bullwhip across his back. We were also unhappy victims of too little food. The guards ate well enough and had protection from mosquitoes and polluted water but not us. Some men had festering sores on legs and feet and were missing toes that had fallen off from disease or rot. Convicts were dying slowly each day even as they were compelled to work each day.

Charnéle had an inmate who was unhinged, driven mad, I believe, by what he had endured there. However, he was sane enough to concoct a condition that would send him to the hospital. His name as I recall was Abner Sigaut, and his age was fifty or fifty-five. One rainy afternoon as we were locked in the barracks after a watery lunch, he came up to me holding a blunt needle in a calloused hand. I knew the man only by reputation and couldn't understand why he was asking for some kind of a favor from me. Then I remembered he wasn't right in the head. So that made me willing to listen. I have a weakness regarding that matter, I guess. I tend to be patient with impaired people.

"Take this," he said, looking fiercely at me, "and punch me in the eye with it. Just a quick jab! Do it!"

"I don't even know you, man. How can you ask me to do something like that even if I did know you? One jab of that needle could leave you half blind. Is that what you want?"

"Yes, goddamn it! That's exactly what I want! Just do it, man, just do it! No talk, from you! No time to weasel out. Just do it!"

"I can't and I won't."

He scowled at me and went up to a more willing man

who took the needle and stabbed at the bulging eyeball. It was either too slippery or the needle too blunt. After the third failed try Sigaut himself grabbed the needle, drove it deep into the Samaritan's cheek, and ran away laughing hysterically. The next day with others looking on, with his own hand he jabbed a long needle into his eye. Blood spurted from it to spill on the floor and soak a dirty rag. He was hauled off to the infirmary by two cursing guards. Two days later with a patch on the eye, he was placed in a blockhouse to await trial for "self affliction." He had hoped to spend time in a comfortable bed in hospital. Instead he got a ruthless sentence and died half blind in solitary confinement

Another fellow spread sperm mixed with toxic mud into his eyes to get them infected. He overdid it and suffered complete blindness. For self-affliction officials gave him fifteen months in a solitary cell. Within two months a guard delivering bread and water to the doomed man found him sitting stiff and upright, eyes wide open, against the concrete wall. Rigor mortis had set in to make a statue of him. His bulging puss-ridden eyes appeared to be staring intently at something he couldn't see. A cursory investigation was quickly launched. The administration never found out with certainty whether he starved to death, or was able to kill himself. He was twenty-seven and had been a schoolteacher. The sexual instinct got him in trouble.

Incorrigibles in Camp Charnéle were treated worse than any farmer known for cruelty ever treated his animals. I've heard of rural people forcing horses to pull up stumps until they dropped dead. I've heard of brutes driving animals so hard they fell to the ground, couldn't get up, and for their trouble received lashes from a bullwhip, or were shot. I've heard of dogs tormented and starved by their owners. Our treatment was harsher. At Charnéle they forced us to down gigantic trees with dull axes, working all day without rest. After felling a tree every man had to chop off its limbs and stack the heavy wood high. For a strong man in good physical condition the work was hard enough, but most of us were suffering from malnutrition and disease. When a man fell and couldn't resume work, he lay there to bake in the sun, drown in putrid water, or die of disease. In all the time I was in that Charnel House not once did anyone in authority show us kindness or mercy, and no medical person ever saw fit to pay us a visit.

Every day began at five in the morning with the blast of a bugle. At night I tried to sleep on a hard board in a fetid room with leg irons around one ankle. The shackle cut into my flesh to disturb sleep, and I couldn't wait for the morning guard to remove it. For breakfast I ate a lump of bread washed down with black coffee. A few minutes later with all the others I was marched off to work. We walked in single file with our tools slung over bare shoulders. Guards armed with rifles strolled along beside us prepared to shoot any convict who broke the line. Swift-footed Arabs, ranked as trustees in the system and paid for their service, were in every detachment. They were there to chase down with rifles or machetes any man who tried to flee. I reflected how unlike was this situation to the one where guards left us on our own to walk several miles into the jungle to a notorious camp called Hollow Reed.

Near six o'clock in the morning the tropical weather was cool, and we worked without a struggle. By ten or eleven the sun was burning hot. Sweat flooded every pore of half-naked bodies. Yet it wasn't so bad to sweat profusely. It sapped our strength and required additional salt, but it tended to keep us cool and the mosquitoes at bay. At noon we had a half hour to rest in the shade and eat something watery and tasteless. Then back to work. At the end of the day, exhausted, we straggled back to camp. Any person who hadn't filled his quota of work got no supper and was locked in a special room. Even though the sustaining food was almost inedible at times, the ration was just enough to keep us working. Unlike other cooks in the penal colony, the cooks at Charnéle never pilfered supplies intended for us. I never quite understood why. Maybe the stuff they fed us wasn't good enough to sell to anybody.

Shortly after supper each day the irons went on raw ankles. As darkness came on fast — there is virtually no twilight in the tropics — talking was prohibited. Even so, we talked but in low voices just above a whisper. And what did we talk about? In one word: *escape*. It was in the thoughts of every man among us. Each of us had tried to escape at least once, and each of us was absolutely determined to try again. It was just a matter of finding the right conditions at the right time. When I say that it sounds simple and easy to pick a time and go. It was not easy because the right time was never right for all freedom seekers. The time to flee came only after careful preparation and after a man felt he had to go.

I was asked if I had heard the story of a convict respectfully called Gordo the Sapient. He was called "the Sapient" because his speech was like that of an ancient oracle and because he knew the jungle like the back of his hand. For him it was a friendly place. He had been sentenced to five years hard labor in French Guiana shortly after the turn of the century, had gained many years more, and was there when I arrived. He had tried many times to escape, and each time he failed he was given more time in prison. Altogether thirty-eight years were added to the initial five. He declared in one of his oracular speeches that he would try again and expect to make his sentence fifty years.

It would be fifty years if and when he was captured. His final escape lasted thirteen years before he was caught. Even the wily administration believed he was never coming back. But one dreary day he did come back, all bloody from a severe beating delivered by brutal, vindictive guards. He got his additional years and was labeled "Incorrigible." I knew the meaning of that term all too well. Gordo may not have suffered under its weight but I did, and the memory even now is painful.

From the camp named after medieval Saint Godeberta, old Gordo escaped into the jungle naked as a jaybird six times. The guards fired a fusillade of bullets at him, even turned a machine gun on him twice, but couldn't bring him down. One bullet ripped off part of an ear. Another disfigured his buttocks, but the old guy asserted later it didn't matter a whit to him. He stuffed a banana leaf against the wounded ear and sat in a cool creek to ease the wounded buttocks and stop the bleeding. Then barefoot he ran on through the jungle. With every escape he melted into the forest like salt in water. Most in the prison community assumed he was dead. Then everybody heard the chasers ran him down and brought him back from as far away as Venezuela. Any guard on duty when Gordo escaped was suspended a month with no pay.

A Corsican guard with a grain of humor pleaded with Gordo to tell him precisely on what date he would flee again. "Will you escape today or tomorrow, Gordo? Please tell me. I want to know."

"Not any time soon, you old bastard," Gordo replied, cackling and dancing a little jig, "But don't you worry old fellow [the guard was 23] I'll let you know when the time comes."

And he did let the man know. He bashed him in the head with a shovel one day when he wasn't looking and was in the jungle before he or two other guards could fire a shot. All three were suspended without pay and swore they would kill the dog who was causing them hardship and misery. Gordo was captured after thirteen years and returned but never tried to escape again. Three angry guards tried to kill him but failed. He was sixty-two when all this was happening, and by the time he reached sixty-seven he had found an easy life on one of the islands. I was told he had his own little house and cooked his own meals, and for most of every afternoon he lay in a hammock nestled in the shade.

He made a fairly good life for himself living alone on Devil's Island. I say he lived alone because the political prisoners who inhabited the island were celebrities of a different class and background and had little in common with the old man. Then one day a young newspaper reporter showed up to interview Gordo for a story. Three days later he left with a story that received a large audience and made Gordo a celebrity. Five days later Gordo passed away in his sleep. The prison authorities liked the story because nothing irregular was said about the prison. Accounts that tried to expose it as a terrible place were few in number and rare. At a later date most accounts tried to get the prison shut down.

On Devil's Island life was easier than in the Charnéle barracks. Yet at times, as on a night I remember clearly, a semblance of camaraderie emerged at Charnéle. In the darkness after the lamp was snuffed, a man lit a cigarette and passed it along from one person to another. The idea was to take one draw on the cigarette, savor the smoke in the mouth and lungs, and pass it on while exhaling slowly. Of course the cigarette didn't last very long even though several men got a taste. Half an hour later all was quiet, only a whisper here and there. Exhausted from the long day's labor, we began to fall asleep. The only sound was the clank of shackles on the metal bar as tired men sought comfort.

Then suddenly someone screaming at the top of his lungs pierced the quiet. Just about every night every person in the barracks was jolted awake by the moaning, or screaming, or sleep talk of some prisoner in nightmare. When I heard the eerie racket for the first time, I thought come morning the offender would be severely punished by comrades. It didn't happen. Among the habitués in a barracks as brutal as that of Charnéle was an unspoken understanding of the mental agony some of us suffered. It was there in addition to the physical misery and had to be tolerated. Some men lost their humanity in that prison, in fact many. Some did not. In the worst of places a tiny bit of human goodness could be found. Too soon the night went by to bring another day of hard labor and pain. It was not a good life for even the strongest among us. It was, in fact, no life at all.

Chapter Eleven
The Hospital on Isle Royale

Not a single convict in French Guiana envied my life as an "Incorrigible." Everybody knew we suffered daily but somehow endured all that was thrown at us and had the courage, or foolishness, to try escaping again. Even though the guards hated us and tried to find excuses for killing us, the prisoners in the sprawling penal system to a man were in sympathy with us. They heard our stories, and emulated "the brave Incorrigibles" with disastrous results. If I may tell the unvarnished truth, we were not worthy of emulation. Quickly I learned there was very little regarding our situation that could be called admirable. It was in many respects a deferred death sentence, for when a man was labeled "Incorrigible," he seldom outlived the label. With good luck, which seldom came my way, I managed to get rid of it.

I existed in that identity only three months, from the beginning of June until the end of August, and I must admit the months seemed like years. Then when a new Director of Administration heard my case, I had the good fortune of becoming an ordinary convict. I sent a letter to him describing in detail how poor my health was becoming, how I was liable to drop dead at any moment, and to this day I believe the man saved my life. I was unwell, anemic, and worn out when I wrote to him. I would have died before finishing my sentence. He replied in a brief but pointed note in blue ink that he was releasing me from the Incorrigible class. I would be leaving Camp Charnéle for Isle Saint Joseph for a term of six months. Afterwards I would be sent to Isle Royale where life was much easier than on Saint Joseph. Because I was not a political prisoner, I would not be going to Île du Diable or Devil's Island.

Even though I managed to escape Charnéle, I would continue to face harsh conditions on the island reserved for those who had committed serious offenses. Most of the time when a convict murdered a guard, his fate was the guillotine. A few, however, managed to escape the blade and were sent into solitary confinement on Saint Joseph. It was the island where convicts were kept in small solitary cells in silence and darkness. I wasn't happy to hear I was going there but took comfort in knowing I wouldn't be subject to overwork there. On adequate rations — I heard the food was passable there — I thought I might be able to get some rest and restore my strength.

I went to the island on a coastal boat containing more than thirty convicts. More than a dozen were too sick even to walk unaided and so were not in restrictive shackles. They suffered from severe dysentery, wore soiled trousers, and exuded a stink that knocked a man down. It put a barrier between them and all other inmates. They were going to the solitary confinement cells in spite of their condition and expected to die there. Another man was suffering from a fatal disease and was being sent by a doctor to the hospital on Isle Royale. That was where I wanted to go. I sorely needed rest in a good hospital but had no money to bribe a guard to send me there.

In late afternoon we were loaded onto an old night steamer two at a time chained together. My partner was a bald man short and square in appearance and no bigger than me. I couldn't help but notice he had blisters on his face and neck. His eyes were bloodshot and bleary. He spoke in a very low voice that sounded like a woman's. I noticed most of his teeth were missing, and the sight reminded me of my own bad teeth. Also a strange though not unpleasant odor came from him. It appeared to be a kind of perfume entirely out of place. Guards shoved us into the hold, and within minutes the vessel was picking up speed in the river. As we entered the ocean, our shackles were removed. I heard joking and banter as they came off and got a farewell from my partner.

The ship's hold was damp and dark except for a dim oil lamp that cast grotesque shadows as the men moved about. Tossed into the hold with bags of cement and other freight, we were going to Isle Royale, Saint Joseph's, and Devil's Island for a long time. While some of us had achieved a good life before being sentenced to hellish French Guiana, only one had gained a bit of fame.

A prominent judge widely known in Rouen, where Joan of Arc was burned at the stake, was on his way to Devil's Island as a political prisoner. I heard conflicting stories as to how he got into trouble, but one more believable than the others involved a very light sentence for a woman who had murdered her husband. The judge's enemies brought suit against him, claiming the sentence was a miscarriage of justice because he was having an affair with the young woman. When he denied the claim, calling it ridiculous, they produced intimate photos of the two that won their case. On hearing all this, my thoughts centered on Captain Alfred Dreyfus, an innocent man once confined to Devil's Island for treason and eventually acquitted.

We got to the islands early in the morning just as the sun peeped over the horizon. They lie only ten miles off the mainland but as many as thirty miles west of Bella Vista. So we endured several hours of tossing and shaking as the old boat chugged along at five knots through the night. On arrival I elbowed my way to a porthole and got a view of the "salvation islands," as they were once called. All three were beautiful, postcard lovely, typical and tropical with palm trees swaying in gentle breezes. That image dissolved never to return as soon as I touched foot on shore. We were ferried ashore in a large rowboat to land on Royale, the largest island and most developed. Devil's Island, the smallest and the one that journalists dramatized because of its name, was little more than a rock with coconut trees.

It was customarily reserved for upper-class convicts, professionals who had broken the law. The men lived in huts on the island. They were required to do no work except collect coconuts for the administration from time to time. They had to cook their own food, mostly good stuff brought in by boat once a week. Their confinement was more humane than on the other two islands and the food was better. It was an easy life for prisoners on Devil's Island compared to elsewhere, but judging from all I heard, it was a lonely existence that took its toll on a man. Most of the prisoners sat in the shade and fished all day, or lay in hammocks reading or snoozing. As each day ended they didn't gather to socialize with each other, but went off to sleep alone in their crude little huts.

I would soon discover that life on the islands was different than on the mainland. In the camps every convict sentenced to hard labor got exactly that, forced to perform excruciating labor many hours each day. On the offshore islands no convict worked at a job so hard as cutting down gigantic trees with dull axes. A few trustees were actually paid by the administration to keep an eye on things, and a literate man could earn enough for tobacco by writing letters. Most of the convicts on Isle St. Joseph spent their time hoping eventually to get back to the mainland where they might escape. Just about every night, because there was little else to do, they gambled away anything of value they owned. Many, however, in spite of their wealth in civil life, had little more than the rags on their backs. Poverty-bitten, they could only watch the games.

Approaching Saint Joseph, I suddenly became very sick. I thought it might be seasickness, but just as the boat was docking I fell into a swoon and lay unconscious. When I couldn't be easily revived, the chief guard decided I should go instead to Isle Royale. At the island's dock I was placed on my feet, and an orderly rousted me immediately to the nearby hospital. I had a fever and vomited on the way. The orderly, himself a convict, slapped my head and neck hard when I spewed thick amber vomit all over the pavement. Cursing under his breath, he threatened to make me lap it up with my tongue. He relented when the skies opened for a downpour to wash it away. In the hospital, soaked to the skin and shivering, my temperature rose to an alarming 105 degrees. My head swirled as if on a circus swing and my vision blurred.

A tired-looking doctor showing genuine concern examined me and gave me a bed reserved for the very sick. I couldn't swallow. I could only sip a little water that refused to go down. Anything I tried to eat came up explosively from a sour stomach. He prescribed milk and eggs to ease my condition, but even that I couldn't keep down. I suffered from severe diarrhea and began to stink horribly. I lost weight rapidly, grew weaker and weaker, and became a bundle of bones. Early each morning I got a raw egg in a small glass of milk but couldn't keep it down. Later the egg came slightly cooked, sunny side up, on top of buttered toast.

I could eat and digest a meal like that and slowly got better. I remained so weak, however, I couldn't walk or even turn over in bed.

Mentally as well as physically I was sick. After all I'd been through I was certain my body and brain had just given up. Three and a half years had passed since my coming to Guiana. My former life, all that I held dear, was fading from memory. The streets and clubs of Monmartre, the pleasant boulevards of Paris, even the pretty girl I had loved so dearly were becoming insubstantial shadows. I tried desperately to hold on to her name, Gabrielle or was it Giselle? At times I struggled to recall and savor the good things of past years. I tried to live in the past as a way of keeping at bay the bad things of the present.

Only on rare occasions did the remembrance of past activities seem to comfort me. Most of the time it didn't because I felt the pain of all I had lost. My mother left me when I was a toddler; my grandparents died when I was a child; my uncle and father disowned me when I was very young; and possibly the girl I loved more than life itself had given up on me. I thought of those who had come with me on the convict ship and had to admit that many were dead. I didn't view any of them as friends; yet knowing they had died in so short a time left me feeling numb. Why did they go within a year or two while I lived on? It was a question I often asked myself. As I mulled those thoughts, I was in a hospital bed and very sick. Would I be dying before the day ended?

Lying there in the best hospital the penal colony could offer and slowly getting better with each passing day, I understood for the first time that I had become a seasoned convict. I had learned all about the underbelly of the prison system, the graft and corruption among the guards running upward to the bigwigs of the administration. I knew about the rackets dear to the hearts of most guards and the abuses of the administration. Also I had gained a good understanding of the prison population. I divided convicted men with whom I lived into three simple classes: those who thought only of escape; those who didn't think of escape; and those who didn't think about anything beyond themselves. The men in the second category were old and tired. Many in the third were animals steeped in degradation. Only the ones bent on escape seemed worthy of any respect at all.

The doctor on duty was a good man. The joke shared by hospital patients was that Dr. Linville was too good for his own good. The sight of strong and healthy men falling into ruin with diseases he couldn't fathom upset him. If a convict came to him with only a slight wheeze, he was diagnosed as tubercular and given a hospital bed. Patients received all the food they could eat, and they got special drugs (when available) for their condition. If a man complained of pain in his chest, it was a sure sign of heart trouble to be treated with care. Anyone complaining of pain in general got expensive painkillers that were often addictive.

When the administration got wind of what the doctor was doing, it clamped down on the man with an iron fist. In fewer than three short months Dr. Linville was sent back to France and replaced by another medical man with a different mindset. Dr. Fabroni found a hundred men in the facility and decided it could hold only fifty. So he emptied the hospital of all patients who were ambulatory. He also cut back on food and medicine for all patients, and he refused absolutely to administer painkillers to any man. Some of the men protested but soon realized, as some of us began to get better, that his practice was based on sound training. He wasn't a likable man, Dr. Fabroni, but competent.

When I left the hospital after three and a half months, thankful it was far superior to the one in Bella Vista, I was sent to the Cochineal Barracks. The unit was located on Royale six miles from the hospital. I had never heard of the place and had to ask a fellow inmate about it. He said it was named after a tiny insect that leaves a crimson stain when crushed. And then he added that *Cochineal* was nothing more than a fancy name concocted by the administration to replace *Bloodstained Barracks*, the name given the facility by convicts. He told me about a savage fight between two convicts with their vital blood soaking into the wooden floor. Those who witnessed the event said the men fought each other half an hour with sharp and pointed knives, stabbing and slashing until they both died in a bloody heap at the same time.

Prisoners selected by guards tried to remove the bizarre stain with soap and water and later with strong chemicals. It proved stubborn and remained imbedded in the floorboards for a long time. Inmates coming later viewed the stain with apprehension as a symbol of prison violence. It remained visible for a long time because not a person dared to walk across it. Men on their way to the latrine invariably walked around it. The story was anecdotal and not entirely believable; yet some of us wanted to believe it. We had seen enough of raw and brutal violence to last a lifetime. With no invitation we had witnessed man's inhumanity to man in all its disgusting and degrading forms, and we yearned for calm and peace. Even though not a person in our group was afraid to die, we wanted as little violence as possible. It was a small thing to ask, and yet we never got it. I can remember staring at that bloodstain just before the call came for lights out. I felt incredibly tired and very sad.

Chapter Twelve

The Cochineal Barracks

The men who occupied the Bloodstained or Cochineal Barracks were to a person the most dangerous and merciless convicts in the entire prison colony. They were known to slit a man's throat simply because they didn't like his looks. The inhabitants of that most depraved of barracks were there mainly because of crimes against officials. Offenses were as petty as slapping a guard's face or calling him an idiot. Others included torture of an innocent victim and murder. Some of the worst criminals ever spawned by the French Republic were quartered in the Cochineal Barracks. While I didn't view myself as a criminal of that magnitude, my record showed I had recently been an "Incorrigible," something of a troublemaker. Also I had tried to escape twice. There was little doubt among officials that I would try again. It was only a matter of time.

So in the mind and conscience of the man who signed the order of transfer, I was justifiably sent to Cochineal. Everybody knew it was a place of pernicious reputation. Dangerous is a mild word to describe it. If I wanted to avoid trouble, I would have to sleep with one eye open through every hour of every night. In the daytime I would have to lose myself in a protective group. Any man foolish enough to be seen alone, regardless how big and strong he might be, was a target for predators. They worked as a gang and hit other prisoners with vicious efficiency and regularity. Afterwards, any investigation trying to get to the bottom of what happened was met with a wall of silence.

Cochineal was a large building about a hundred feet long and thirty wide housing about fifty convicts. The windows had enormous iron bars and the one massive door was made of iron. Every evening after the roll was called, guards bolted the door and didn't open it again until early morning. If a fight broke out in the middle of the night and a man had to be taken to the hospital, they grudgingly made an exception. Then the door was opened and quickly banged shut. Always when the great door was closed, activity sprang up within that even the guards knew little about. In the darkness after all lamps were extinguished, tiny personal lamps were brought from hiding places and lit. In flickering light some of us played cards while others read or wrote letters.

The men bought kerosene for the crude, handmade lamps from the official lamplighter who stole the kerosene from his supply for the three regulation lamps hanging from the ceiling. It was a lucrative business he had on the side that made for the good life. His boss knew all about it but turned a blind eye. That's because once a month in a clean envelope the boss would find a sizable kickback in his desk drawer. Prevalent everywhere in the prison colony was this unspoken code of behavior: *"Si tu me grattes le dos, mon ami, je te gratterai le tien."* To put it in English, the second language along with Spanish often heard in the prison barracks, *"If you scratch my back, friend, I'll scratch yours."* That silent injunction was a way of life on all levels.

On entering the building a guard directed me to a rusty and rickety cot where I deposited my meager belongings. When settled I looked around at my surroundings. Across the aisle was a man in ragged shorts with blue skin. The blue came from tattoos covering his entire body. His face was blue; his chest, arms, hands, and baldhead were blue. Intricate tattoos on his head resembled hair. On each cheek was an ace of spades. On his forehead just above the nose and between the eyes was an ace of diamonds. His back and legs and perhaps his buttocks had scores of tattoos in that one bluish color. Some were writhing snakes so delicately done one could see their scales. I thought of the pain the man must have endured when the tattoo needle was active. Then I heard many inmates eagerly wanted a surfeit of tattoos because they craved the pain. The needle piercing the skin many times had become a source of pleasure for them, a soothing medication.

Near him another prisoner, mumbling to himself and cursing when his world didn't go right, tediously carved a face on a coconut. On the floor sitting Red Indian style were several inmates playing cards. Most of the battered cards were so dirty it was hard to read them.

A very thin man, wearing nothing but a loincloth and glistening with sweat, sat on his bunk writing a letter to his lawyer in Paris. He asked the group how to spell a certain word and got curses in return. In the passage between the cots a man with an audience was talking about his last escape and his plans for the next one. He sounded very serious when speaking of money and his need for it to fund his next escape. The one thing on his mind and on those listening was finding a way to obtain money for their next escape. Anyone who couldn't raise the funds to escape never got the chance. So squirreling away plenty of money was the first step.

From time to time above the chatter came the cry, "Pascarelli, two coffees!" Bennie Pascarelli was the keeper of the barracks. He was sent to French Guiana to serve six years for molesting a child. Seven attempts to escape cost him twenty-one additional years. So he quit trying to escape and went into business. Exactly how he did it no one seemed to know. The coffee he sold came from kitchen leftovers, its nutty taste only slightly the taste of coffee. Later I learned he sold tobacco, candy, cigarette paper, matches, oil, toilet paper, and vinegar stolen from island supplies. He earned a premium on vinegar. It was always in demand, for many convicts drank it as a substitute for alcohol. The candy he got from a liberated convict who stole it from the shops on Main Street.

On occasion Pascarelli was able to buy a case of rum from a man on the mail boat, and that he sold by the ounce at sky-high prices. Also he owned the only "library" on Isle Royale, books on all subjects collected over many years. He rented the books for a handsome fee, payment in advance. In his library Charles Dickens rubbed elbows with Victor Hugo, Maupassant, Nietzsche, Tolstoy, Cervantes, and Jack London. Also the library boasted newspapers and magazines in English, Spanish, and French. A few were in Italian and even in Arabic. The old scoundrel, envied by some, had become so busy with his profitable enterprises that he gave up trying to escape. "C'est la vie, mon ami, c'est la vie!" he often said when inmates asked him about his past and how he managed to become a trader in so many items.

As night came with darkness demanding personal lamps, several groups of men began to gamble. A group in a corner shot craps with wooden dice. Others spread a blanket on the floor and played poker for small stakes. Instead of trying to sleep, a well-known group of men often gambled through the night. Hard labor, as I've said, wasn't required of them, and so they could get their rest in the daytime. While stud poker was the most popular game, several were played simultaneously, and quarrels broke out. The conflict was usually settled by a strong-armed Corsican who called himself master of the games. The job required a commanding person with strong arms and hard fists. Pascarelli, keeper of the house, sold candy, chewing gum, and cigarettes to the players at a profit better than 100 percent. Near daybreak when bright streaks were appearing in the sky beyond the window bars the personal lamps were snuffed, and the card players slept.

When reveille sounded at 0500, three guards unbolted the heavy iron door and tramped inside. Their boots beat a tattoo on the wooden floor loud enough to waken everybody. Though few in the barracks had slept more than an hour or two, we clambered half naked from our cots to stand at attention for inspection. The guards looked for weapons, drugs, contraband, anything suspicious, and found nothing. Cards, dice, and lanterns had disappeared. Any weapons were well hidden in the rafters. The men paid to look made no effort to search closely, and they ignored Pascarelli when he shuffled off to make coffee.

However, before leaving they were careful to check the privy at the end of the building. Every morning they made it their duty to inspect the latrine, expecting to find something amiss. More than once they had found a body sprawled on the floor. The Cochineal privy, or toilet, had gained infamy as one of the deadliest places on earth. In that one room with its wooden floor replaced with tile, countless murders had taken place. Although in subsequent years the tiled floor itself revealed no bloodstains, the grout between the tiles was reddish-brown instead of white. Anyone remaining in the Cochineal Barracks longer than a month found himself hearing sharp groans that quickly became a death rattle. Grisly sounds taught me never to relieve myself at night even if I had to run the risk of waking up with a damp mattress.

There were times when the privy was the scene of

three killings a month or even five. And did the neck of the murderer touch the blade of the guillotine for his crime? The answer, I gathered, was almost never. When the assailant was discovered and tried, he had nine chances out of ten of being acquitted. An unwritten law among those in the barracks was to blame the dead man. Let the victim become the villain. After all, he was dead to all suffering and not able to speak. Let the victor live even when guilty. His enemy would take care of him in the privy or elsewhere when least expected. Never, to my knowledge, did any man speak out for the victim or dare to name the murderer. To do so was to seal his fate as a snitch. That meant a quick slashing of the throat in the privy without delay. Every man I came to know, myself included, hated a snitch. Invariably the snitch was a cowardly little man trying to gain acceptance from the guards and the administration at the expense of his comrades. The criminal code didn't allow that behavior.

As soon as the guards left, Pascarelli came back with weak coffee, mincing down the aisle with a steaming copper kettle and humming a tune. He had diluted the issued coffee to accumulate a stash of beans that he could make coffee with later, and he was very pleased with himself. A measuring cup was attached to the kettle, and every convict wanting coffee to begin the day dipped the cup in the kettle and drew out enough hot liquid to fill his own pewter mug. No person without paying could have a second coffee and was urged to make it quick when taking the first. All of us knew the little thief was cheating us with coffee weaker than water but did nothing about it. He was running a business, and we depended on him to acquire hard-to-get items that made life tolerable. So while most of us merely tolerated Pascarelli, we respected him as a businessman. In a dangerous world of high cliffs, he knew exactly how close to stand safely near the edge. We admired him for that.

Instead of "Bloodstained Barracks," some denizens of the building called it "Blood Barracks." That epithet sounded more formidable than bloodstained. Others called it the red box, *la case rouge* in the French they usually spoke. It was a stifling, stinking, very uncomfortable red box. It was a box filled with despair because no convict residing there could even think of escaping. We were on an island surrounded by an ocean brimming with deadly sharks, and we had no boats. All one could do was dream of a distant freedom on the mainland and make nebulous plans for it. In time I would be able to leave Cochineal and be quartered in a safer part of the island. In the meantime I had to watch my back day and night. I endured sleepless nights there simply because I feared an attack. I suffered almost as much there in Cochineal Barracks as in the formidable jungle where I stood in leech-ridden water under a blazing sun to chop down gigantic trees.

And yet in a way I was lucky. I managed to keep on living while some around me spurted blood in the privy, or in their beds, and died. I managed to keep on living without appreciable damage when the man in the bunk next to mine was beaten so fiercely he lost his front teeth, his right eye, and the use of his left leg. Inmates talked about that beating as being the worst in many years. I managed to keep on living when another man two bunks away from mine was pinned face down on the dirty floor and burned all over with a metal spoon heated in the flame of a personal lamp. I kept a silent mouth and a low profile and made no enemies. After seven months, in relatively good health I was lucky enough to leave the infamous Cochineal Barracks for the other side of the island. It was a safer, more comfortable place for a man grown infinitely tired of prison life.

My life in the new place poetically named Blue Moon was never on the line, as I now recall. Life there was appreciably better. I fell in with a group for personal protection and in time became friends with some in the group. In the Cochineal Barracks where every man kept his distance, friendship was a foreign concept but not in the new place. Also in relaxed Blue Moon I had the leisure to write letters. To Gabrielle in France I wrote, affirming my love and promising to return. Day after day I waited for her reply but received nothing. Not hearing from her puzzled me. It was out of her character not to respond. I worried about the girl. Was she sick? Had something unspeakable happened to her? I wrote to one of her friends asking for information. I took pains to make the letter as polite as possible. She did not reply.

Gabrielle might have answered every letter I mailed. Her delicate letters to me could have been lost, sent to the wrong place, or deliberately disposed of by the administration. I know I heard nothing whatever from her. So in time with feelings of loss and futility I ceased to write. Years later I wrote to one of her sisters, hoping to get a full account of what had happened to Gabrielle. I waited impatiently for a reply however brief but got nothing. A number of years passed by, and I received no mail whatever from anyone. I am not able to describe how lonely that made me feel. I was in a world with not one caring person even aware of my existence. Even now as I remember those days and what was happening, I firmly believe prison officials chose to destroy all the mail addressed to Arthur Maurice Bonheur, the malcontent and troublemaker. It could have been their idea of just punishment of a more subtle kind. My name with those of many other inmates who had ruffled the feathers of the mighty was perhaps on a NO MAIL list.

Chapter Thirteen
A Tryst and Trouble

All the time I was on Isle Royale no official saw fit to supply me with a new shirt or a new pair of trousers. I wore the same ragged clothing day and night. When it began to smell, I tried washing the skimpy clothing under an outdoor shower. I was wearing it as I soaped it down, and I rinsed it as I if it were my body. At first it seemed a good idea, but then I discovered I had to choose between keeping my clothes tolerably clean or my body clean. I chose the latter, and so after several days of soaking up sweat in the tropical heat, my clothing once again assumed the odor that pervaded the barracks. That's when I wrote to the Commandant, Colonel Rousseau, the man in charge of everything on the island. I told him I had nothing to wear and was in dire need of new prison garb. To my surprise, my letter and the entreaty it contained was not ignored. His aides delivered a change of clothing including underwear, a blanket, and a pair of sabots. Later I traded the shoes, worthless as footwear, for enough tobacco to make a dozen cigarettes.

In another letter to the Commandant, sent only a few days later, I urged him to find work for me, something to fill the dreary hours of each day and eliminate depressing boredom. Two paragraphs presented a convict formally pleading for work! He thought I was joking and shared the joke with other administrators who found it ironical and refreshing. They persuaded him to give me a job as a bookkeeper of food supplies for all the barracks. It wasn't exactly the kind of work I wanted. Entering tiny figures into a ledger several hours each day paled in comparison to writing letters or reports or a book detailing the strange and twisted history of a French penal colony in South America.

Yet I enjoyed with the job an amazing amount of liberty. I spent my afternoons near the shore looking at the sea and dreaming of lands beyond the horizon. Even though I lacked a formal education, having left school at fifteen, I became known among men of little schooling as a literate, well-educated man. Then hearing of my qualifications, a guard of the first rank asked me one day if I would be willing to tutor his daughter. He offered generous payment for daily lessons to be held in his home. The subjects would be French, which I knew well enough, European history, geography, mathematics, and astronomy. I felt I didn't know much at all about the other subjects but decided to fake it. Two days later I walked to his house in the evening for the first lesson. His daughter was sitting primly at the family piano. She played a lively little tune for me. It removed the social barrier and we began to talk.

Ella Louise had recently turned 17. She had lived all her life on the island and had grown up near convicts.

From early childhood she had seen convicts in her home working as servants, and she viewed them as ordinary men. So when her doting father introduced me to her I was just another man come into the house and into her life. I was twenty-eight, small of stature but well built, and apparently attractive in her eyes. She was young and fresh with a pleasant oval face, large and pretty eyes, and abundant dark hair. Even though her body was a bit on the plump side, she was nubile, sexy, full of life, and curious.

She had a soothing way of talking and loved to talk even as I tried to tutor her. I got the impression she knew more about the birds and bees than a sheltered girl on an island had a right to know. After three weeks of lessons in which she proved herself a fast learner, she began to turn the discussion away from Europe and geography to human anatomy and risqué topics. I hadn't been in the company of a female of any age for several years, particularly one so desirable. Instead of teaching her as I was paid to do, I yielded to impulse and became an ardent admirer. Really and truly I should have known better.

I did know I was taking a feckless and stupid risk. Her father was hot of temper, and if he had gotten so much as an inkling of what was going on, he would have put a bullet through my skull with no fear of reprisal or consequence. Losing all control, I put myself in grave danger for a few minutes of pleasure every time I saw Ella. I knew the cost was high indeed, knew it shouldn't be happening, knew I could die if found out, but couldn't help myself. The girl seemed not worried at all. She even came to the office where I worked to whisper sweet phrases in my ear and run away. One evening when no moon was shining, I suggested we walk along the path near the sea to a grove of palm trees. She didn't resist, and as we lay on the grass close to each other, the chief man on the island came upon us. I won't describe the scene that followed.

The next morning I had orders to see the commandant in his office. He was sitting stiffly behind a big desk, impeccably dressed in white, and twirling a yellow pencil. He stared at me for a moment, a look that made me feel very uncomfortable. He didn't invite me to sit, and so I stood and grew more nervous with each passing moment. I could see he was angry and I knew he was powerful. My destiny was in his hands. He had the power to throw me to the wolves, to solitary confinement for a year, or even the guillotine. He could charge me with indecent conduct with a minor, even with rape, and see my head bounce into the basket. I waited for the verdict. Sweat began to dribble down the sides of my neck, and my palms were cold and clammy. Making no attempt to hide his displeasure, he deliberately made me wait to find out what he had in store for me. Then directly and firmly but without any show of anger he invited me to sit and spoke to me.

"Look at me and listen, Bonheur. I'm sending you to Saint Joseph. You will go on the nine o'clock boat. You are lucky it was I who found you. Had it been the girl's father, you wouldn't be alive now. The sharks would be feasting on your bloated body even as we speak."

He put the pencil down, laced the fingers of well-manicured hands, and eyed me sternly. "What do you have to say for yourself?"

"I'm very sorry, sir," I mumbled. "I'm real sorry to disappoint you. I can't defend my behavior. I was stupid."

"How did you come to know the girl? He demanded. "I'm told she is the daughter of the chief guard on this island."

"I've been her tutor for a couple of months, sir. Her father asked me to prepare her for schooling on the mainland. I did all I could to earn my fee, but things happened, sir. Things got out of hand."

"And so they did! You were tutoring the girl in the dark, in a grove of palm trees in the dark! You were sprawled on the grass very close to her. As far as I could tell, you were lying on your back looking upward. Is that the way you tutor astronomy? I have one major question for you. Did you violate that girl? Don't lie to me, Bonheur!"

"I did not, sir. I swear I did not. She told me she was a virgin when I met her. As far as I know she's still a virgin. We fooled around, sir, but I didn't have intercourse with her. I was crazy enough to cross the line, but all she wanted was smooching and kissing and being close."

"I believe you for now," the Boss said in icy resignation, "but if you lie you die. I can't have a convict romancing the daughter of one of my guards. That's conduct not to be tolerated. I cannot and will not allow it! I've a mind to tell the girl's father what you were doing with his young daughter, but I won't. I'm sure you know this island has endured enough scandal without you adding more to it. Get your stuff together, Bonheur, and make ready to leave. You'll be going to a lesser island."

So without delay that very morning, in the company of two brawny guards, I left Isle Royale for Saint Joseph. At the dock we had to wait for the shuttle boat to take us over. We were told the boat would return in half an hour. An hour and a half later I was still waiting. In the meantime the guards had gone off to enjoy a cold beer. I didn't mind their doing that. I would have done it myself in their shoes. But while they enjoyed their cold beer I suffered anxiety, hunger, thirst, and the hot sun. It was a tableau of life in prison at French Guiana. Not fair, of course, but not meant to be fair. I knew St. Joseph had become notorious as being worse in the way it treated convicts than either Devil's Island or Isle Royale. I didn't know what the island held for me. In the days that followed, I learned enough to stay with me for the rest of my life.

On lethal Saint Joseph the man in solitary confinement suffers most. Set against a slow and painful collapse of body and mind, he can do very little to improve his condition. He finds himself entombed in a dark and tiny cell with a narrow bench to sleep on and a foul-smelling bucket for waste. The bench, bucket, and the clothes on his back are all the items in the cell. If the prisoner is lucky, he will get unsafe drinking water with coarse food twice a day but not every day. For forty minutes every morning, after he discharges the contents of the bucket or slop jar, he enters a silent courtyard where he walks in solitude. He is able to see the sky at that time, but for the rest of the day he exists in semidarkness and damp silence afflicted by insects and the tropical heat.

The man in solitary confinement has nothing to occupy his time, nothing to read, nothing for writing a letter, not a thing for any kind of positive activity. He paces back and forth or circles his cell for hours on end, just for exercise or to fight boredom, and his mind wanders into a strange dimension unlike anything sane persons have known. He sees in front of him nothing but damp and dirty walls, hears only the rumble of the sea and the howling of mad convicts in another building. Alone with his thoughts, he tries to remember the past. Yet many poor souls lack the imagination to grasp the past. In many others the past is too painful to remember with satisfaction.

A cautionary tale inmates in good health were hearing about the dangers of solitary confinement was about a man in solitary who had managed to hide a small mirror on his person before entering the cell. For several weeks he was happy to have the mirror. The reflection he saw every morning as light filtered into his cell put him in touch with himself. Viewing the image was almost like having another person with him. But as the weeks passed the mirror turned against the man and made him spiral downward. He came to believe the person he saw in the mirror was a real person. When that person wouldn't respond to his questions or talk to him, he grew sicker and sicker. One rainy morning when he didn't emerge from his tiny hole with stinking bucket in hand, a guard went to check on him. What he saw as the light flowed in caused him to cry out for another guard. There on the dirty floor in a pool of blood lay their prisoner. He had slashed his throat with the mirror he had used so lovingly, its edges sharp as a knife.

Most prisoners in solitary confinement cells turn to the future and try to visualize an ideal life. They begin to dream of long and lazy days, surrounded by loved ones. Life for them becomes a shining mirage of lovely scenes, a fertile garden of green lawns and gorgeous flowers. They live in a house beside a lake, and their table sags with rich food and drink. They listen intently to the music of the spheres, and slowly they find themselves going mad. Desperate to be near other human beings, they cut and gouge themselves to merit a hospital stay. They risk killing themselves to rest in a clean bed, talk with another man, smoke a poorly rolled cigarette, and read. They know in time they will have to return to their cells, but with a genuine memory of a few pleasant hours in Utopia and a small stash of tobacco.

I feared I would be confined in a solitary cell, but I had misjudged the Commandant's anger. Close to the pounding sea and surrounded by a high wall was the camp for prisoners sent to the island for offenses not meriting solitary confinement, and there I was placed. About forty of us, maybe fifty, were imprisoned there. As in my case, most of my comrades had done something on Royale to upset authority and get themselves punished on devilish Saint Joseph. Their offenses could be as innocent as merely looking at a white woman crossing the street.

Our walled seaside camp, called Tranquil Ocean by some wag in the administration, was more brutish than anything on Royale. Not far from us was the "Howling House" where demented prisoners were kept. The barracks was called that because in the middle of the night, sometimes all night long, an ugly screeching or howling kept the convicts in our camp awake and cursing and threatening to kill the vermin who robbed them of sleep. It was a new experience for me, a terrible one. I would awaken in the middle of the night drenched in sweat with my ears hot and ringing. When day came I couldn't get the howling out of my head. Yet to some degree I felt sorry for the poor creatures.

"Don't pity them," a man with hideous sores on his neck and face said to me. "They have escaped this god-awful prison. They live insanely now in another and finer reality. They do no work. They do not listen to authority or to stories of suffering, dying, and death.

147

They eat and sleep and howl. I believe deep down they are better off than you and me."

"Do you really believe that?" I asked. "Do you really believe they are better off than the sane and suffering?"

"Yes, I believe that. Why shouldn't I? In their condition they feel no pain. They feel no responsibility. They feel nothing." I, on the other hand, feel terrible nerve pain night and day. Shingles, you know."

"Then why do they howl, my friend? Tell me. Why do they howl?"

I got no answer. The men were not in a finer reality. They were not better off than men who claimed sanity. They were hollow replicas of what they once had been. I couldn't believe they were better off. They were helpless and exploited, and they were miserable. Unscrupulous guards, so the rumor went, stole a good portion of their food supply. The little left for them barely kept them alive. Few of them had clothes, even dirty or ragged, and stumbled about naked chittering and chattering as in a horror movie. Doomed human derelicts, they suffered keenly as we all suffered in that detestable place. I was never in the presence of the crazy convicts but heard many stories about them, anecdotes often told with bright eyes to bring laughter. Man's inhumanity to man, the poet Robert Burns has written, makes generations moan. On Saint Joseph it made for hilarity and cruel jokes but maybe a moan too.

One man in the Howling House counted during all

his waking hours, counted even when trying to eat 31, 32, 33 . . . 31, 32, 33. Another in the one hour he had in the courtyard threw pebbles at the sun. He shrieked when required to stop. Still another was an inmate with a distinguished degree, a man said to have taught the classics at the Sorbonne in Paris. He spent every hour of each day verbally composing a letter to be sent to authorities in France. Even the guards were moved by the sound of his rhetoric, nodding their heads in agreement with some of his claims. Because at an earlier time he had written letters of complaint to figures outside the prison system, a sane man was driven insane and sent off to die. He probably died after I left Isle Saint Joseph, and nobody in France or anywhere else bothered to inquire about his death.

If for some reason someone did inquire, the immediate response on official stationery that looked like parchment would have gone like this: *"Subject was made crazy by the tropical heat. Now deceased."* That blunt and unfeeling explanation wouldn't have satisfied the man's loved ones, and yet it would have ended all further investigation. Any private citizen expecting to find out more was doomed to discover nothing whatever behind the scenes. Powerful political committees had tried and failed. A group of newspaper reporters from England and America once spent many weeks and a fortune trying to *expose* the penal institution. They found rampant *corruption* and bruited their finding in huge headlines. Perhaps it briefly caused a stir in

France but not in America or England or anywhere else. That's why once the evil got a foothold it lasted a long time and was very difficult to root out.

The infamous ravages of Saint Joseph I endured for three months. Each day I carefully planned, almost as an intellectual exercise, how I might escape. Then from the mainland, dressed as if to attend a party, came the local Tribunal. These were self-important judges who would review my conduct on Saint Joseph and decide my fate. I was told I had two serious reports against me. I would have to stand before the Court of Justice, politely state my case, defend it, and hear my sentence. That I expected to do without delay. Instead I was compelled to wait an entire week even though the judges were on the island and ready for work.

It was the waiting that confused a man and left him vulnerable in the court. Any defense the man might have made, depending solely on memory, was rendered useless by waiting. A literate man could have used the time to prepare a good defense in writing, but neither writing paper nor a pen were available to prisoners on trial by the Tribunal. Deliberately those items were carefully rationed to prisoners who could read and write. The penal administration didn't want disgruntled men writing letters to friends or relatives or the newspapers. As in my case, when I managed to prepare a letter, very often it was destroyed.

Chapter Fourteen
Solitary Confinement

To make a person wait and wait and wait, as often happened in the prison colony, was another and more subtle form of punishment. The judges were housed in comfortable rooms with plenty to eat and drink and were not in a rush to get down to business. It didn't matter to them if the inmates to be tried had to wait. They were in control and would conduct business as they saw fit. At length on a rainy day that left water in the streets, they got their ducks in a row and began the proceedings.

"Bonheur! Arthur Maurice Bonheur!" an officer of the court called.

"Here, sir!" I answered, stepping forward and standing at attention.

Behind a makeshift counter sat three judges in comfortable chairs. Their leader, a round and fat little man sweating under a thin shirt, was thumbing through sheets of paper, looking for the accusations against me and having trouble finding them.

"Ah, here they are," he said in a monotone and then began to read. "Bonheur, Arthur Maurice, 51080. Spoke with insolence and impudence to a well-meaning guard who tried to advise him to accept his condition without rebellion. To the guard he reportedly said, 'I don't want to hear your stupid remarks. Get the hell away from me! Get lost!'"

The judge shuffled the papers, looked over the top of his eyeglasses at me, frowned and asked, "What have you to say about this? We want to hear an explanation of your conduct. Why did you speak that way?"

"I have nothing of substance to say, sir, nothing at all to explain. The day was hot. I was hungry and hurting. I spoke out of line."

He looked at me in silence for what seemed a long time, and then he read the second accusatory report. "Bonheur, Arthur Maurice, 51080. Asserted in vulgar language he was being cheated on his ration of food. Insisted the food be weighed. His complaint was heard with patience but deemed grossly out of order and ultimately denied."

Again he shuffled the papers in front of him, looked over the rim of his spectacles, and frowned. I stood waiting as he sat back in his chair, sipped a glass of cold water, lit a cigarette, and began to converse with his colleagues on either side of him.

"What do you say to that?" he finally asked, clearing his throat and staring at me again. "Would you call it unseemly behavior?"

"They refused, sir, to weigh my portion of meat. They knew as I did, just by looking at it, that it was too meager a serving and wouldn't meet regulations. They could have quickly added an ounce or two more."

"You must surely know, 51080, the stewards do not weigh every portion of meat or anything else that is served to you daily. On some days, depending on the way things go, you will get more. On other days, less. In my view you are fortunate to get any food at all here."

"That may be true, sir. But closer attention to what the regulations say appears to be necessary and might solve the problem."

"It might indeed, but who are you to say? As a condemned man you have no say whatever in this matter, nor any other matter regarding the way this institution is run. You should be thankful you receive any food, shelter, and clothing at all. Moreover, if you know what's good for you, and I think you do, you will not make a habit of insulting guards. Their lot is hard enough without hearing insults."

He stopped talking, shuffled papers, and consulted with colleagues. For several minutes they appeared to be having animated conversation. Then once more he looked at me sternly as if required to follow a script in a drama. He was scolding me again before passing sentence, and he was taking his time. Then came the gavel and the gibberish began.

"By unanimous decision, Number 51080, we have decreed here that you are to spend thirty days in solitary confinement for your first offense, and thirty days for the

second. Should a third offense be recorded against you, let it be known that it will bring you another thirty."

I moped out of the room crestfallen, knowing my mistake was to offer instruction to the round little judge. I might have received a lighter sentence had I remained calm, polite, and tight-lipped. They viewed me as confrontational and cocky, an arrogant prisoner with too much self- esteem trying to instruct or intimidate veteran members of the court. So it was necessary to use their power to put me in my place.

"How many, Maurice?" asked a fellow convict when I returned to my bunk in the barracks. "Five months in solitary for cussing a guard?"

"Not quite as much, Broussard," I answered while making ready to leave. "Two months only, but believe me, two very long months."

A good friend filled my suppository with tightly packed tobacco, cigarette papers, and matches. That way on the sly I could smoke in solitary. A guard came to take me to my cell just as I went to the privy to conceal the suppository. It was a device universally owned and used by convicts in Guiana, a small aluminum or bamboo cylinder. Thievery was rampant, and no person had a trunk or chest that could be locked or bolted in place. So hiding one's money inside a personal cavity was a necessity. In the stall I jerked on my pants and left with the guard. For several minutes I was in sunlight, and then the iron door closed on me.

I would have to endure sixty days away from the sun, away from light and life. I would have nothing whatever to do to while away the hours, nothing but a crude bench to sleep on, a foul bucket assailing my nostrils, and a slimy floor attacking sore feet. I should also mention the damp, clammy, grimy walls that seemed to close in on me at times. The medical profession called the condition *claustrophobia*, and I thought it might get worse. That worried me. Outside the cell and certainly within was dead silence. Try as I might I couldn't hear the slightest sound. I thought I might call up memories of the past to console me, but even those were slipping away. I dared not think of the future.

Coming in from the bright sunlight, my vision had to adjust to the somber darkness that cloaked the cell. Then as the darkness dissipated, I heard a key rattling in the lock. The guard wanted to know if he could bring me something worth money to him. I gave him some coins to get me coffee and bananas. Half an hour later he returned. Even though the coffee was weak and the bananas over-ripe, I felt better after eating and drinking and began to pace my cell. In late afternoon the same guard ordered me to go into the courtyard for exercise. It was cooler there than in the stifling cell, and the air was fresher. But I was there only half an hour before ordered to return. Some watery rice on a tin plate was shoved into the cell, and the iron door was locked until morning. Soon afterwards the blackness of night fell heavily upon me.

I lay down on the crude bench, the hard board my bed, and tried to sleep. Thoughts of the present, the past, and what could have been the future flooded my mind and kept me awake. I thought of how it came to pass to find myself in so dire a situation. I thought of people I knew in the past and wondered whether any of them were still alive. My old flame, the girl I knew before I met Gabrielle, returned to my thoughts now that I was so completely alone. Monique was her name. So young and fresh she was, so much in love, and pretty too. Then quickly my thoughts centered on Gabrielle, my one and only love, the person I dearly wanted to marry. I thought of what our life might have been together. Sadly I remembered what I did to cause trouble, how I wanted to please and impress her and make her smile with a special joy.

Would Gabrielle wait for me? Probably not. Perhaps she had fallen for another young man even before the convict ship dumped me like a sack of garbage in the tropics. And for that I couldn't blame her. She had but one life to live. She couldn't throw it away or damage it severely as I had done. One mistake had seized my life to destroy it. Even so, I would survive solitary confinement and find a way to live again. The next day my supper was two slices of bread smeared with bacon grease. The stale bread and rancid grease attracted flies, but I quickly flicked the flies away and washed the stuff down with gulps of bitter and metallic water. An hour later the guard brought coffee. I paid him with my last coins.

Without names the tedious days passed one after another. Was it Tuesday or Saturday? It didn't matter. Slowly I became accustomed to the routine and monotony of isolation. Today would be a few ounces of rice topped with molasses on a tin plate. Tomorrow would be dry bread and metallic water. If I happened to be lucky, I would find no insects on the bread or water. Night again and the cell was pitch black. It was a time not for sleeping, but for pacing back and forth like a caged animal. With all the pacing on the damp and dirty floor, the soles of my feet became soft and sticky. I had no water with which to wash them.

Ignoring the pain, in vivid fantasy I thought of how I would cope with the future. I spent an hour buying a suit in Chicago, or was it New York? Impeccably dressed, I waited in the lobby of an elegant hotel for a graceful girl, impatient for her to arrive and joyous when she did. We dined in a five-star restaurant, ordering the most expensive fare on the menu. Sipping champagne after the dinner, we agreed on the size of the tip. As the waiter glanced at the tip, I saw surprise and satisfaction on his pale face. Rising to leave, I could see and feel the happiness in my love's pretty eyes. I could hear her musical laughter as we stepped into the street. My fertile imagination was allowing me to live a dream of life not entirely beyond a realistic view of life, and it kept me sane.

It wasn't long before I made up my mind to get out of that place. I was getting weaker by the day and had to go soon. I could no longer tolerate the stench, the bad air, and the dampness that damaged my feet. Then as I desperately sought a solution, I remembered an old trick used by clever convicts and hoped it would work. I mixed saliva with the dirt and dust on my cell floor and made a paste. I rubbed the gray-brown mess into my eyes to get them infected. When the doctor came the next day for his weekly visit, he found both eyes puffy, red, and watery. The paste had done its job and I could barely see. Without delay he sent me to the hospital. Under guard but confused and anxious because I was seeing double, I left Saint Joseph for the hospital on Isle Royale and a clean bed. Nourishing food, clean water, something to read, a cigarette now and then, and people to talk to made all the difference. I hoped to remain in the hospital a long time, but that didn't happen. My fake condition rapidly diminished and disappeared.

The doctor believed his medicine coupled with his expertise as a well-trained physician had saved my sight. I was in no position to argue with him, and to this day (if the old fellow is still alive) he tells the story of saving a young convict's eyesight only hours before he would have gone blind. Saving my sight was the pivotal triumph of his career. Until then he believed there was little he could do to help the sick and dying men he saw every day in that hellish place. Believing he had saved my sight changed his attitude and made him more confident. He took under his wing any number of living cadavers and slowly restored them to health. He left the penal colony a contented man respected by inmates. In France, as I learned later, he gained prominence as an eye doctor.

In the hospital on Royale I soon discovered that during my absence on Saint Joseph a scandal of large proportion had occurred. It was a scandal far more juicy that anything the guard's daughter and I might have brought about. It involved two notorious convicts and the wife of an administrator, André Corbin. Convict Jean-Paul had once been a chef in one of the finest restaurants in Paris and was something of a celebrity in the penal colony. On one of the islands, or so the story went, he had worked in the kitchen of the Commandant with two other cooks doing his bidding. Then one afternoon in fierce altercation, he split open a subordinate's skull with a heavy frying pan. Subsequently, he gave up cooking altogether and became a dissolute denizen of the Cochineal Barracks. His life centered on a young prisoner named Ethan Price who had become his lover. One day Ethan was ordered to work as a servant in the house of André Corbin. His wife, Lena, found herself attracted to the young man, and within days they were having an affair.

She knew Jean-Paul was Ethan's homosexual lover but wanted the young man for herself. She called Jean-Paul to her house one afternoon and gave him an ultimatum: "See no more of Ethan Price if you don't want to go to a cell on Saint Joseph."

The crusty old convict laughed in her face and turned to walk away. She shot him in the back at close range.

The bullet lodged in his spine and paralyzed him from the waist down. It all came out in sordid detail at the trial. Corbin's wife was charged with adultery and the attempted murder of a well-known and accomplished prisoner. In the hubbub of noisy proceedings, a skilled lawyer proved guilt beyond a reasonable doubt, but she was acquitted. It wouldn't look good for the wife of an administrator to have her life and reputation, and that of her husband, damaged by a convict. Lena Corbin left her husband, a man two decades older than she, and went back to France. Fewer than four months later André Corbin was promoted with an increase in salary.

That brought an end to the scandal. Not even her husband ever found out what happened to Lena in France. Yet for weeks the scandal gave us something to talk about. We wondered what happened to the woman, and we wondered what events were swirling around paralyzed Jean-Paul and Ethan Price. We heard Jean-Paul was given additional prison time on Devil's Island after being judged guilty of "improper behavior with one of the same sex." Ethan also was given additional time because of "suspect behavior with a lady of rank." The young man spent a month in solitary and was sent to Devil's Island where he and paralyzed Jean-Paul eventually got back together. It was a story with a happy ending, rare in French Guiana.

Chapter Fifteen
Americans With Carte Blanche

In the hospital on Isle Royale I completed my sentence of sixty days in solitary confinement. I spent only seventeen days in solitary and forty-three in the hospital. I'm amazed even now how I managed to get away with that bit of subterfuge. I saw my doctor only once a week and only for a few minutes. He was too busy tending other patients to remember how long I had been his patient. Also any time I saw him I had new ailments for him to consider. So after more than a month of hospital care I was already in peak condition and wondering whether I should stay longer. Then one morning without notice, I was told I would have to leave the hospital and return to barracks near Bella Vista. My doctor had discovered I was malingering.

Returning to the mainland was fine with me, for there I could put into motion another plan to escape. However, the bosses gave me work as a bookkeeper without a cent of pay. I needed to accumulate money for an escape. But how could I get a fat purse working each day at a job with no wages? There seemed to be only one solution. I would give up sleeping and gamble all night. I tried that but it didn't work. After two nights of no sleep, I became aware it wasn't a good idea. I thought I might stow away on an old freighter bound for Venezuela. I believed I could hide in the stacks of firewood stowed in the hold meant to feed the steam engine. Then a well-meaning comrade told me the stacked wood could fall and crush me if the ancient ship were to run into wicked weather. That got me to thinking, and reluctantly I gave up an escape plan that might have worked.

A couple of weeks later, a co-worker asked me what I thought of the American couple taking pictures of activity in Bella Vista. His question came as a big surprise. In all my years there I had seen nobody taking pictures of anything, and certainly no Americans. Foreign visitors in the town were rare and carefully supervised. Bella Vista was not a tourist attraction. Prison officials discouraged photography by anyone. Years earlier a handful of photographs showing skeletal, half-naked prisoners dragging a huge log in a swamp were leaked to the press. It caused a hue and cry as far away as France. The scandal drove administrators to keep a wary eye on anyone who might want to take pictures. So how could two Americans appear to have carte blanche to ask questions and take many pictures in a town so carefully supervised?

"They surely must be reporters from an influential newspaper," my friend suggested, "people of importance with special permits. I hear they've been asking ordinary citizens a lot of questions and taking photographs of them. The two seem to be exploring the entire town, walking about everywhere though apparently not in or near the prison. I heard they have a room at the Commandant's house in the square. If that's true, they must really have clout."

"Staying at the Commandant's surely means they have permission from higher authority," I said. "Maybe the Governor or even the Board of Supervisors in France. I'm thinking they're here to write propaganda, a glowing report with pictures for European and American newspapers. Propaganda, you know, to improve the image of the place. But maybe, just maybe, they'd like to hear the truth."

On the spot I decided to meet the Americans and offer them some stories I had written about prison life in French Guiana. Because I had found no way to publish or promote my stuff, I saw them as offering perhaps an opportunity. Early the next morning, saying I would return soon, I left my job with a small bundle and walked to the house where the Americans were staying. As I had done for him on more than one occasion, my co-worker Clement covered for me.

When I knocked on the door, another convict employed there as a servant left me shifting my weight on the stoop while he went to inform the couple of a visitor. He said he'd been told they represented a major magazine in America. In a few minutes a man of thirty or thirty-five appeared and asked me what I wanted. In broken English, I told him I wished to sell him a few authentic stories about the place he had come to visit. As he examined my bundle of papers, a tall and slender woman in her early thirties appeared behind him to look over his shoulder.

"How much do you have in mind for this material?" the man asked. "I'm not able to read most of it. My French is terrible. But it seems to me it reveals stuff about the prison we might be able use."

"Whatever you think is fair," I replied. "I've never sold any of my writings, never had a chance. So I can't put a figure on them."

"Just a cursory glance tells me your work deserves a closer look," said the woman. "Geoffrey and I will read through the material this evening. Come back again tomorrow, will you?" She slipped into my hand a folded American bill with a value of 100 francs!

Expecting no money from them unless they bought my stories, I couldn't believe my eyes. I went immediately to a Chinese trader where I bought a few items to change the note into local currency. After paying off a debt that had nagged me for weeks I had eighty-one francs left, a small fortune for a convict. The next morning I went again to visit the young woman and her husband. They were having breakfast and invited me to join them. I can taste even now the delicious cold orange juice in little glasses. For half an hour I felt like a free human being.

With a sense of gladness I hadn't felt in a long time I told them my story. Happily the woman was skilled in French and jotted down notes as I spoke. She gave me a list of questions about prison life in the colony and asked me to supply the answers. Then as I was leaving she slipped another American bill into my palm. It too was worth 100 francs! Until the administration began to take notice, I met with Ellen and Geoffrey Thornhurst several times. For each document I gave them, she paid me generously. I was having a wonderful time, but one afternoon Geoffrey told me they would be leaving in two days for New York. They would be taking passage on a ship berthed nearby in Dutch Guiana.

I thought if they were willing to help me, I might be able to get to New York on that ship. On the eve of their departure I went to see them about it but lost my nerve and couldn't ask for help. I wanted all the help I could get, but stubborn pride intervened and left me on my own. After wishing them *bon voyage* I went to the shack of a liberated convict and bought from him a white suit, a good pair of shoes, and a pith helmet. Then I asked him to find me a man to take me to the Dutch side of the river. A person named Malcolm would do it for a reasonable fee.

At high noon the next day when officials were taking their siesta, I went to Malcolm's little skiff and pushed off. Within an hour we were in Dutch country near a small town. I gave Malcolm more than he asked for, and the man shoved off as I stood on the bank. Later I went to an open-air bar and ordered a beer. It was native beer and known to be rather bitter. Yet I remember even now how delicious it was to a tongue that had not tasted beer for many months. I sat around and had a few more, waiting for night to come. When all was dark I left for the seaport seven miles to the north where the ship lay in harbor.

I had plenty of money and my intention was to book passage as an ordinary, well-dressed traveler. Perhaps in that identity I would meet up with the Thornhursts and travel with them. Somehow I would have to get to the port and get on the ship without causing attention. It didn't happen. I never made it to the ship. I was on the road fewer than fifteen minutes when I came face to face with the Dutch police escorting a work crew back to their prison cells. A white man on the road at that hour seemed out of place to them. They asked me where I was headed, and I answered politely. They asked for identification papers, which I couldn't produce. That aroused suspicion; something wasn't right. They insisted I come back with them to the town. Within minutes I was branded a French escapee and thrown in jail.

What a sad situation that was! As I recall it years later and reflect, I feel the same old sadness as then. My high hopes of freedom, my dreams of fleeing the nightmare of French Guiana to live with dignity again were instantly dashed. And not because I had failed to see the worth of some detail in my plan, but because of sheer bad luck. Three times I had tried to escape and failed. The third escape, better than the first two, seemed a winner. But not so. The Dutch treated me kindly but sent me back to Bella Vista on the same motor launch the Thornhursts had used to cross the river. For a moment as a strange sense of loss swept over me I could have sworn I got a whiff of the lady's perfume. It lingered in my nostrils as I stepped off the boat to be escorted away.

Guards placed me again in the blockhouse. Officials wanted to add another three years to my sentence. I had heard of a new regulation that said a man had to be away for twelve hours to be considered an escapee. I decided to fight the charges. Quick thinking told me I was absent from my work only ten hours. In a letter to Colonel Rousseau, Commandant of the colony at Bella Vista, I explained my situation. For several days I waited for a response. When it seemed I would hear not a word from him, I got a handwritten reply on fancy stationery. He had brought my situation before the Disciplinary Commission and had made it plain to them that under the new regulation I could not be given more time. Notwithstanding, they classified me as "Incorrigible" and gave me sixty additional days on Isle Royale. They could have sent me to solitary confinement on Saint Joseph, but in deference to the Commandant they settled on Royale. I protested the treatment — that was expected — but everyone in authority ignored the protest.

So I found myself once again in Cochineal, Bloodstained Barracks of hardened Incorrigibles, and watching my back. Sweating and stinking but snickering and scornful, the habitués wanted to know why I was with them again. I didn't want to get on their wrong side by saying it was none of their business, and so I told them. Even though I left out some important details, they laughed and laughed at what happened. I can hear their merriment even now. The scornful cackling of brutes burned my ears then and even now. I savored the tantalizing taste of freedom for ten hours. I remember the agonizing loss of it through no discernible fault of my own. Every detail of my next escape next escape would have to be carefully scrutinized. It would have to be meticulous to the last degree. I wouldn't be walking down a road with traffic to attract the attention of anybody.

Chapter Sixteen

My Raft Before My Eyes

In that tropical prison where men came to suffer and die a condemned man would do anything to get away, anything to taste freedom, and I was no exception. I told myself this fourth escape would have to be longer than just a few hours. It would have to be longer than a few days or months, even a few years, for I was not coming back. I was on record as one having endless determination and a penchant for giving officials trouble. So when I found myself once again in a notorious and deadly barracks, I had but one idea: to escape one more time and make it final. It quickly became an obsession.

I had to find a way to get out of Cochineal on Isle Royale and into the hospital only a few miles away. From the hospital the doctor might decide to send me back to the mainland as he did once before. So for several days I smoked cigarettes stoked with quinine supplied by a greedy guard charging me too much. When the doctor examined me, he found a nasty rash on my neck and face and a towering temperature. I thought that condition would get me admitted, but the shrewd doctor sensed the sham and sent me back to the Bloodstained Barracks. He was a very perceptive man and I despised him.

A day later I stuck a needle through my left cheek, rubbed fecal dirt into the wound, and got my face so inflamed and swollen I appeared to be on the brink of death. When the doctor came on his weekly visit and gave one look at my face, he decided it was not a sham and sent me immediately to the hospital. The first step in my scheme to escape had succeeded on the second try. I had managed to get away from the red box, the barracks of brutes, to a place of ease and safety. Sprawled on the white hospital bed in clean underwear after a long hot shower, I now pondered how to get away from the island and do it before the doctor pronounced me well.

Isle Royale was thirty miles from Bella Vista though only ten from Cayenne, the capital of French Guiana. Everyone knew the island lay in waters filled with sharks. From it very few inmates had escaped. Scores had tried only to die or be caught and given additional time. I would have to construct a shark-proof raft to get to the mainland, but out of what? The island had but one material used invariably by would-be escapees, bamboo. One desperate man had tried to escape on a large canvas bag filled with coconuts. A hundred yards offshore the water-soaked canvas became so heavy the bag began to sink. A feeding frenzy turned the blue-green water crimson. To escape with my skin intact, I would need something better than a sack or flimsy raft.

One afternoon my eye fell on a pile of boards in the corner of the ward, twenty of them stacked on the floor.

I knew at a glance they were used on the bed frames to support the mattresses. Made of hardwood and strong, they were six feet long, an inch thick, and seven inches wide. My raft was there before my eyes, the essential component waiting to be assembled. I would have to find a way to connect the boards tightly to form a unit that wouldn't fall apart. Under the pretext of changing the grimy boards on my otherwise clean bed, I was able to put aside just the ones I needed for the raft.

The problem now was how to get the planks out of the hospital and hidden in a safe place. As I thought about it I realized how difficult the task would be. The ward was on the second floor, and that made the job even more difficult. However, when I found out that beneath my bed was a room on the ground floor in which old mattresses were stored, I knew exactly what to do. I would drop the boards through a hole in the floor to the next level, but how would I make a hole in the thick floor? That too seemed a problem defying solution.

However, on examining the space around my bed, I found a square foot of soft wood caused by decay. Every night for a week I patiently dug away at the decay with the knife I always carried for protection. I made a hole just large enough for each board to slip through. Then working silently I dropped twelve selected boards through the hole. Landing on the mattresses, they made not a sound. I rolled up a blanket and a sheet and dropped them down the hole also. When everyone in the ward was asleep and the orderly was busy in the toilet, I raced downstairs and gathered up my boards. Within minutes I was in the yard running for the wall. I folded the blanket and threw it to the top as a cushion against the pointed pieces of glass, barbed wire, and nails. Then I made six bundles of two boards tied with strips of cloth from the sheet and threw them over. I climbed the wall where the blanket lay across the barbed wire and slithered down the other side with blanket in tow.

Working rapidly in half-light, I lashed the raft boards together with strips of strong blanket cloth. An hour later I was struggling against waves, trying to get the raft through the surf. Away from the building the night without a moon was very dark, and so I didn't have to worry about being seen. As I struggled in the surf, a big wave lifted the raft, and suddenly I was away from the shore and in the sea beyond the breakers. Away from the shore that far, the sea was calm.

Even so, I was in water where hungry sharks had grown fat on human bodies. I tied myself to the narrow raft so as not to be separated from it by rough weather should it come. I was daring night waters on a clumsy contraption in a sea filled with circling sharks, and I couldn't swim very well. One false move and I could drown or be torn apart and eaten. I looked back at the shore, thinking maybe I had made a mistake. All was dark except for one flickering light, and all was quiet except for the pounding surf. I took comfort knowing the night was calm.

The tropical morning came suddenly, stark and hot, and I knew as soon as a check was made the guards would find me missing from the hospital. They would question every convict in the ward but would get nothing from anyone. Not a soul had seen or heard me leave. Only one man had seen me dropping a board but wouldn't talk. A posse would comb the island looking for me but to no avail. Through binoculars they would scan the ocean and see nothing. The news of my escape would run like wildfire through the prison population. Luck was on my side. The storeroom that held the mattresses had a door but no lock.

Every person who heard the story would have his own theory as to how I made off. Then wild rumors would start. Word would come from a so-called official source that a battered raft had washed up on the rocky shore of Devil's Island. A wild rumor grossly untrue would claim that my corpse, partly eaten by sharks, had also washed ashore. As every man in the prison community discussed my daring attempt to escape, I became a celebrity. Yet the other side of the story reduced me to nothing more than carrion on a sun-washed beach. Even as I felt my throat becoming sore from the salt air and exposure, I laughed at that.

When day broke, the islands were out of sight and it appeared I was only a few miles from the mainland. My mouth was dry and the sun was already scorching my skin, but that was small change to pay for the cloak of freedom. All day long under a hot sun the raft drifted slowly toward shore. In late afternoon I was fewer than a hundred yards away. Then I noticed the contraption that was keeping me alive had come to a standstill. It was no longer moving toward shore but was beginning to spin a little and drift seaward. Low tide was setting in and taking me out! With oars I might have fought against the tide but had none. It took me so far out to sea that I lost sight of the mainland. I lay on my stomach sick and desperate. I wanted to curse the cruel gods who controlled the sea. I wanted to sob like a little child but couldn't even do that.

The next day, weak and thirsty but not feeling hunger, I drifted back to within a few hundred feet of the shore. Had I been able to swim well I might have made it to the beach in a few minutes, but dared not try. Despair set in to compete with desperation. I pried loose a board at the risk of having the raft fall apart and began to paddle. But the tide was pulling the heavy structure back to sea again, and I was too weak to fight against it. Once more I found myself far out on the open ocean and staring exhausted at the stars in a black sky.

Day came and I was sick with thirst but not hunger even though I knew I needed food. Also the sun had burned me torrid red. Four days passed and then seven. I grew dreadfully sick and slipped into delirium. I lost consciousness for a day or more and lay baking in the sun. Sharks bumped against the raft, trying to tip it over. They caused no harm, but I was slowly dying of exposure. When the raft came within a few yards of the coast one night, I thought I might wade ashore. I struggled to get off but was too weak. The tide, relentless and indifferent, swept me to sea.

On the seventh day, though I couldn't be sure of the count, a group of Indians fishing off the coast near Cayenne saw a white man burned severely by the tropical sun. He was lying unconscious on water-soaked boards about to fall apart. The fishermen silently approached and with their paddles drove away two circling sharks. They found the man half conscious but just barely alive. All they could get from him as they asked questions was a series of moans and a stare from bloodshot eyes. They placed the half-dead man in their canoe and brought him to their village north of Cayenne as a curiosity for the tribe to see.

Except for soldiers who came sometimes to their huts looking for escaped convicts, they tolerated no white persons in their village. They expected this sorely burned wretch to die before sundown. But an old Indian woman named Peche took it upon herself to care for the stricken man. She applied cooling wet cloths to his blistered skin, dribbled water down his parched throat, and fed him a mush of sea-turtle eggs to quell his hunger. In a few days Peche watched the stupefied man awaken. I found myself in the midst of strange surroundings but stronger.

A week later an Indian girl named Leywa helped me climb into a hut where six women and four men were living. She hung from the rafters a hammock wide enough for two people. I lay in the hammock for only a few minutes before she came and snuggled beside me, careful not to rub against my blistered but healing skin. Though I couldn't understand her language, she let me know her village had adopted me, and she was my keeper. I had come to them from the sea almost dead, but a woman of her tribe had made me strong again. That woman, her mother, had given her to me as my wife and keeper. She touched my face, ears, eyes, and mouth gently with both hands. Her fingers were long and tapered but rough with small cuts from the coral where daily she dived for oysters.

I kissed her full lips and she returned the kiss with a painful bite, her way of kissing. After my sunburn healed we found an empty hut, set up housekeeping, and lived as man and wife. Leywa cooked meals for me in earthen pots, and in time I gained the weight I had lost during my ordeal on the raft. As the days passed, we bathed each other in seawater. Then we lay in the shade of palm trees to dry off. Speaking softly Leywa began to teach me her language, pointing to an object and naming it. Strong again and understanding some of their language, I went hunting and fishing with the men of the tribe and earned their respect. The women liked me too; my savior Peche made sure of that,

I had escaped the brutal penal colony in French Guiana to struggle against natural forces and almost die. Then as miracles would happen I found myself living an idyllic existence with a beautiful young woman who called herself my wife. It was beyond belief, a wild dream of sorts, and yet existence that continued without pain for several months. Each day we would rise as the village came awake to build the fire that would cook our breakfast. I had to get used to the food she fed me. Often even the breakfast food had a fishy taste, but the beverage I drank with each meal was delicious. Later I learned my comrades depended on the sea for most of their food. Also they had wild and cultivated fruit.

The chief of the village was a young man who went by the name Owahu. He had acquired the position of leadership after the death of his father. Circumstance and tradition made him a hunter and a warrior. I was told the people of the village tried to live their lives in peace in spite of a tribe to the southwest who sometimes made raids upon them. So even though each day seemed pleasant with children playing happily in the big and open common ground, a lookout was always on duty. Owahu told me, with Leywa translating, that the tribe to the south was the bane of their existence. He and his tribe wanted to live in peace. His enemies wanted the excitement of battle. They had killed men and carried away women. It saddened me to hear this story. It confirmed in my thoughts a fact I didn't want to believe: no place on Earth can ever be perfect.

We made love and Leywa found herself pregnant. I could see how proud she was to be carrying my baby. Her younger sister grew jealous on seeing her swollen belly and wanted the same. One day Leywa placed her nude sister next to me on the beach and waited for natural impulses to take over. I made it known to her in the native words she had taught me that I was unwilling to have her sister as a sexual partner. To hear that made her joyous, for she was thinking because she was no longer slender I was losing interest. With all the native words at my command, I assured her that pregnancy made her even more beautiful.

She liked to hear that and for a time she was very happy. Then one day as the rain poured down in torrents, invincible and total grief struck my lady down. Soldiers on the prowl barged into her settlement with rifles ready and hauled her husband away. They didn't allow me to say goodbye to her, and they would not allow her to come near me. They tied my hands together, put a rope in them, and made me trot behind their vehicle when we reached it on the road. In good physical condition, I was able to trot more than a mile before becoming winded and tired. I called out for them to stop. They didn't. When they saw me fall to my knees and then to my belly, they stopped, placed me in their truck, and drove onward. I never saw Leywa or the baby I fathered ever again.

Two days later I was back in prison. Two weeks later I was again on the island of Saint Joseph in soul-shattering solitary confinement. Three additional years had been added to my sentence. Eighteen months were to be served in the damp and darkness and total isolation of a solitary cell. There I would eat a handful of cockroaches, patiently collected each day, to supplement my tiny daily ration of bread and water. My fourth attempt to escape had failed miserably. How many more times would I run away only to be caught? How many more years would be added to my sentence? How many more days or weeks would I manage to live?

I thought of my loving wife and her gentle relatives and wanted to return to her village, but it never happened. Even worse, I didn't learn anything about the incipient life within her that we had created. When the soldiers wrested me away from her, she wept with her head low and between her knees. Her shoulders trembled, and I ran to comfort her. A soldier threw himself against me and knocked me down. I shook the dirt from my clothing and tried again. Two of them knocked me to the dirt again and wouldn't let me go near her. The fracas had become almost a game for them. They hit me with their rifle butts, made crude jokes in gibberish I couldn't understand, and laughed at my pain like hyenas. The cruel laughter I did understand.

Later on I came to terms with what happened and began to realize apart from the violence of it that my leaving was probably for the best. I rather liked living in that pleasant Indian village with Leywa and all her relatives, but I doubt I could have remained there longer. All the time I was a condemned man I had a hankering for civilization and the city. I sometimes thought of city lights when walking with Leywa on the beach in moonlight. From the time the pale French judge pounded his gavel to pronounce sentence, I firmly believed I would return some day to a big city. I would not remain in exile forever. On Isle Royale I often sat on the rocky shore for hours to look across the water and dream of New York, Chicago, Hong Kong, Singapore, London but never Paris. I knew I would never return to Paris, but living in another city wasn't impossible. It was the dream that sustained me.

Chapter Seventeen
Corrupt Cayenne

During my long isolation on Isle Saint Joseph, I bribed a guard to let me write a letter to the Governor of French Guiana. Politely I explained to his Excellency that I was very sick and suffering and would soon die in solitary confinement if I couldn't secure help from some humane person in authority. My letter must have touched a sympathetic chord because soon afterwards he persuaded officials on Saint Joseph to transfer me to the penitentiary at Cayenne. Within a week, wheezing and coughing, I was again on the mainland and seeing the capital city for the first time. It wasn't much to look at because to see the town beyond its multi-colored buildings, red rooftops, and lush vegetation, was to see human misery on every level one can imagine.

When I was there it was the capital of a colony without colonists. Few people wanted to establish themselves and their families in a place peopled mainly by unpredictable convicts. Hungry and bedraggled, they roamed the streets like demented phantoms or lost souls. The so-called "liberated convicts," had served their sentences and were free of prison jurisdiction, but a heinous French law demanded they remain in Guiana for the same number of years as their sentence. They were pariahs with no support from any person or any organization, and no visible way to make a living. How they managed to live from day to day was a puzzle for the entire town. Every year a fair number would try to escape to another country. Trained dogs would track them down, and the guards would bring them back to serve more time in prison.

In those days not a single street in the entire city was paved. The main street with a few struggling shops was sprayed twice a month with used motor oil. When pedestrians, would-be customers, tracked oily dirt into their shops, the merchants complained, but nothing was done about it. Nothing could be done about it. Without the oil, a thick layer of dust would have settled on all surfaces, and no customer would buy dusty merchandise. All other streets were raw and muddy when it rained and dusty soon afterwards. The rain poured frequently from the skies, but the tropical sun made a street dusty within hours. On the streets leading away from Main Street were brightly painted little houses built to stand very close to one another. Here and there were finer houses inhabited by people of means: prison administrators and businessmen.

The town stretched along the seashore for six or seven miles and was surrounded by sea and rain forest. Pelted by tropical rainfall just about every day of the year, it was equatorial and hot. Flowering plants were abundant, but tall weeds and grass choked any street not tended by convicts. Stagnant water lay in ditches to breed gigantic mosquitoes. Buildings were made of wood, mainly one story in height, and painted whatever colors that happened to be available. In a town where fresh water ran through the streets with every downpour, households had potable water only twice a day. The water works was primitive at best, electricity scarce and unreliable. Convicts ran the machinery of the plant and were known to cut the power to throw the town in darkness when an inmate willing to pay them money tried to escape.

Believe it or not, sweltering Cayenne as late as the 1930s had no modern sewers. Collecting sewage for disposal in a creek that emptied into the ocean was a job done by convicts at night. They went through the town on wagons drawn by oxen. They crawled under the houses, took away the full buckets of waste, and replaced them with empty buckets. To fleece their pockets with extra coin, they employed a simple scam. Regulations called for the buckets not to be entirely full, the aim being not to soil the carrier with human waste. But dropping a heavy stone into the bucket filled it to the top. People in the house were awakened and told the bucket was too full to be moved. The man of the house would have to pay extra to have it taken away. I shuddered to think the job had to be worse than any other one could imagine. Yet I soon discovered that hauling away the sewage was eagerly sought after. Numerous inmates wanted the job. Practicing the scam, one could earn ten francs or more in a single night. Any job that allowed a man to make a little money was viewed as a good one.

Convicts were in charge of garbage collection and disposal. Every other morning two trucks with three men on each truck went through the town to pick up the trash left in front of houses. Their eyes were carefully trained on every item they tossed into the truck. While they didn't expect to find treasure in the trash, often they saw value in what others threw away. Sometimes they found a lamp, table, or chair that could be repaired. Those items went to a penitentiary workshop where they were refurbished and sold to the owners of shops on Main Street. The shopkeepers in turn resold the items to the public.

One day right after a shower, the scavenger convicts picked up an old piano on the curbside. It was severely out of tune and missing some keys, but they managed to sell it to a Chinese trader at a good price. He restored the piano, giving it a coat of varnish and a gleaming keyboard. A friend of the shopkeeper was able to tune it to make tolerable music. When a city employee saw it one day in his shop and was amazed at the low price, the trader soon afterwards sold the piano at a profit to the city. The convict collectors also got a good return for an old washing machine and trombone. Clever wheeling and dealing was the order of the day in Cayenne. Enterprising men made enough money for small luxuries they bought from guards. Garbage was dropped in a tributary that ran into the ocean. Ebb tides carried it into the sea.

The population of Cayenne when I was there was far

less than it is today. The town had only a few thousand people, and of those more than a third were convicts. Half of them were liberated convicts living in exile. The other half were condemned men who had committed crimes ranging from petty theft to murder. They mingled with citizens of the town when not at work on assigned jobs but had no say in the way the town was run. Liberated convicts had no work at all unless they were lucky enough to pick up a handyman job here and there. They were so-called free men but had no social or political standing and no homes in the city. They were compelled to live on the outskirts near the jungle. In some ways the condemned prisoners were better off. They had at least a roof over their heads when attempting to sleep at night.

The civilian population was made up of four classes. Political and prison officials, exclusively white, were at the top of the social ladder. They lived well on comfortable incomes in houses often with servants. They enjoyed status and social prestige and a good deal of power. Their women were invariably accompanied by a servant when in public. Their children were often tutored at home, for Cayenne had only two public schools. A few white merchants were placed under the officials even though many of them were poor and struggling. The merchants had the right to hold political office, and some sat on the City Council.

Below the white merchants were the Chinese merchants, larger in number and often more industrious.

They operated most of the shops on Main Street, including the town laundry. They were responsible for importing goods consumed by the citizens of the town. But they had little say in the way the town was run. On the lowest rung of the ladder were the native blacks, largest in number and seen everywhere. The men scratched out a living on small farms, labored at odd jobs in the town, worked as carpenters for the one construction company in town, or did no work at all. Their women worked as servants in the homes of wealthy officials. Although their way of life was thought to be more difficult than that of others in Cayenne, most black citizens seemed to be satisfied with their condition.

A few Chinese merchants lived better than some officials. One man in the town owned a laundry, a Chinese restaurant, a filling station, and a trucking company. All these were enterprises that made him rich. He lived outside Cayenne on two hundred acres close to the sea. His large house was impressive as were his stables. He bought and sold horses, thoroughbred horses, for additional income and could be seen riding a splendid white horse as he inspected acres of banana growth. He was one of the few people in Cayenne who owned a late-model car. Some thugs in the town envied his wealth, and spoke of breaking into his house, but it never happened. His property was well protected.

In the bustling market down by the waterfront all classes merged into one. There in the early morning people of every stripe mingled in a chatty crowd. I was not able to see or be a part of this scene until I was given leave to walk the streets of Cayenne as a prisoner. Then I went there every morning to enjoy the noisy spectacle. Shapely black women oozing sexuality from every pore stood in groups chatting, laughing, and swaying their hips. Free convicts wandered among the booths looking for a bargain and often snatching a vegetable or fruit when the vendor wasn't looking. Condemned convicts in their signature straw hats and prison garb — I was one of these — were there to buy something tasty to eat with their prison ration. A few white women could be seen in the crowd, some with their maids and others with a male escort.

Also I noticed several well-fed cooks in civilian clothes but wearing the convict's wide straw hat and customary sandals. Later I learned they were the cooks of important officials. One of those before he got into trouble had been a celebrated chef in the kitchen of a famous Parisian café. Another came to French Guiana as a political prisoner and spent two years on Devil's Island before being enlisted in the service of the lieutenant governor. A convicted man who could prepare tasty, well-cooked meals was sought after by officials regardless of his crime.

The men who pretended to be trained cooks, and there were many, were quickly found out and punished. A good example was a Corsican who tried to pass as an Italian chef. He had studied the culinary arts in school before getting into trouble. Prison brought an abrupt end to his studies, and in prison he had no chance to gain experience as a cook. Yet he applied for a job, claiming wide experience, in the house of a leading judge. In less than a week he proved a severe disappointment and was fired. He could have been sentenced to hard labor for impersonation. But the judge's little daughter, who liked the Corsican because he was funny, persuaded him not to file charges.

I was surprised to see convicts at liberty to blend in with the town's population anywhere they chose. The penitentiary on the shore with its back to the rain forest and other parts against the sea had no walls, only a tall metal fence with gates left open after 0700. So the inmates had free run of the town during daylight of every day. However, most of them answered to roll call and spent their nights in the prison. They were required to spend several hours each day on a work gang in or near the prison but worked in shifts. Some with special privileges didn't return to their cells at night. They slept in the houses of their employers and enjoyed a vast amount of liberty for prisoners.

Those employed often had plenty of time on their hands and money to spend. The storekeepers were told not to sell alcohol to prisoners, and yet each day those who could afford it had glasses of rum or wine with Cantonese food in a Chinese restaurant. On occasion, with special permission, employed inmates threw parties in the town square. Tables were loaded with food to be eaten by less fortunate convicts, including the poor men who called themselves liberated. Prisoner squads cleaned up when the party was over. At one time Cayenne had numerous strong slaves to do the dirty work their masters wouldn't do. In time the slaves were freed and the penal colony was established. So when I was there in the 1930s, a reversal of fortune had taken place. Convicts did the dirty work and a few descendants of slaves had good jobs that allowed for a good life. Later these same people held key administrative jobs.

I couldn't believe inmates in the penal colony of French Guiana had the liberty and the means to throw a fantastic party in a public square. And yet they did. Although I was never present to see it, they did it not once but many times. Everything in lawless and poverty-bitten Cayenne was to my way of thinking unbelievable, but in time I came to accept the things I saw. I recall an old-timer whose sole pleasure was narrating a good story. His name was Albert Fein, and he wore a white beard that covered most of his face. In a gravelly but clear voice he told me of an incident I found hard to believe but worth recording here.

Six miles from shore on a rock with no vegetation stood a beacon tended by convicts. Its purpose was to guide ships into the harbor at night. By day its bell emitted a clang that could be heard for miles, and the sound often disturbed the three men who lived in a hut near it. Then one day one of them began to scream that he was losing his hearing and also his sight. Fearing that the man was either very sick or going mad, his comrades quickly got him returned to shore to be examined by a doctor. A day later the man died of a fever and a brain aneurysm. Formal regulations called for replacing the essential worker immediately, but that was never done. A week later the two convicts remaining on the rock grew worried when the launch didn't bring them food supplies.

So they covered the white light with red cellophane to raise the distress signal. They expected those on shore to respond without delay, but the light shone red the next night and again the next. Anxiously they watched and waited for the launch to put out from shore, but it didn't move. After several days they had nothing to eat. In desperation they had to scrape shellfish from rocks. Several more days and nights went by, and the beacon ran out of fuel. That meant a main navigation light along the coast was dead and shrouded in darkness. Three more days passed and still the port launch was nowhere in sight. For three nights an important light no longer appeared on the sea. Two weeks went by and the boat at last came to the rock. It approached to within hailing distance of the famished men but turned back in a stormy sea. The men on board felt their boat would hit the rocks if they tried to make fast to a dock that was already falling apart.

Knowing they had been left to die, the two stranded men stood on the rocky shore and watched the launch grow smaller and smaller. Now their concern was to save themselves any way they could. Rather than die on the rock, although one of them couldn't swim, they decided to dismantle the hut and make a raft of its wood. They waited all day for the sea to grow calmer. When night came, they pushed off into a wild surf that almost flipped their raft. After struggling for hours in angry waves and shark-infested water, they reached the mainland. Half naked and bitten bloody by mosquitoes, they sprawled in a heap on the beach and slept through the night.

As day began they set off through the jungle and finally reached a settlement of soldiers. The soldiers transported them to Cayenne. One might expect they were celebrated for their bravery and persistence, but not so. They were arrested and sentenced for deserting their post. But the story doesn't end there. In a room in the hospital at Cayenne I saw five large bottles on a shelf. In them, preserved in clear alcohol, were the heads of five executed criminals. I looked at the heads closely. After the guillotine blade cleanly sliced the neck, the hair continued to grow. The faces of three grotesque heads had readable expressions and stubby beards. The bulging eyes of two were wide-open and staring back at me. I saw a glint in the eye of one face but no sign of pain or anguish. Passing a mirror as I left that room of horror, I couldn't help but see plenty of anguish on my own face.

The third head belonged to none other than one of the brave light keepers. In a rage after surviving the ordeal of rock, sea, and jungle, he had strangled a guard who had taunted him. After a month in solitary confinement, he was brought before the Tribunal of Justice. Less than a week later the blade of the guillotine severed his head. The public, some with children, attended the spectacle. Surely some saw the heads as symbols of the inhumanity that pervaded every nook and cranny of the prison in French Guiana. I couldn't believe and cannot believe even now how a civilized nation could have condoned and supported so barbarous a system as that prison.

Once more the words of the Scottish poet came back to haunt me: *"Man's inhumanity to man makes thousands mourn!"* That was presented as unequivocal fact, a universal certainty not to be questioned by the wisest among us. But have thousands ever mourned the inhumanity of man? Millions have surely suffered injustice, cruelty, and the general barbarity of those who for centuries have called themselves leaders of men. But has any person, unless caught in the crossfire, ever mourned the maltreatment of people he doesn't know? Perhaps the masses have never cared about what happens to unknown persons. If the disaster doesn't strike them or their loved ones down, they mourn not. The creature we call human is surely a work in progress.

Chapter Eighteen
A Victim of Circumstance

Most of the condemned men in French Guiana had but one consuming desire — to escape as soon as they could. Within days I learned of four ways to escape: 1. through the unforgiving jungle; 2. across the river to hostile Dutch Guiana; 3. a passenger or stowaway on a Brazilian pirate's boat; and 4. by sea in a canoe or sailboat. Escape through the jungle into Brazil was difficult and deadly. An attempt by way of Dutch Guiana was easier, but Dutch authorities soon began to send escapees back for more prison time. To brave it as a stowaway on a vessel sailed by pirates was a big gamble. The pirates were known to abuse luckless stowaways and even throw them overboard to drown or become shark food. Going as a paid passenger was safer, of course, but only if a runaway could afford the exorbitant fee. Even then he had only a fifty-fifty chance of making it to his destination alive. Escape by sea was also risky. Yet it offered the best chance to convicts strong enough to endure the ordeal and foolish enough to try it. All would-be escapees knew fleeing was a gamble.

At the time I began to think of my next escape, I had served more than six years in French Guiana and knew how the penal colony worked. In a few more years with good behavior I could have become a free man. I record "free man" for lack of a better term. Because of a draconian law passed by French sages in all their wisdom, I would never be free. The cruel law demanded I live the remainder of my days in that tropical hell (unless I lived to become very old). Finding that gravely unacceptable, I began to think about escaping by sea. I asked around if anyone bent on escape knew how to navigate a boat but had no luck.

That was no deterrence because I had the money to embark as a passenger on a coastal ship moving southward. In Brazil I would be able to get on a mail boat for farther passage but would need a passport. I had heard that certain people in Cayenne had the equipment to make fake passports and knew exactly how to perform the procedure. What I didn't know was how secretive were the men engaged in the lucrative enterprise. A friend said a man called Raoul had made fake passports for two escapees, and they looked really good. Raoul was an old ex-convict working in an office with a printer, and he charged me 100 francs for a passport. Also he made up false papers that looked genuine to show I had once been a convict but was now a free man.

The ship was scheduled to leave on a Wednesday afternoon, and I had everything ready by Monday. At the appointed time I would leave my work gang, dress in civilian clothes bought in secret from a Chinese trader, and walk casually up the gangplank and board. Later I heard a problem with the engine would cause the ship to be delayed until the next day. That troubled me. It meant I might have to follow a different timeline that could make prison officials suspicious. Under supervision, as every prisoner knew, one had to be in the right place at the right time all the time. Otherwise an order might decree a severe penalty.

I was facing a predicament, a serious problem, but thought it might be resolved in the end. If a gendarme didn't arrest me moments before the ship sailed, I would gain freedom down the line. At the fishing village on the Brazilian border where the ship was scheduled to land, only one policeman would glance at my papers and find them in order. My plan would work, I told myself, and to falter would be to lose everything. The only wrinkle in all I had planned was the change in the ship's departure time. Although apprehensive, I had to go forward anyway. After all the preparation, I couldn't make changes at the eleventh hour.

Wednesday afternoon near four o'clock I left my street gang as we worked at pulling up weeds beside the road. I told the guard I was dying of thirst and had to find something cool to drink. He pointed to a nearby gas station and said I could go there for water. I wouldn't have to return because our work was done for the day. I ambled off in that direction but circled back and went to the hut of my friend Charles, a liberated convict. There I had stowed my civilian clothes and there I spent the night too restless to sleep. As soon as first light, I sent Charles to the pier to find out the exact time the ship would sail. I paced the floor and waited. He seemed to be gone for hours. Then suddenly returned, he advised me to get to the ship right away. It would be leaving at eight o'clock.

"Go now," he advised, "before the streets become full of guards. You know as soon as breakfast is over they scram into the streets. And the people of this town, they fill the streets early every morning to escape the blazing heat that comes before noon."

I got dressed in a clean shirt, a white suit, a good pair of shoes with dark blue socks, and a pith helmet. Wearing sunglasses, I crossed the town with Charles in tow and arrived at the pier. Waterfront activity was already buzzing, and the morning seemed quite normal. We stood at the gate. Beyond it was the long and narrow pier. At the end of it sat an impressive ship, her bow pointed southward. I shook my comrade's hand warmly, turned on my heel, and strolled nonchalantly past the gendarme at the gate. He glanced at me and nodded.

Beyond him my knees seemed to buckle under excitement. I was on the pier, my runway to freedom, approaching the ship resting languidly in the morning sun. I managed to put down all feeling and draw from within a pervasive calm. Though I walked briskly, the ship seemed far away and the long pier endless. Then of a sudden almost trotting I was mounting the gangplank.

On the ship's deck I casually presented my ticket. A smiling steward in uniform directed me to my cabin.

I breathed a sigh of relief when the steward closed the door and left me alone. Mentally I went through all the details of my escape to see if anything was missing. Everything seemed in place. This time I would be absolutely acquiring the freedom I had dreamed of for so long. I stood behind my locked door and chortled with joy.

"It worked!" I said to myself. *"I did it, by god, I did it!"* And speaking in my native tongue, I muttered out loud, "Vive la liberté! Vive la vie!"

I had risked everything, life and limb as they say, five times. I was caught four times but not the fifth. This time the world was my oyster; fickle Lady Luck was finally on my side.

Moments later I began to ask why the ship wasn't already moving. I looked through the porthole and saw only little eddies of water glinting in the sunlight. If the ship had been moving, I would have seen a bow wave rushing by and turbulence in the turgid water. I grew nervous. Maybe somehow prison authorities had found out what I had done, knew I was on board, and were delaying departure. Then from on deck came a blast from the ship's horn, the signal that her mooring lines were being cast off. Beside myself with excitement, I found a secluded spot on deck to watch the departure and the boarding of late passengers. Again the horn sounded. In minutes the ship would be free of the pier, and I would be free of French Guiana. A feeling of intense joy welled up inside me, an emotion I had not felt in many years.

Standing there and looking down at the long pier, my gaze fastened on a gendarme running at full speed toward the ship. He flew up the gangplank, saluted the ship's officer at the top, and rapidly began asking questions of the steward. Winded and breathing hard, gesticulating, and speaking loudly. I saw him point to a piece of paper he held in his hand, and I heard him ask if a man named Raoul had come on board. I couldn't believe my ears! Raoul was the name of the convict who had made my escape possible. Somehow his name had gotten on the passenger list instead of mine! When they ran below to check my cabin, I knew it was time to make myself scarce. In seconds, or so it seemed, I was down the gangplank and on the pier. Trying not to attract attention, I walked as fast as I could. Again the pier seemed endless, and the little gate stood miles away. Suddenly I heard someone call out to me, a polite but urgent "M'sieur!" I pretended not to hear and kept walking.

I heard rapid footsteps behind me and glanced over my shoulder. A slender man in uniform, the gendarme, was catching up with me. He was suddenly walking beside me and asking me to slow down.

"Where do you think you're going, sir?" he cried, huffing and trying to catch his breath. "And why so fast?"

"To the town before the ship departs," I replied as calmly as I could.

"But you are leaving the ship," he said, gasping. "Why?"

"I forgot something important and have to go back and get it. I must hurry, or the ship will leave without me. That explains why I'm walking so fast. Wouldn't you be doing the same?"

As a competent officer doing his duty, he asked to see my papers. He glanced at them and saw the name Raoul.

"Oh! You are not Raoul!" he exclaimed. "I arrested Raoul yesterday. He was dead drunk and stumbling down the street. We put him in a cell overnight. I myself put him behind bars. What exactly is this?"

In a moment I realized what had happened. That old sot Raoul had bought a pint of alcohol with the money I had given him, had stumbled away from his hut, and got himself arrested. Now the same officer was about to arrest me! I sought for an opening.

"Oh, let me explain, it's simple. It so happens Raoul is my name also. I have the same name, but I'm obviously not the gentleman you arrested yesterday for public intoxication. Did you let him go or is he still in jail?"

"He was in jail to sleep it off. Released him early this morning."

The ruse might have worked. But when he looked at

the full name on my papers, he smelled something fishy. Raoul Bouchard was the full name on the passenger list and on my papers. I couldn't possibly have the same last name as the old drunk in custody. That would be too much a coincidence. At the police station I was quickly identified and hustled to the penitentiary. Once more the fates had turned against me. I had come so close, so very close, to escaping French Guiana forever only to have circumstance wallop me hard.

Some mental quirk had driven Raoul to put his own name on my papers instead of mine. Then drunk from rum bought with the money I paid him for the papers, he had run into this particular gendarme and got thrown in jail. On a desk in the jail, for reasons no one could explain, was the ship's passenger list. On it was Raoul's name readily seen, and the policeman concluded the man he had just released had plans to escape the colony. When he ran out to the ship as fast as his legs would carry him, he was there to arrest Raoul Bouchard. Instead he caught me. I had only myself to blame. If I had chosen another forger to process my phony papers, maybe nothing of the kind would have happened.

"Oh my! What a tangled web we weave when first we practice to deceive," wrote a disgruntled poet, lover, or politician some years ago. Despondent and suffering the sting of another failure, I was in no mood to disagree. I had tried to deceive, no defense whatever, and had become a victim of circumstance. I was never a child of fortune, never a friend of fate. During all the years of my youth that inimitable force dogged my footsteps and was doing so when I hoped with all my heart and soul and sinew that all would go well. Simply put, I was grievously unlucky. Fate, or whatever one calls it, struck me down moments before I was to leave Guiana. If the ship had sailed as shown in the printed schedule, my fifth attempt to escape would have succeeded. If old drunken and dissolute Raoul had put my name on the papers instead of his own, who knows what might have happened? Oh, well. C'est la vie!

Chapter Nineteen

The New Governor

I wanted to avoid several years added to my sentence, and yet I knew any chance of that was slim. The police had found my false passport and had caught me in the act of using it. They looked at other papers in my possession and claimed I was trying to escape with false identification. It meant I would go on trial again and could receive a harsh sentence of several months in solitary confinement plus three years added to my sentence. But when I was summoned to court on Isle Royale a month later, the esteemed Tribunal added only two years and meted out no solitary confinement. For once a person with influence gave me a break. My reputation as a literate man had reached the new Governor who asked me to write an essay describing alleged abuses in the prison. I had sent him some of my work before the trial, and those seven pages he must have read. He most certainly brought about the lesser sentence. By his direction, I prepared to leave the island shortly afterwards.

When I departed Royale to return to Cayenne, I was in good health. An earlier attack of dysentery was gone. I had a canvas bag stuffed with clean clothes, toilet articles, and a stash of money. The boat reached the mainland in late afternoon. I entered the penitentiary and found most of the convicts I had known when there earlier. We had a little party to celebrate my returning from the islands so soon. We drank pints of rum as we played cards. I was glad to be a prisoner in Cayenne where most condemned men had more freedom when compared to Bella Vista or the offshore islands. But I worried when the chief guard told me the Commandant wanted to see me. I asked him why but got no answer. So thinking I might be in serious trouble, I walked without a guard across town to his office. He greeted me affably almost as if we were equals and friends, but I knew better.

He wanted to ask me why the Governor would want to see me. Why would a man of high rank specifically ask for a lowly convict? He didn't use those words exactly, but what he said meant the same. Moreover, he couldn't high the condescending tone that characterized the man. As I stood to leave his office, he said if I behaved myself he would try to find a good job for me in Cayenne. It would be my reward if I gave up trying to escape. In the meantime I was to go to Government House to be interviewed by the new Governor. He didn't know why the Governor wanted to see me in person, and neither did I.

Walking rapidly in the tropical heat, I got to his residence wet with perspiration. It could have been the dank humidity causing me to sweat, but excitement was a factor too. The doorman, clad in red and white and not much older than twelve, required me to wait at the entrance. After a few minutes that seemed more like half an hour, he returned and said the Governor was ready to see me. I climbed the long stairway, mopping my face with a handkerchief to look my best. The boy led me down a narrow hallway to an office with the door ajar.

Outside in the hall was a cushioned bench where I sat and waited another fifteen minutes. Slowly I managed to calm myself by thinking the Governor liked what I had sent him and perhaps wanted more. Then standing at attention and dramatizing his patter with a snappy salute, the boy announced in high-pitched cadence that I might go inside the chamber. I wasn't sure of the protocol governing my behavior, and so I quickly rose from the bench and stood in the doorway.

"Come in, Bonheur!" a man almost hidden behind a huge desk called out. I could barely see the flecked gray hair on the top of his head.

I dropped my straw hat on the bench and sidled into the well-appointed office, trying to be as unobtrusive as possible. The Governor was shuffling papers on his desk and didn't look at me immediately. The office smelled of lavender and was very quiet.

"Have a seat, Bonheur! Make yourself comfortable. Be with you in a minute," he said in a mellow voice, speaking educated French.

The gentleman behind the desk was in his middle or

late fifties. His shoulders were square, his neck strong, and his lined face rugged. As for weight and height, he was even smaller than me. His greenish-gray eyes depicted high intelligence but appeared too small for features accenting a large mouth and strong jaw. His hair, perhaps reddish-brown in youth, was already gray. His hands were clean and capable. I looked him over as he did me and instantly liked the man. Maybe I liked him because he was a little guy who had made it big in the world. He pushed the desk papers aside, filled his meerschaum pipe with tobacco, sat back in his chair, and began to puff on the pipe. Even before he spoke he impressed me as a man of intellect, will, and energy.

"I wish to thank you for that interesting document you sent me from the islands," he said cordially. "Your style is honest and clear and you write with frankness. You seem to have a good ability to see things in this place as they really are, and that's important. How long will it take for you to complete your sentence?"

"Only a few years now, your Excellency," I stammered. "Not more than another four or five if memory serves me right. "

Many times before falling asleep I had counted the years, months, days and even the hours that would bring me to the end of my sentence. But not used to being in the company of a man highly placed, I was too nervous to remember details exactly. He saw my discomfort and tried to put me at ease, asking another question.

"I see by your record that you've tried to escape *five times*. Are you planning another any time soon?"

He chortled as he said this and puffed on his pipe. I could see a glint in those gray-green eyes as he puffed vigorously. It was a satirical glint mellowed with amusement. Or so I thought so. I answered quickly.

"Oh no, sir. No sir! No, your Excellency, I won't be trying to escape again. I've learned my lesson after all the failures. I'm done trying."

I knew I was lying and I believe he knew it too. But he was a kind and generous man willing to give me the benefit of the doubt.

He shuffled the papers on his desk as if looking for something. I waited patiently for the man to speak. Pausing to look at me, he asked, "What kind of work can you do, Bonheur?"

"I can do just about anything you assign me to do, Excellency. I'm not highly educated as you must know from reading my stuff, but I try. I was a bookkeeper on Isle Royale but got into trouble. In Bella Vista on the mainland I worked as a bookkeeper without pay."

"Yes, I can see by your record the kind of trouble you fell into on Isle Royale, and the punishment on Isle Saint Joseph could have been worse. You have to guard against that sort of thing, Bonheur. The girl could have her little adventure and receive only a slap on the wrist. Not so with you. It could have been a deadly game for you."

"I understand, sir. It won't happen again, sir. It can't happen again. The girl is now gone to France to finish her education."

"Good! That takes you away from temptation. Now about the job. I think maybe you'd like working on the waterfront. You will keep track of the supply ships that come and go. No work as a stevedore, no heavy lifting mind you, just a bookkeeping job with pay."

It wasn't the kind of job I could really like but tolerable. I worked with an old convict named Sidney Bechet, a man who had been in prison so long he couldn't remember being free at any time during his adult life. The one thing that kept him alive and breathing was a slim hope that in time he would find a way to escape oppressive Guiana and die a free man. Getting away was the only thing on his mind, the only subject he could talk about as we entered figures into ledgers.

I had been on the job only three weeks or so when he came to me in the middle of the night all excited.

"Maurice! Wake up! Wake up, goddamn it! Let's go! You coming?"

"Coming where?" I grumped.

I was sleeping soundly and suddenly the silly man was shaking me by the shoulder and asking questions I didn't remotely understand.

"With me and Bruno to free living! Two men left a sailboat at the dock, and Bruno knows how to sail it!

She's a sweet little vessel just sitting there waiting for us! Too good to pass up, Buddy Boy! We're ready go! More than ready! So hop to it, ol' buddy, and come with us." Bechet's tired old eyes blazed with excitement.

"I can't come with you," I said as clearly as I could. "The Governor was good to me. I made a promise. I promised I wouldn't try to escape."

"Have it your way!" old Bechet replied. "It's your choice, Buddy! But me and Bruno are gonna make a run for it. We gonna go! When they question you, just say we was gone when you woke up."

I watched them gather water in some empty cans and push off in the darkness. A mild breeze was stirring and the little sailboat caught it and moved quickly away into the night. I wanted to be with them in that boat. It wasn't big but looked sturdy and seaworthy. But I had said I wouldn't try to escape to a man who had treated me kindly. For the first time in many years an official had asked me a question expecting me to reply truthfully. All the others were certain they would get from me a string of lies. The new Governor was anything but gullible. He knew I would seize any opportunity to get out of Guiana. Nonetheless, he had spoken to me almost as an equal and I felt beholden to him.

Daybreak came suddenly near half past five. With very little dawn, the tropic sun rose fast with heat that burnt like a poker. The waterfront quickly became busy with commerce. Then near 0700 the owner found his sailboat missing and set going a hullabaloo. He complained to the harbormaster who had already heard that two waterfront convicts were missing. Assuming the two had stolen the boat, he sent a high-speed powerboat in hot pursuit. Three hours later the men in the speedboat, armed with high-powered rifles, came back claiming they had not seen any sign of the sailboat. How they could have missed it puzzled me. The day was bright and clear, and the men couldn't have sailed far offshore. The boat was white on a blue sea, and they missed it?

An Inquiry was held to look into the matter, but nothing came of it. Some of us believed the men in pursuit murdered Sidney and his friend and sank their boat. If so, Bechet died a free man. Because I was Bechet's partner on the waterfront, investigators assumed I knew all about the escapade. Within days I was summoned to be questioned by a panel of three administrative officials. They asked a horde of questions I tried to answer honestly. I gave them the full truth as far as my knowledge went. Bechet had come to me in the middle of the night asking if I wanted to make a run for it in a small sailboat left at the dock. His friend Bruno had agreed to navigate, he said. Half asleep, I mumbled I wouldn't be going with them. I went back to sleep and when I woke up the two men were gone. The owner discovered his boat was missing, raised a hue and cry, and a powerboat was launched to find the stolen sailboat and bring it back. The officials let me go. That ended the Inquiry.

No one ever knew whether Bechet and Bruno lived to gain freedom. No committee was established to investigate the incident further. Not a single person asked why the men in the speedboat couldn't find a little white sailboat in good weather moving slowly in near-calm water. The owner of the sailboat demanded compensation for his loss but got nothing but trouble. Every official he talked to referred him to another official until he finally gave up, came to terms with his loss, and went home to Bella Vista.

For another month I did the job of two men instead of one. Ships came and went, and dutifully I kept track of them. Several hours each day I recorded their movements in my ledgers. I tried as best I could to be meticulous and accurate. The auditors liked my work and put in a good word for me with their superiors. Somehow their report got to the Governor, who read it with interest. Believing I was qualified for work more challenging, he used his influence to get me a job I came to like more than any I ever had. It was a job that gave me more than a birds-eye view of French Guiana's prison system. I saw it from the inside.

At a time when things were looking up for me, I wondered whether Bechet and Bruno after many years of trying had finally escaped. What happened to those two men and their stolen sailboat made for rumor and remained a mystery. Later, looking at penitentiary records in my new job, I was not able to find even one mention of their names. They had made a desperate run for freedom on the deep blue sea in a small craft and were never heard from again. All knowledge of their existence simply evaporated. I believed then as I do now that the two lost their lives before their adventure began. They were murdered.

Chapter Twenty

"Take This Form and Fill It"

For decades the records of the French Guiana penal colony existed in miserable disorder. Papers and important documents were crammed in desk drawers and cardboard boxes that went into corners and closets, nooks and crannies. The filing system was broken. It was impossible to find anything without searching for it all day. The messy records irked the new Governor, and he thought I might be the one to bring order out of chaos. So with his characteristic energy he ordered the chief guard to release me from my waterfront job and send me to Government House. I need not tell you I went there with alacrity. That same afternoon I began to sift through hundreds of files, examining some with an eagle eye. It was interesting work that piqued curiosity. I had access to all the prison archives and was at liberty to read any of them, even the ones labeled classified or confidential.

On occasion the Governor would put aside his daily labor to ask about my work. It pleased him to see I was truly interested in what I was doing and didn't view it as work. I had become, believe it or not, an archivist. I liked reading detailed reports meant only for high-ranking eyes. Administrators were required to act on some issues and promptly report to their superiors residing in Paris. These were sensitive reports on matters kept secret and stamped "Classified" in red letters. Often they referred to political prisoners who were appealing their sentences. Also some spoke of overcrowded camps and barracks, prison conditions in need of repair, and hospitals without medicine.

Governor Egremont had come to his post eager to reform abuses so old they had become tradition. He labored many hours each day when he might have accepted chaotic conditions and done nothing as other governors before him had done nothing. However, he was an idealist believing application on his part could change the colony for the better. With very little support from any person in the administration and none whatever from the citizens of the town, he struggled alone to improve the penal system. At first corrupt officials ignored his proposals, making excuses for not acting and mocking him among themselves.

Later when he persisted, they began to hate and fear him. He visited the camps in the early morning, one by one without notice, and found conditions even worse than expected. In one camp the chief guard had not bothered to show up for work. When asked why, he was told the man had been drunk for three days. In another he found four guards drunk and passed out while convicts cooked their own breakfast. In still another he found convicts in loin cloths laboring in the sun and gasping for brown water not permitted them.

He catalogued all the abuses he discovered and reported each one in detail to members of the high court in France. Alarmed by what he was doing, civilian officials in Cayenne joined the administration to charge Philip Egremont with misbehavior in office. They sent their grievance by courier directly to Paris. Following the complaint, they demanded the Governor be recalled and replaced. They charged him with malfeasance and wanted him put on trial. Nothing came of it. The Governor remained to the end of his term. By the time it was over, he had probed so deep and wide into a hill of dung authorities smelled it as far away as France. Officials there grew increasingly worried about what was going on. They believed that at any time Egremont would uncover a scandal that would give the prison a worse reputation than it already had. They quickly made it impossible for the Governor to serve a second term.

A paunchy little man calling himself Bernard Lambert replaced him. His mission was to make no changes whatever. The man was totally out of his element, apprehensive of his position in relation to the people he worked with, and unsure of his duties. He closed his eyes to the ugliness of the place, was seldom seen by anyone, and did no work. He quickly returned to work in France. Among the shakers and movers in Paris, he was celebrated as a very efficient civil servant. Within a month Lambert was given a lucrative position in the Treasury Department where he did very little work and was soon promoted. Governor Egremont, shunted aside, retired from politics and bought a vineyard in Burgundy. He and his family made a select wine they called *Soleil d'Or* after the sun that ripened the grapes. He lived to a ripe old age, dying at eighty-nine.

For nearly three months I worked at sorting and filing hundreds of documents in the Archives Room of Government House. I worked at my task all day long, stopping only to eat. I went back to the barracks often as late as ten in the evening, telling the guards the Governor had kept me working late. In that musty old room I sat at a long table reading files and reports as old as the colony itself. I found books that no one in French Guiana had ever read, books in different languages about the notorious prison sent there to be studied but ignored. I examined every item carefully before filing it away and came to know the horrors of the penal colony as well as the shenanigans of many officials down through the years. Then one morning Governor Egremont called me into his office and announced he was under considerable pressure to dismiss me and send me back to the barracks.

The next day I was summoned to the office of the Commandant. That double-dealing man leaned back in his chair, and with a wide grin on his pockmarked face he smirked: "So, Maurice, you no longer work for Egremont? Did you quit all of a sudden or did he fire you?"

I hesitated before answering, for I knew he had something up his sleeve and wanted to tease and mock me. Then slowly and calmly I replied, "I finished the job I came to do."

Of course I was lying and from his reaction I could tell he knew I was lying. There was much more to do at Government House, enough to keep me busy for another six months, but someone of higher authority had persuaded the Governor to let me go.

"I have a job for you as bookkeeper for the penitentiary here in Cayenne," said the Commandant. "The man currently doing the job is incompetent, and I'm told he's drunk three days out of every week. It'll be a lot of work for you, but you can earn some money and sleep in the office if you wish and not have to worry about abuse."

Of course I took the job, for to turn it down would have brought punishment. Even so, I was bitter at having lost the labor I really liked, the all-absorbing work with the archives. Later I learned I was removed because of warnings from the Commandant sent to his superiors in France that Governor Egremont had hired an inmate who was ready to expose abuses he had found as an archivist. Scandalous information about the prison, if published in leading newspapers of the United States, could harm the prestige of France itself. So Governor Egremont, eager to bring about reform, was put under pressure to pry me away from the records and drop his investigative work.

However, neither he nor the Commandant appeared

to know that as the bookkeeper of the mainland prison I had an open avenue to many corrupt schemes lurking in the tiny figures of my ledger. A guard, for example, would order food for a work party on a jungle mission lasting five days. He would dole out to the convicts maybe half the food ordered and sell the remainder later to an unscrupulous merchant. Schemes like that I ferreted out and reported. As a whistleblower I made no friends, but guards of every rank left me alone. They feared I might expose an unsavory or illegal activity that would cause them harm. Officials in the administration were forced to pretend I was doing a good thing. But one official sent a warning through a subordinate to back off because I was "stepping on too many toes." I knew from experience that those were the toes of people who could punish me severely should the occasion arise. So not being a hero I backed off for a while.

One sultry afternoon after heavy rain, I was called upon to register the untimely death of a convict with special privileges. I learned when I entered the hospital with its strange antiseptic odor that the dead man had been for years a citizen of some renown in France. His name was Merle Pantoppian, and he had authored enough books that criticized political schemes to become famous. When he was sentenced to French Guiana, his supporters in the hundreds protested in the streets. He had become wealthy, influential, and powerful but had gained enemies as well as supporters. In Cayenne he quickly exerted his influence among highly placed persons. They responded by offering him the comforts of home. He wasn't obligated to work or even consort with other inmates.

Now he lay dead after drowning while swimming quayside at the waterfront. He had been condemned to five years on Devil's Island after trying to poison a powerful politician who wanted him dead. The victim with his legal team was invited to a sumptuous dinner at the author's chateau where he hoped to settle the matter. He lived luxuriously as Inspector of Forests for eastern France. It was an honorary position that demanded little of his time, for most of his time was spent performing tedious literary labor. Rather than put the famous man on trial, several prominent lawyers suggested he pay the politician, now fully recovered, a handsome sum for his suffering. When the author renounced the deal as outrageous and said he wouldn't pay the crook one sou, his victim's powerful cronies pulled just the right number of strings to have him sentenced to French Guiana.

In their conflict his adversary had shown himself as stronger. Yet Pantoppian wielded influence wherever he went. He spent only three weeks on Devil's Island before his transfer to Cayenne. With plenty of money at his disposal, he bought with generous payment any number of favors from officials of the administration. To show their appreciation, he was given free run of the prison and town. So on the day he died he was eager to enjoy a refreshing swim in tepid water. A day later it was my duty to register his death by drowning and notify relatives in France. Minutes before the official letter was ready for mailing, I was informed that a legal pardon had arrived from France. The pardon should have been delivered to Pantoppian the day it was received, but delivery of any sort in Cayenne was often delayed. The letter was lying untouched on the Commandant's desk at the moment Pantoppian was drowning. Had it been delivered at the proper time, in all certainty the man would have been preparing to leave the prison rather than going for a swim. The pursuit of pleasure and prison incompetence cost him his life.

Of course no one but Pantoppian himself could be blamed for his death. Administrators took the event in stride as always. They required me to send off the usual insincere notice of death just as his prison term was ending. I could scarcely believe it, but in time my own prison term began to get closer and closer to ending. For trying to escape five times, seven years had been added to my sentence of eight years. Although I have never viewed fortune as a friend, I must say in a way I was lucky. I had managed to endure fifteen years in that place while so many others, including some of the men I had shipped with, had died after one or two years. Also some who tried to escape got many years added to their sentences while I got, using my wits as a weapon, only seven. I know full well if I had suffered more time in one of those horrendous solitary cells on Saint Joseph, I would have died before my time.

When the time finally came for me to celebrate my prison release, I played cards in the barracks with old comrades well past midnight. A guard on duty sold us some rum, and we got a little drunk and noisy. I wanted to play poker all night, just to celebrate and because I was winning, but they were tired and had to be up at six to meet the prison grind. So I crawled into my cot too but couldn't sleep. I liked to think I had seen too much of the world to become excited by anything, and yet the prospect of prison release brought a pleasant stream of thoughts concerning my future. I lay awake into the early hours feeling happy and imagining what the future might hold.

Then as the day broke at five-thirty with reveille sounding, all of my comrades gathered weary-eyed around me to say goodbye and wish me luck. For the last time I watched them go out to labor in the sun. Then I went to the commissary to turn in my convict clothes though dirty and ragged. In exchange they gave me civilian clothes that hung on me like scraps on a scarecrow. I complained but they laughed and made jokes. I was also given a small sum of money and my "free-convict" certificate. That certificate I had to have on my person should a gendarme stop me. The moment I received the certificate I was told that by law I had to stay in French Guiana for another fifteen years. Also I couldn't remain in Cayenne as a resident but would have to live outside the city limits. If I tried to escape, I would be sentenced to five years hard labor in a jungle camp. Feelings of happiness were quickly replaced with numbness.

"Look at me and listen. If you are not out of the city by tomorrow morning," the police captain admonished, "you'll be arrested and tossed into a prison cell. Now get the hell out of my sight."

I had been a free man for only a couple of hours when a pompous official was treating me like something less than human and threatening to lock me up again! Angry and confused by what was happening, I went directly to Philip Egremont's office and found him working with many documents as usual. He looked up from the mound of papers on his desk and cast a friendly smile in my direction.

"Well, Maurice, you are now a free man. Congratulations!"

"Yes, your Excellency," I replied tense with emotion. "But I must live like a stricken animal somewhere on the edge of the jungle. Even though I can roam the streets by day, I can't lodge anywhere in the city. I'm told I must get out of Cayenne as soon as tomorrow morning."

"Well, maybe not. Do you have money to leave Guiana by boat?"

"I do indeed, sir, but if I try to leave I'll be arrested and sentenced to five years hard labor, cutting down trees with a dull axe. Like all the other so-called liberated convicts, I'm expected to remain in Guiana for the rest of my life. You know and I know that isn't freedom, sir."

221

"Indeed it isn't, and I've been trying to get that law abolished from the books. I face opposition at every turn, but I'm hoping some right-minded person will give me a hand. No civilized country has so brutal a law as that. It places a life sentence on a temporary sentence and kills. I find it hard to believe my countrymen devised that law."

All the time he was speaking to me he was rummaging through his desk drawers looking for something. An old proverb tells us the best things in life come in small packages. He was a good example, a little man with a big heart, kind and compassionate. He found a printed form, looked it over, and handed it to me.

"Take this form," he said to me, "and fill it out. It's a formal petition asking permission to leave the colony for one year. Say in the Comments Section you have found no way to earn a living as a liberated convict in Guiana. You, therefore, wish to go elsewhere to find a job, save some money, and live free of abject poverty on returning."

I couldn't believe what I was hearing. The Governor, who within months would be called back to France, was offering me a way to leave French Guiana. Two days later he called together a council to approve my carefully prepared request. Since he supported the petition, there was little the council could do but approve it. I was given a passport and formal permission to leave the colony for one year. With that document in hand I went to the Consul of the Venezuelan embassy to request a visa.

To my surprise the Venezuelan, a portly gentleman with an aloof and distant manner, flatly refused my request. Thinking fast on my feet, I told him it wasn't my intention to take up residence in his country. I merely wanted to stop over on my way to Panama. All I needed was a visa that would allow passage. Reluctantly he offered no argument and stamped PANAMA on my passport. Within a few days I was breathing the sea's salt air among well-dressed people who couldn't know the value of human freedom until they lost it.

I booked passage on a small ship called *Poor Butterfly*. It was a curious name for a run-down coastal ship transporting cargo and a few passengers to the tip of Brazil, and I inquired about it.

"Oh, I think the name has something to do with the opera by Puccini called *Madama Butterfly*," said the booking agent. "I've heard it's about a Japanese girl who falls in love with an American naval officer."

Years later I had the rare opportunity to attend a performance of Puccini's opera. Because I knew Spanish, the Italian wasn't altogether foreign to me. The music was striking and memorable, the story sad.

My cargo ship was scheduled to leave the next day at two in the afternoon, and I made myself ready to be on board. I laid out for wear on the first day of the voyage my natty white suit, a clean shirt of light blue, and a narrow black tie. I wanted white shoes and socks to complete the outfit but had to settle for black. My ticket I tucked away in the pocket of my coat. I knew in the tropical heat I would have to remove the coat, but I intended to wear it until I could relax in my cabin. On the morning of my departure I went to the office of my generous benefactor to thank him again for all he had done. He shook my hand, wished me well, and said I had to remember three things of high importance.

I should make myself known to the French Consul in Panama; I could not extend the time given me beyond one year; and above all, I would not publish any article whatever that might damage the prestige of France on the world stage. While I had no problem keeping two of the requirements, I had doubts about returning after one year. Nonetheless, I quickly promised the Governor I would certainly comply with all three. I couldn't know what the future held. I didn't know whether I would voluntarily return to captivity.

Precisely at two o'clock I heard the bosun's whistle, and within minutes the *Poor Butterfly* was leaving the shores of French Guiana. For the first time in a very long time I felt relaxed and happy. I was on my way to the free world and a future. I was free at last, free at least for a year. I looked out across the shimmering water, acutely aware of the problems I would face but ready to meet them head-on. A diminutive but powerful friend, whose power would soon end, had granted me the gift of freedom for an entire year. Though I felt I would have to return, I viewed the leave of absence as my sixth escape. Just the thought of returning left me dazed and discontented. How could I return to that heinous prison after living free for an entire year? It was a question not the wisest among us could answer.

Chapter Twenty-One
Heavy Hammer of Justice

My first night aboard the *Poor Butterfly* was creepy. The gentle motion of the vessel allowed me to sleep comfortably in a clean bed, but I was soon wide-awake in a cold sweat and bolting upright. Thugs from the Bloodstained Barracks had somehow come on board and were trying to rob me. Between two worlds and having trouble adapting to the new one, I was experiencing nightmare. After a few hours of fitful sleep, I left my cabin and paced the deck to greet the day. When sailors on the early watch found me lurking in the shadows to smoke, they began to call me "that crazy gringo." I made no effort to correct them.

They thought I was American and crazy to leave a cozy bunk for a cigarette on a dark and damp deck with a chill wind blowing. I stood at the rail slightly seasick to watch the new sun push away the gloom of a moonless night with pink and gold. Under blue skies made bright by the sun, I paced the deck constantly reassuring myself that my passport and stash of money were safe. I went to breakfast in the ship's dining room and sat with the other guests to exchange banter, the news of the day, and polite conversation. We shared our laughter as good friends. I liked that. However, I couldn't relax and feel at ease around them. I had not yet entered their world entirely.

The ship put into a Venezuelan port and spent one night there. I went ashore to feel freedom under my feet but didn't go into town. In the old Customs House an official glanced at my passport and nodded. A pleasant sea voyage the next day took me to Colon in Panama. Wearing a big smile too wide for my face, I strolled down the gangplank in breezy weather with hat in hand. Though my heart was racing and I was a bit apprehensive, I felt ready for a new adventure. It would require me to use each day the rudimentary Spanish I had picked up in Bella Vista and Cayenne. From the ship I went to a cheap hotel and rented a room.

The next day, as Governor Egremont advised, I visited the French Consul. He appeared to be a typical Frenchman with a sharp nose, sharp eyes, and a little oily mustache. I expected to speak to a Parisian, but the gentleman spoke a northern dialect, which I didn't understand entirely. Even though I missed the meaning of some of his remarks, we got along well enough to complete my business there. After leaving his office, I had lunch at a sidewalk café and began to adjust to new surroundings. The next day I went job hunting. After a few days of searching for work in Colon and being rejected, I decided to try my luck in Panama City. I was ready to take a bus to the capital when the night manager of the hotel suggested I go with his cousin. The man would be leaving early to travel there in his own vehicle.

"Ah, his name is Tomás, a capital fellow and colorful. You will like him and remember him. Just buy him some gasoline. He won't ask for much. He will take you anywhere you want go with no problems. It's more pleasant and less expensive too than riding a crowded bus."

I had heard what it was like to travel by bus in Panama, and so I gladly accepted the offer. Tomás said he would meet me at the hotel early in the morning. I got my shower, got dressed, ate a quick breakfast, and waited. He didn't get to the hotel until nearly nine. As the sun was rising high in a blue sky, the two of us set out to cross the isthmus in a cranky old truck that put my nerves on edge. It swooshed around sharp curves with its old tires squealing. Its rusty radiator began to boil over, spewing out plumes of vapor, and we had to stop for water. I had filled the truck's gasoline tank in Colon. Now in the new place I filled the tank again (a gesture Tomás didn't expect), and thanked him for the ride with a tip. He called me a saint and recommended a small hotel where I could sleep comfortably at low cost.

Panama City was bustling, noisy, and prosperous. In a few days I managed to get a job in the Records Department of the local hospital. I could have served as an orderly there, for I had the experience, but the records job was more desirable. In my possession were papers falsely showing I had worked as a bookkeeper in France. Also, truthfully, they indicated I had been an archivist in French Guiana. The latter got me the job.

After my interview I worked in the hospital without incident, living comfortably in a small apartment and making friends of my neighbors.

A friend I could tell you about in detail was a Greek with intense blue eyes. He was in his thirties, well built, and sporting a shock of very black hair. He spoke several languages, I learned as I got to know him, but none very well. He called himself a citizen of the world and laughed loudly as though he had made a delectable joke. His name was a musical Georgie Popadopoulos. He was something of a braggart and claimed he had lived well with a number of beautiful women in several countries. Though a little hard to take, I liked the guy. I didn't believe half the stuff he said about his life, but I liked him. I never revealed much about me.

It was a pleasant and productive year for me. My position at the hospital, filing medical records, was hectic at times, especially when a missing record couldn't be found. A doctor treating a woman for goiter was certain he had given her papers to me and got all excited when I couldn't supply them. In anger he threatened to have me fired. It was about to happen when he found her chart hanging at the foot of another bed. He apologized and offered to buy me dinner at the best restaurant in town. I politely declined the offer. The incident was forgotten until he sent the woman home wearing an amber necklace. He thought it would cure her condition, but it didn't. Within a few days she was dead. I was thankful I didn't have his job, for the hospital was not without drama. In my spare time, usually in the evening after dinner, I began to write about my prison experience. The thick notebooks I filled became source material for the present narrative.

Although my year of freedom was fruitful, time in its flight weighed heavily on me and distressed me. The days and weeks came and went much too fast. Before I knew it the year was gone. As the last week approached, I decided in anguish to travel to France and petition for a permanent passport. I reasoned if I could do that, I wouldn't have to return to French Guiana but could live free just about anywhere. Later I was forced to admit I had made a destructive and impulsive decision. The expensive voyage meant I had not broken my promise to Governor Egremont. Yet in Brest the authorities placed me under arrest as soon as I touched French soil. As a liberated convict I had returned prematurely to my homeland. Though a free man and a Frenchman, I was breaking an important law. I tried to argue my case but failed.

Two months I languished in jail before being hustled southward to the infamous convict ship lying at anchor in the Bay of Biscay. A guard from French Guiana, one who knew me when I was imprisoned on the island of Saint Joseph, prodded my back with the butt of his rifle to shove me along. Having heard I was returning after tasting freedom for an entire year, he snickered and snorted in derision. He appeared to be envious of my great adventure, envious perhaps of the freedom I had enjoyed for a year. He was a guard of rank and free to live anywhere he chose, but his job robbed him of true freedom. He would never return to his village in Corsica, and he knew it.

"Well, if it ain't little Bonheur! Did you buy a round-trip ticket when you left the colony, little maggot? And of all the places in this wide world for you to go, you went home to France. Oh my God, you poor little runt, how could you be so stupid?"

Aware I'd be punished if I made a reply, even one clothed in a joke, I kept my silence and joined the other luckless convicts boarding the ship. It was the same old scene of almost two decades ago, the same old rust bucket of a ship with its filthy cages in the hold, and its frequent stops to dump the dead. I lost count of the times the ship cut her engines to drift so the crew could heave another corpse overboard. We heard as general knowledge that a brief religious ceremony took place before "the burial at sea." If a ceremony with the chaplain presiding really did occur, most of us believed it was phony and hypocritical.

After seventeen days of rolling and rocking, the old tub dropped anchor off Bella Vista near the mouth of the river. The men in my cage rousted each other to get a view of the jungle from a dirty porthole, but I didn't bother. I had seen it before, and I knew it to be a very unfriendly place. I tried to remain calm but was ablaze with anxiety and anger. In a few hours I would again be under the thumb of the administration in

French Guiana, a very heavy thumb. Three pompous judges would call me before the Tribunal of Justice for a hearing. They would require me to stand before them and explain why I was there. They expected me to plea for a lighter sentence which I wouldn't get.

Unable to sleep in the stifling ship's hold, I lay fuming with rage and drowning in self-pity. I cursed myself for being so stupid at a time when I should have been keenly logical and reasonable and cogently aware. I had freedom and life in the palm of my hand and stupidly threw it all away. So while I hated the vile institution about to engulf me again, my anger was directed mainly at myself. Fierce mosquitoes came through the open portholes and tormented the wretches around me. They had a feast on my flesh too, but bitter thoughts made their attack less painful. I had convinced myself, as they buzzed in my face and ears to bite, that I deserved the pain they came into the world to inflict.

As the hot and humid day began, we were herded into small boats to stand and wait on the wharf at Bella Vista. I had but one thought in my aching head, and I mulled it over and over. It became an obsession. I would escape again and make it my final escape. I had no promises to keep, no feelings of loyalty any more to anyone, no thoughts of "doing the right thing" as the Governor had said. I would simply bide my time, wait for the right moment, and walk away from that god-awful place to become human again. They had made of me an animal at bay, but it wouldn't last. I would find a way to taste freedom again. I would make it my one and only mission. I would lie awake at night parsing every little detail of a complicated plan. At the right time, with zeal and precision, I would carry out the plan. I would not be recaptured. I would find a way to die rather than be recaptured.

Because of our number, we were forced to stand on the long wharf in blazing heat for more than two hours to be processed. Some of the men fainted while others begged for water. My knees were beginning to buckle when a sweating guard marched me away to a blockhouse and locked me in a solitary cell. On the grimy floor was a tin cup filled with water. I grabbed the cup and drank the brackish water in one gulp. In a stupor I slumped against the wall. That moment was absolutely the end of my year of freedom. Again I was a prisoner among dying men.

During my year of freedom I had been a model citizen. I had found a job and worked industrially at it. I had behaved myself and lived soberly in a town that had pulled out all the stops. I had broken no laws. But when the year ended I made a mind-numbing mistake: *I went to France seeking justice.* I thought I would be able to receive justice in France. I must have been sick to do such a thing, must have lost my mind. I can't believe the stupidity of it even now. I should have remained in Panama. I would surely have stayed there except for a pressing need to keep a promise. One man had treated me kindly and I couldn't betray him. But on returning I learned Governor

Egremont had been recalled to France. Now I owed nothing to him. Come hell or high water, *I would escape.*

They added three more years to my sentence and imprisoned me in a solitary cell on St. Joseph. Except for the guards who had become more brutish, the island hadn't visibly changed at all. Even though suffering convicts were constantly in conflict with the guards, I managed to hold my peace and stay out of trouble. Three months went by in slow motion, and the only way I kept my sanity was to pace the tiny cell all day long and often at night. Sloppy food with flies on it was shoved through an opening to rest on the floor. My toilet was a chamber pot I had to empty during my half-hour of so-called exercise in the courtyard.

Day by day I did all I could to keep my muscles firm. I found a way to chin myself, and I did pushups. I lay on the dirty floor, put my hands behind my head, and did sit-ups until my abdomen ached. Finally a year closed in behind me, and I realized with satisfaction that I had managed to keep my body sound and my mind sane. I did it in spite of being shut up like a rat in a stinking box. They gave me solitary punishment for a year just for entering France, my homeland, as a convict who had served his time. That I cannot believe even as I say it.

The guard reported I was growing weaker in harsh confinement. Prison officials thought surely I would die before the year was out. But to their surprise I remained alive. *I'm alive, haha. You didn't kill me. I'm alive, haha.* That was the refrain of the song I sang in my head over and over again. I had not died, had not gone crazy, and had lost no part of my body, except for crumbling teeth, to disease or lassitude. I was a walking skeleton, having lived on nothing more than black bread and bad water, and yet every part of me was functional.

I was thankful I had possessed the presence of mind to exercise in that tiny space. They gave me a chance to exercise in the courtyard on some days, but the courtyard had no shade. Activity beyond a slow walk couldn't be done under a tropical sun or relentless rain, and they knew it. They didn't know I would find a way to stay fit even if I had to do it in darkness. I was determined to survive in confinement, and I would find a way to survive when finally released too. That meant only one thing: I had to escape again and make it stick.

It was a well-known fact in French Guiana that no man could escape the prison without money. Most of the money I had earned during my year of freedom went to the guard for little favors, such as coffee now and then, that were expensive. I was broke and needed money merely to survive. I tried catching butterflies to dry, preserve, and eventually sell their iridescent wings. Other libérés were doing the same, and so the money that came of it was just enough to buy cigarettes. I had to forage in the jungle for food or steal it from the garbage bins in town. Once I dug an armadillo out of its hole and boiled it for dinner in a clay pot. I looked in vain for turtle eggs, recalling how they once filled my empty belly. Hard cash was the thing I needed most.

Money was necessary to buy a canoe, to buy a sail for it, and to supply it with food for a couple of weeks. I was reminded of an old liberated convict who had found a way to live well. Just about every day he paddled his old canoe across the river to Dutch Guiana to bring back duty-free goods for the guards. Sometimes he brought them opium from China, cocaine from Colombia, and good whiskey from Scotland. Once he delivered to his delighted customers a mulatto girl. Where she came from and how he got her no one ever knew. I shouldn't have to mention he demanded a very high price for her. The old rogue had found a way to survive and prosper. On the proceeds of his lucrative adventures he lived well while keeping a low profile. I would follow his example.

However, my survival depended on a final escape. I had six behind me and was thinking night and day of a final one. Three failed attempts had taught me that escape through the jungle was impossible. Escaping by sea was the way to do it, but it required the assistance of competent partners I could trust. Also there was the matter of finding a sturdy boat, food and drink for at least two weeks, and supplies such as fishing gear, a lantern, and a stove. Also we would require some kind of canopy to shield us from the sun or suffer terrible sunburn. The boat would be at sea for a dozen days or more and would have to hold up against bad weather at times. It would have to be seaworthy.

I could hope for good weather, a steady breeze, and

moderate seas, and yet I knew the vessel had to be ready for heavy weather. Realistic thinking told me all those requirements could be out of reach, figments of wistful dreaming. Many young men in my position had fashioned a similar dream to have it crushed by reality. I was no exception surely, but somehow I would find a way. I couldn't spend the remaining years of my life living in abject poverty and shunned by decent people as a social pariah. Thoughts of eking out a hand-to-mouth existence year after year on the edge of an unforgiving jungle troubled me deeply. I would find a way out, escape once and for all, or I would die trying.

Chapter Twenty-Two
The Village of the Damned

As it happened, I was able to carry out my seventh escape much sooner than expected. One typically hot day in Cayenne I was walking down a dusty road that led to the sea looking for a place to fish. I was thinking if I were lucky I might catch a sizable fish and make a good dinner of it. Of a sudden from behind me, came a man's voice calling out to me. A lanky young man caught up with me on the sun-baked road. He was dressed as a tourist, wearing a blue knit shirt, white trousers, white shoes, and a pith helmet. His hair was blonde, his eyes a brilliant blue behind horn-rimmed glasses. After an awkward and silent hesitation, he struck up a conversation with me, his blue eyes blinking in the bright air. I stopped walking to hear what he had to say.

"I think you might have the means to help me, sir. Thank you very much," he said in textbook French. "I am looking for a man the powerful people say is still a prisoner here. Do you speak English, please?"

His French was atrocious and made me chuckle. I knew if I had to listen to more of it, I would burst into riotous laughter and offend him. So quickly I replied, "I speak a little English. How may I help you?"

"I'm an American journalist, from the States you know," he said in hesitant English. Sweat dribbled from his forehead down to cheeks and chin of a face that appeared honest and open. He cleaned his sweaty glasses with a white handkerchief and spoke again.

"I'm here on assignment for a well-known magazine in the States, and I'm looking for a good story. Sadly no one wants to talk to me. All the prison officials rebuff me."

"If you are looking for something sensational," I said, "you've come to the right place. We call this wicked town 'the village of the damned.' In its streets so-called free convicts mingle with condemned convicts. They also have the leisure to mingle with the town's citizens, but they become sad victims of ill treatment wherever they go. They are ghosts, pariahs reviled and persecuted by everyone. They are called free men but they are not free. I know what I'm talking about, sir. I'm one of them. I am what is called 'a liberated convict,' a libéré, but I am not free."

"I'm so sorry to hear that, sir. Maybe you have heard of a man they call Maurice? From what I know, his situation is similar to yours. I do hope you've heard of him and can tell me where to find him."

"In that loathsome prison in back of you are scores of men called Maurice. This hot little place, as you must know, is owned by France. Maurice is a very old and honored name among the French. It's a very common name in France, much like James or John in your country."

"His full name," the journalist added, consulting his notebook, "is Arthur Maurice Bonheur. His last name in French means happiness. I'm told he goes by Maurice, his middle name. If you can tell me where to find him, I will give you five dollars for your trouble."

"I can tell you exactly where to find him, but you must pay me first. I'm not saying you don't look honest, but trying to keep body and soul together in this place makes me wary of promises any stranger makes."

Smiling broadly, he fumbled in his pockets and found a fat leather wallet stuffed with American dollars. I was thinking what a fool he was to be wandering alone in Cayenne with all that money but said nothing. He gave me the five dollars, chortling gleefully.

"Is the man nearby?" he asked. "I can't wait to see him. I do hope he speaks some English so I can communicate with him."

"He is indeed nearby," I answered. "You are looking at him!"

"Ah, no!" he replied, speaking with disappointment. "You couldn't be him. You're too little, too frail. The man I'm looking for has incredible strength of muscle and strength of mind too. I've been told he's famous or notorious, maybe, for constantly trying to escape. Half a dozen times they tell me, and with each time he stays away longer. Now don't con me, little man. I wasn't born yesterday."

"I don't advise you to call me little man," I said with a wink, "and yet I am a little man and so won't take offense. I'm the person you're looking for, the chump known for 'incredible strength of mind and muscle.' I'm guessing you want information about the prison."

"Yes, yes! That's right! I'm eager to pick your brain for details! Sorry for misjudging you, Maurice. May I call you that? My name is Tom. Well, it's really Thomas, you know, but people call me Tom. I'll pay you plenty for a good exposé of Devil's Island or even a story about your time here. Do you think we can go somewhere and talk? I've heard you've tried to escape more times than any other living convict."

"I've tried it a few times," I said, "but maybe not more than others. Years ago an old man they called Popo escaped a dozen times but was brought back defeated each time. When he finally got it through his thick skull that he would never be free, he slit his throat in front of the judges prepared to send him into solitary confinement. He spun around like a whirling dervish as the knife did its work, and his blood spurted in all directions. Before he collapsed he stumbled as close to the judges as he could get and left a bloody mess on the floor. The ugly scene appalled the three men who were there to judge and sentence him. They thought they had seen it all but not so. Ah, not so. All sorts of interesting and unexpected events happen in this prison. We can talk wherever you're staying, but I have to go before nightfall. I'm not allowed to spend my evenings or nights in town. Can't be caught in Cayenne after dark. It's a little rule they have here that most of us free convicts obey."

We spent the night in his hotel room hunched over a table as I did most of the talking. He jotted down in a little notebook many notes in a crabbed hand. I told him the story of my life, how I made a destructive and brainless mistake, and was sent to French Guiana. I narrated in detail my attempts to escape by sea and jungle. Time and again with a look of fascination he asked me to slow down. He didn't want to miss a single fact, not one syllable. When daybreak came he was too weary to write another word even though I had more to tell him. He opened his wallet and flicked some bills on the table. I didn't bother to count them until he left Cayenne. Within an hour he was on a plane heading out. I would have given my right arm to be in his position, free to soar through the heavens to exotic places, free to make a living asking questions.

He had seen me not so much as a suffering human being, but as a source of information. On that table, however, as he shook my hand and hurried away, he left a hundred American dollars! I counted it more than once and was amazed. With so much money to finance a final escape, I could feel absolutely it would go down right. I wouldn't suffer recapture as with all the other escapes. I would gain once and for all the freedom I had sought for so many years. Should I not accomplish that goal, I would die rather than return to French Guiana. So my lucky coin had two sides: one for winning and the other for failure.

I found a Chinese merchant doing business on the

waterfront who offered to sell me as one package a good boat provisioned with food and water for a month. I was certain I could find men who would gladly join me, but knew I would have to search carefully for the right kind. We would make our way first to a Caribbean island for a taste of freedom, and then to the United States. Thousands of miles lay between French Guiana and the southern-most town of the United States, but with each mile gained we would come closer to civilization and liberty. I believed the American authorities, appalled by the reputation of the prison they called Devil's Island, would accept us as *free men.* W had paid our dues.

Methodically for several days, I searched for three men who would go with me. Each man had to meet several requirements though one in particular was paramount: each of the chosen had to assure me that *either freedom or death lay before him.* There could be no turning back, no decision to surrender to anyone or anything. In time I selected Jules, a young man who had just completed a five-year sentence for robbery, and Ludo who had served fifteen years for killing a friend. Though both were capable men, neither knew anything about navigation. So after days of searching I found a third man who had been a sailor. Cluseau in his late thirties had served five years for stealing a car. It was a crime he claimed he didn't commit. All he needed, he said with a confidence that impressed me, was the sun and stars to guide us to wherever we wanted to go. He knew how to sail a small boat in fierce conditions, and he could navigate. Sailing to the Caribbean and beyond would pose no problem.

As the sun was setting on a sultry day, the four of us met at the merchant's shop to put the plan in motion. As night came we crept into the jungle and made our way to the hidden creek where the Chinaman had assured us a boat with ample supplies would be waiting. It proved to be smaller than the craft we had bargained for, only twenty-six feet in length. Also, like most rowboats, it had no keel to keep it upright in heavy seas. In the light of a half-concealed lantern I inspected supplies stored in the cuddy and found they were lacking too. In particular the best food I ordered and paid for, canned meat for example, was missing. The "reputable businessman" as our benefactor was calling himself had cheated us severely. It was a heart-rending discovery.

I had paid for something I didn't get and had a feeling my grand adventure had been dashed even before it began. My comrades spoke of beating the man silly to teach him a lesson and trying again at a later date. In such a craft, little more than a modified canoe or rowboat, we could die at sea. Yet I was determined at all cost to carry through with my escape plan. I sat down in the wobbly boat and urged my comrades to come along. With no little misgiving they gingerly took their places and we shoved off. Within minutes, or so it seemed, we were out of the creek and paddling down the river in darkness. We kept to the center of the river to be as far from shore as possible.

The current was with us and we moved swiftly. Before reaching the ocean we passed a long and slender canoe moving upstream. In it were several strong Indians, rowing the craft expertly. They called out in their language expecting us to sing out, but we didn't answer. At the mouth of the river we hoisted sail. The "reputable businessman" had promised the sail would be strong and sturdy, but even in the dark it seemed worn and flimsy, too thin and weak for a working sail to work. A feeling of anger mingled with despair rose in my throat, but I said nothing. There could be no grumbling to disrupt the adventure. Cluseau seized the tiller attached to a crude rudder, and the craft began to skip across the water as if alive. He pointed to a star and said it would guide us northward. He called it the pole star. Ludo knew it as Polaris.

Although the sea was fairly calm, we took on some water and began to bail it out. Another man sat beside the man at the helm to be certain he didn't fall asleep. As the hours passed all of us began to come to our senses, to know we were flirting with disaster. Four men were on the open ocean in a sailboat with a shallow draft, only twenty-six feet in length, and too slender to be seaworthy. Its beam or width was less than five feet. We thought the first wave that hit us would capsize our craft. Yet in spite of the danger, we were driven to put penal servitude behind us and secure freedom at any price.

All through the night the heavy darkness was thick

with an overcast that blotted out the North Star chosen to guide us. I found in the cuddy a small compass and gave it to Cluseau. Reading it now and then in the light of a single match kept us moving northward. The silence was like no other silence I had known. Like a heavy fog playing tricks on sounds, the heavy silence played tricks with hearing. Some of us tried to sleep. The two men not sleeping spoke not a word. When the black night surrendered to a bright and sunny day, we could see no shore in any direction. We complimented Cluseau on his navigational skills, and Ludo relieved him at the helm. I volunteered to cook.

In a saucepan I boiled some coffee on the alcohol stove and passed it out to the crew. The coffee was strong and bitter. It tasted awful but stoked us with energy. The Chinaman had cheated us grievously on the food supplies, but at least we had a stove and spare fuel. We ate very little that first day at sea, and nobody grumbled. As the sun was setting we made certain our supplies were safely secured should we encounter rough weather. It came with a vengeance in the night. The wind howled from the southeast, and the little boat whooshed across the water at breakneck speed. Cluseau was on the tiller all night, singing snatches of French and Italian popular songs to drown out the wind and boost his morale. Ludo had to relieve himself and without thinking began to stand up and lean over the side of our ship. Fearing the craft would capsize, we demanded he use a can. Jules and I had to do the same and it became the rule. All night not a man dared move about even a little. Then as daylight was breaking quite early the wind died.

We sang a nostalgic little tune of Paris in the rain to welcome the calm and set about repairing the sail. Several old pillowcases with their double thickness had been used to make it. The wind had ripped it at the clew, the corner of the sail attached to the line or "sheet" that controlled it. We repaired the sail with cloth from a tough old prison shirt, thankful we had tools for the job. The sun was soon high in the sky, and casting no shadows. We took care to cover our bodies but had to leave face, neck, and hands bare. With tired and anxious eyes we swept the horizon all day but saw no sign of a ship. We were alone on a wide and merciless ocean and yet relieved to be alone. Night came and the wind blew hard again. Jules manned the tiller when he learned Cluseau's right palm had a big blister. He steered through the night, the boat riding the waves and sliding down them just when it seemed it might capsize. In strong winds we made no attempt to keep a course.

The black canopy above us had not a single star, and a rogue wave washed the compass from my hand. At first light after a night in which no man slept, we found ourselves soaking wet, stiff and exhausted, but hungry. And we were not at all so optimistic as the day before. I dipped some water out of the water keg and discovered seawater had seeped into it and turned it salty. I mixed the water with condensed milk and passed it around in tin cups. My companions agreed it tasted like parrot piss. I wondered who among them had ever tasted parrot piss. Already we were having a hard time of it but could still laugh at a vulgar joke.

Near noon a school of porpoises sprang above the water's surface and began to amuse us. We were sailing fast, but they were swimming faster. They came at us as if they were ready to ram the boat and tip it. At the last moment they dove under it to come up on the other side. Bobbing and bouncing and making whistle-like sounds, they seemed to be laughing at us. Ludo wanted to toss them pieces of stale bread tainted by seawater. I cautioned him not to do it. The bread was eatable, and we had so little of anything edible left. Then Ludo remembered he had read about dolphins not being hungry when playing. And these were playing.

"The porpoises are fun to watch, but we'd better try to reach land somewhere," said Jules backed up by Ludo. "We can't drink salty water, it'll kill us. We can probably get some good water and shove off again."

"The water isn't all that salty," I replied, hoping to persuade. "It isn't "100 percent, maybe only 10 percent at most. It won't kill us."

"Let's try the jungle," inexperienced Jules offered. "I'd rather take my chances in the jungle. At least we can find water and shade there and not have to worry about sharks or drowning,"

"In the jungle you won't have to worry about sharks or drowning. You'll have to worry about snakes and nocturnal animals. We've been gone how long? Three days?" I asked the question as my lips drew tight across my teeth and my jaw tightened.

"Three very long days," Jules retorted.

"And you tell me you already want to go ashore? Didn't we agree that under no circumstances, for no reason whatever, would we turn back? If we land on the Colombian coast, we'll be arrested and put on a road gang until they send us back to Bella Vista or Cayenne."

"Well, even if the water isn't all that salty," Ludo argued, "we could die out here from plain exposure. I'd rather be in prison serving more time than dying painfully and slowly of exposure or worse."

"Don't speak nonsense," urged Cluseau. "You're the oldest among us and should be the wisest. Relax, take it easy, we'll be all right."

And so we quarreled off and on all day. Any friendly camaraderie that had developed among us earlier had turned sour and melted away. We endured long periods of silence, and then suddenly without notice a fiery outburst would come from Jules or Ludo. Our navigator Cluseau was on my side, and so we were split down the middle. The fourth night was cruel. Subsequent nights were equally hard to bear. After a week we were clearly losing strength. Our hands and grim faces were swollen and tender from too much sun. Our lips were parched and swollen and our throats were painfully dry.

We gave up speaking to each other. When eight more days slipped by, we had managed to stay inside the rowboat rigged for a sailboat but were scarcely human. The boat remained upright as it rode the crest of an angry wave and plunged downward into a deep trough to be lifted and thrown against another wave. Dazed and half delirious, we began to lose feeling in our legs and feet and lost all desire to eat. The sea had become monstrous, and the sun that gives light, warmth, and life to the planet had become an angry monster ready to slaughter us. The agony we all felt would have to end soon. Ludo said all four of us would be dead in three days. No one spoke to disagree.

Chapter Twenty-Three
La Isla de la Trinidad

The first day at sea I told my companions we were heading for Trinidad. I didn't tell them it was more than 700 miles beyond the horizon. That little nugget had to be kept under wraps. To reveal how far we had to go in a boat designed for a small lake or pond would have brought doubt, indecision, and complaining. As a schoolboy I loved geography, and as we sailed I remembered Columbus gave the island its religious name. He called it "The Island of the Trinity" in 1498. At the time of our adventure Trinidad was under British rule and prosperous. My comrades were surprised to learn that La Isla de la Trinidad was located only seven miles off the coast of northeastern Venezuela. They had thought a vast ocean surrounded the island.

"That's good to know," Ludo ventured. "But wouldn't we be in for trouble if a Venezuelan patrol boat should happen to see us? Don't they send convicts, freed or not, hastily back to Guiana?"

"Well, not hastily," I replied. "Not long ago I heard they took the initiative from Colombia and are now requiring escapees to work on their roads for months before sending them back. It's slave labor, mind you, and not acceptable. But as we attempt to stay on course it's a risk we have to take. If we keep well out to sea and move in from the east rather than from the south we can avoid them. Most of the time the Venezuelan boats stay close to the coast, seldom venture into Trinidad waters, and the Islanders will grant us refuge. They will allow us to rest a few days and replenish our food and water before we move onward. I've looked into all this carefully; did my homework before we left."

"I'm glad to hear you did your homework," said Ludo. "As a former schoolteacher, I'm always glad when homework is done. I just wish I could be as optimistic about our prospects as you, but I just can't. My gut tells me that Trinidad is farther away than this boat can take us. Many miles ahead of us and many days to get there. Not sure we can make it."

"We'll make it, Ludo. Trust me, we'll make it."

For a couple of weeks I had the trust and compliance of all three men. We managed to get along well together, and we made progress on the long journey. Then the complaining began. Four men were finding it hard to live day by day on a tiny boat surrounded by a world of shark-infested water.

"Dammit, Maurice!" Jules at the bow grumped. "We've been on this rickety little boat too many days now, and we're getting weaker every day. I'm ready to go ashore. Point this thing westward! I've had enough! I want my feet on the ground! What's it called? Terra Firma? I'll take my chances on Terra Firma. Even the deepest, roughest jungle is better than a slow and painful death out here. Even prison is better."

He began crawling aft to grab the tiller. I reached into my shirt and withdrew the revolver I had bought without their knowledge from the Chinese merchant. A week or so earlier I had taken it from my knapsack, wrapped it in oilcloth, and taped it to my chest. I pointed the weapon at Jules's head and then at Ludo.

"I'm sure all of you have noticed I'm smaller than any of you. I'm a little man; it's the unvarnished truth and undeniable. But this thing in my hand makes me bigger than any of you, and don't you forget it. Our course is northward to Trinidad, and it will remain unchanged. Believe me, we'll find rest and security there and freedom too."

For a moment all three, even Cluseau, glowered at me fiercely. Then mulling over what I said and respecting the gun more than me, they fell silent. When night came I thought I might have to stay awake to protect myself. I was thinking I had made the men angry enough to pounce upon me when my guard was down. But soon to my relief I realized no mutiny would take place. They were brave men but feared the unknown. Settled down and more in control of their senses, they believed I would lead them to freedom or die trying. That for a time resolved the issue. Their behavior was the product of desperation, not animosity toward me. The sun had roasted every face. Our water was in short supply, and throats were parched. Every person was hungry, thirsty, exhausted, and fearful of sharks that seemed to be trailing a boat too small for the ocean. I tried to reassure them.

"The coast you see belongs to Venezuela, and it's hostile. You'll be arrested and sent back hungry within a day or forced into slave labor. More than likely you'll have to labor in the red-hot sun for months. Venezuela is notorious for exploiting escapees, and so it could be years. Now listen to me, please. Trinidad may seem far off, but we can make it, and we will. The people there will give us safety, rest, good food, and even medical attention. I promise you this: If we don't see the island in a few more days, we'll go ashore and shift as best we can. Suffer with me just a few more days, comrades. Is that too much to ask?"

Jules and Ludo scowled as they heard my words but said nothing. Cluseau glanced at me calmly and looked downward. We sailed on with Cluseau and me at the tiller until late afternoon. The wind was steady from the southeast and filled the patchwork sail nicely. At the helm I sat amazed at how well the little boat, surely built by amateurs, performed. Cluseau said the way the sail was rigged had a lot to do with it. I speculated four men in the boat instead of two made the difference. It might have capsized in a rushing wave with only two but didn't with four. As the day wore on, the wind diminished and I was thinking we might have to start paddling. Then suddenly in the brilliant blue sky we saw seagulls flashing white.

Seagulls whirling in flight! Didn't that mean we were close to land?

"Not necessarily," said Cluseau, our nautical expert, in that studious tone he often used. "Marine scientists tell us the birds often fly hundreds of miles from shore. Depends on wind currents and species. And you know gulls can rest, even sleep, on the water."

"Well, we do know they came somewhere from land," I said. "They are not sea creatures. They live on land. It's a sight for sore eyes!"

The wind had diminished and the ocean was like a lake, so calm it was glassy. We thought of paddling but lay back instead and looked at the gulls wheeling and dipping in flight. In half an hour or less they were gone, and with them went our excitement. Another hour brought cat's paws on the water. Then suddenly Jules at the bow stood up shouting. In his excitement he had forgotten the cardinal rule I had tried to brand on everyone's brain: *Do not stand! You could tip the boat because it has no keel.* Jules was gesticulating wildly and pointing at something in the distance. The boat was becoming unstable.

"Look! Look! It's land!" he cried. "Oh, my god, it's land!"

"Only a cloud bank," Cluseau called, "but looks like land."

"No, no! I see it too," Ludo yelled. "It's land, by god, it's land!"

"It's Trinidad!" Jules bellowed. "Trinidad, Maurice! I find it real hard to believe, but you did it, man! You brought us to Trinidad!"

Crouched over the tiller and behind the sail, I couldn't see that part of the horizon where they were pointing. I pushed the sail to one side and saw bluish-green mountains against a blue sky. It wasn't a joke as I suspected, and no mirage. It was the Island of Trinidad! Our destination was in sight! After intense suffering that almost decimated us, at last we were making landfall. That glorious sight quickly replaced all the ugly backbiting with joyous shouting and laughter. We were friends again, comrades celebrating a glorious victory over forces much stronger than us. We were children of fortune riding high on a cloud. Cluseau took the helm and caught a rising breeze expertly. The little boat surged across the blue-green water like a mare galloping homeward. Water dashed over the side and set us to bailing. Not a soul complained. The good land on the horizon grew larger and more distinct. We could see clusters of white houses with red roofs against mountainous terrain.

A couple of hours later as the sun was sinking close to the horizon, we were close to shore and about to enter the surf. I steered the bow toward the beach. The boat began surfing, and shot through the veil of water well up onto the gently sloping beach. As the surf receded, my companions in a frenzy of excitement tried jumping from the craft to the beach. All three were too weak to make the leap and fell flat on their faces in shallow water. While they lay there sprawled and panting, I climbed out laughing and hooting and stood with eyes shaded to survey our surroundings. It was a crescent beach wide and white with a pinkish color and free of the detritus delivered by the sea to most beaches. In a moment of supreme elation, I ripped away the revolver I had taped to my chest and threw it far into the sea. At that moment it had become an unnecessary burden. We were children celebrating. Joyous children, I said to myself, do not bear arms.

Some islanders fishing on the beach came strolling toward us but gave us a wide berth as they passed. They stared at us in disbelief but said nothing. In their eyes we were strange creatures to be avoided. I called out to them in English and begged them to climb a tree and toss down some coconuts. A lad not more than fourteen scampered up a nearby tree and began dropping coconuts the size of my head to the ground. His companions rolled them like bowling balls in our direction and hurried off. Each of us had two coconuts but no way to get at the meat or milk. Then I remembered the marlinspike in our supplies. It was the perfect tool for splitting the hard shell. Searching the cuddy, I found it and hacked open coconuts for my friends. We drank the cool sweet liquid and devoured the white meat pried off with the marlinspike. We sat in the sand all the time we were eating. Then like drunken zombies we toddled toward a grass hut away from the beach in the trees.

The hut with its thatched roof appeared deserted. No one answered our call, and so we stumbled inside. We found a large kettle filled with something that looked like gray mush. Its smell was sort of strange but not unpleasant. We plunged our sunburned hands into it and discovered fermented rice and pieces of boiled fish. Ravenously we gulped it down, grunting and groaning with satisfaction. On the brink of starvation, we stupidly stuffed ourselves full without restraint. A few minutes later we were rolling on the dirt floor with violent bellyaches. Despite the pain, all four of us fell into untroubled sleep born of exhaustion. Through the night with room to spare we slept on the sandy floor, so different and far more comfortable than the restrictive boat. Ludo was the first to awaken and went outside before daylight to relieve himself. I suggested we go immediately to the nearest town. My companions were disposed to resist that idea, fearing we could be arrested.

"Why can't we stay here for a few days?" they asked as one. "We can eat coconuts and forage for other food and restore our strength. Then we won't look like walking cadavers when we meet the people."

"It's a good argument," I explained, "but not a good idea. It's much better to report to the authorities in person than have the villagers talk about us among themselves and possibly report us. Proceeding openly and methodically in a business-like way, we lessen suspicion. You can stay here if you like, but after I eat a little more mush I'm following that path to see where it takes me."

"I'm all for that, my friend," Ludo exclaimed. "You brought us many miles across a dangerous sea. Now I will walk behind you on that path."

"Oh, I'll go along too," said Jules, hoping to be in my good graces again. I think it's right and fitting that we stick together."

"I can agree with that," Cluseau added. "We have a leader who has proven himself. The least we can do is follow with no complaints."

At daybreak we were walking down a narrow road all dusty with red earth. Later in the morning we encountered a group of black people traveling by wagon in the opposite direction. They pulled over to the side of the road to let us pass and eyed us with suspicion. An old woman in a red top and yellow skirt said something in English that sounded like a question. We couldn't understand her, and they went on their way. In another hour we came to a village with a police station and went to it. The constable, a black man with bulging muscles under a thin white shirt, sat behind a broad and bare desk in a rather crude office. He had heavy golden rings on his fingers and was wearing khaki shorts. Stripes denoting rank were on the sleeves of his shirt.

"Where do you come from?" he asked in good Spanish.

"From French Guiana," I replied in my best English.

"And where are you headed?" he asked in better English.

"We're hoping to get to the United States."

"That's a long way from Trinidad. Why did you land here?"

"Because we were in a boat about to fall to pieces for two weeks on the open sea. We put in here because of sheer necessity and because our chart showed this as the southernmost island in the Caribbean."

He was recording my answers in some kind of ledger. When he had finished he stood up, looked us over, and gave instructions to a deputy.

"Go to the store, James, and buy these tired-looking men some beer and cigarettes. Have the storekeeper put it on my tab."

"You want I should buy somethin' for myself too?" James asked.

"Of course, James, of course! Get two bottles for yourself. Get a loaf of bread and some meat to put on it. Good for your belly!"

The constable gave us bread and beef, bottles of cold beer, and a place to rest. Assuring us we had nothing to fear, he said he would take us in the afternoon to Port of Spain, the capital of the island, to meet his superiors and be processed. We had entered the country abruptly and illegally, but the processing would supply a legitimate explanation as to why it was necessary.

As we made ready to travel a few miles to the capital, the constable, who called himself Donny Adams, decided to recite our rights and legal obligations on the island. Rummaging in a file cabinet, he found a thin pamphlet and read from it: *"No French convict escaping Devil's Island and reaching the shores of Trinidad shall be arrested unless he breaks the law or disturbs the peace. If he arrives by a boat deemed seaworthy, he will be given ample supplies to continue his journey. If the vessel is deemed unseaworthy, a police officer will take him to Port of Spain to petition the Port Authority for a replacement. He may remain on the island eighteen days. At the end of that time the laws of Trinidad require him to leave. If sick as determined by a doctor, he may stay longer."*

"The main thing to remember, friend," said the constable, putting the pamphlet away, "is you won't be arrested. We believe the French are very much in the wrong as they continue to support and supply Devil's Island. It dishonors a civilized nation. The citizens of France should be ashamed of that place and rise up against it. We've heard of the horror existing there and oppose it."

"Horror does indeed exist there, sir. One glance at the brave men who escaped with me will confirm it. All of us served our sentences of hard labor under harsh conditions and were supposedly free, but we were not free. We were not allowed to leave Guiana."

"We on this island have heard of cases like yours

and you have our sympathy. Tell me about your boat, M'sieur Bonheur. Is it seaworthy?"

"It is not seaworthy, sir. Absolutely not! It's a wreck. It brought us to your island, a very long way, but got broken in the sea and surf. "

"I would like to take your word for it, but regulations compel me to inspect it. Do you mind if we go down to the beach and take a look?"

"By all means take a look, sir! We left the craft on the beach, put there by a lively surf, and I hope it's still there. I don't believe it has any worth at all, but some roaming beachcomber might like it."

His deputy gave us more beer and cigarettes, and we went down to the sea in his old car. Our little boat lay on the sand exactly where we had left it. No islander had bothered to touch it. The constable looked it over, carefully poked the hull with his walking cane, found it soft and waterlogged, and shook his head.

"Would you go to sea in that craft?" I asked. "Look! Near the bow it's beginning to split open. The tiller is broken, the rudder is falling apart, and the sail, made of pillowcases and a prison shirt, hangs in tatters. Also, believe it or not, the boat has no keel. It's a rowboat really."

"No, I can tell you for certain I wouldn't go to sea in that boat even on a Sunday afternoon for an hour. I can't believe you sailed that thing on the big ocean hundreds of miles. It looks like it was made for a millpond. You've done a marvelous thing, M'sieur Bonheur. Your story will become legendary among my people."

"Thank you kindly, sir. Thank you so much for the good words. But I assure you, we are not heroes. We merely did what we had to do."

"Well, I myself will take you to Port of Spain. I'm reasonably certain you'll be given a boat far more seaworthy. You will not have to pay for it. When one is fleeing Devil's Island in a boat as shoddy as this one, our policy is to replace it. No one in the capital will disagree when I say this boat is a wreck. I could take a photo of it, but it won't be necessary."

Before we left for the capital we learned the islanders lived by a code of honesty and trust. Donny Adams would need no photograph of our boat to prove it a wreck. Officials would take his word for it. And the boat would remain untouched on the beach until we gave it away. We were also amazed by the islander's willingness to help strangers from the sea. The prevailing attitude we found on Trinidad was the opposite of the cruelty, indifference, and inhumanity we had known for so many years as convicts in French Guiana. I for one had come to believe there were few people in the world who cared about other people: other men, women, and children. I was wrong.

Chapter Twenty-Four
A Boat For the Briny Deep

During the afternoon we drove along narrow roads across the island. En route we passed a group of farmers prodding their slow-moving oxen forward on the road. They wore colorful trousers, wide belts with shiny buckles, but no shirts. Beads of sweat made their skin glisten in the sun. They stood beside the road and broke into good-natured banter as we passed. I couldn't understand what they were saying. They seemed to be cheerful, happy people satisfied with their lives. Native islanders who had never left their island even for a few days, they were openly friendly even to foreigners. I asked if they were as happy and content as they appeared. Donny Adams flashed an engaging smile and nodded.

"They are indeed," he said. "If you could hear their music you would know as I know that blacks on this island have a good life. I'm black, as you can aptly see, and I have the authority to arrest any white man, any yellow man, any man or woman of any color needing arrest. We've come a long way since the days of slavery on this island. When the British took over some years ago, things got better for the people here."

In Port of Spain he drove us to the federal prison. The guards there were friendly but searched our meager belongings carefully for illegal drugs. Finding none, they recorded our names, ages, place of birth, and last occupation on legal tablets. We told them we were freed convicts forced to survive as best we could in French Guiana while carrying a "certificate of freedom." A very tall guard able to read French examined the certificate and said in his opinion it looked bogus. We had to agree it wasn't worth the paper it was printed on even though by law we had to have it always on hand to prove identity. Guards placed us in a spacious cell while insisting we were not under arrest. We were being held only until our case could be resolved. A courteous jailer gave us meat and potatoes with bottles of beer, and we soon fell asleep. The cots were not as good as a bed but clean.

At ten o'clock the next morning an Englishman in civilian clothes opened our cell. He was affable and talkative, asking many questions in fluent French, questions I tried to answer frankly and truthfully. At last he led us outside the prison and down the street to what he called a halfway house. A man named Bernard Bilk introduced himself and his wife Hannah. The time was nearly noon and a table was set for four. Though we insisted she not do it, the gracious lady served us a delicious lunch with good wine. None of us had tasted such a meal in many years, especially one with wine, and humbly we thanked her.

"You have the right to stay on this island eighteen days," said the English officer. "This comfortable house can be your home during that time at no expense to you, or you may go to any place of your choosing. You are not prisoners here. I shall see you tomorrow."

Living in the halfway house, we were free to come and go as we pleased. People came by and gave us toilet articles and clothes and even small donations of money, saying they were in sympathy with our cause. We were amazed at what a simple toothbrush could do for the teeth and mouth, even more amazed that we had never had one during all our years in prison. I have never been able to understand why. Toothpaste and a toothbrush were not expensive. My teeth and those of hundreds of inmates at Cayenne were in bad shape. Brushing them made my gums bleed but left a good taste in the mouth.

We ate heartily and began to put on weight. We showered every other day and wore clean clothing. We had forgotten what a luxury it was to be clean and to wear clean underwear. With so much leisure, we soon began to plan the next phase of our adventure. Cluseau had money to buy passage to Europe to see his ailing mother but no passport. She had moved to England and had found the climate not to her liking. A barber told us to see a man who lived above a drug store. The man, a Venezuelan political exile, fashioned for my friend within three days a Venezuelan passport with visas. The false identity was expensive, but Cluseau gladly paid the price.

Ten days after arriving in Trinidad our navigator boarded a ship for Southampton. I saw him off at the pier, thinking in time I might be able to book passage on a vessel headed for the United States. Jules and Ludo had no money and no plans. Late at night as we talked before sleeping, they said they might petition the government for citizenship and remain in Trinidad. They could learn English and Creole, find work, and live a good life. I spoke of my dream to gain citizenship in the United States and forget entirely my French heritage. Hearing that, my companions expressed a wish to come along with me. When I said I had money for only one passage, they replied we could get ourselves a better boat and continue our quest by sea. After all we had been through, I felt I couldn't desert them. I gave some thought to it and reluctantly assented.

A week or so later I paid a visit to the Chief of Police, the Inspector General of the entire island. A suave British army officer who spoke beautiful French, he chatted with me for an hour.

"Two things about the French I don't understand," he said with a wink and click of the tongue. "Their Foreign Legion and Devil's Island. Their love of women and good literature I do understand."

He got on the phone and spoke rapidly in English to someone he seemed to know very well. Though not intending to eavesdrop, I found myself understanding his English as well as that of Donny Adams. The black farmers we met on the road had spoken Creole, a mixed language. So that's why I couldn't understand them. Even though English was the official language of the island, Creole was spoken by most of the citizens. Native

English men and women (only a few on the island) and those who viewed themselves as the upper classes spoke English.

"You will have your boat, sir!" said the Chief. "All you need do is go to the harbor and look for one that's up for sale. A fisherman's boat, I should think, will serve you admirably."

Before the noon hour the next day we had a boat. It was a ship's lifeboat more than thirty feet in length with a wide beam. It was rigged with a tall and sturdy mast, a long boom, and good sails: a mainsail and a jib. A naval officer enlisted a nautical carpenter to modify it according to our instructions. We wanted a foredeck and a cuddy, and that we got. We could sleep and rest in the cuddy (a small cabin) away from the elements. I was also given a chart showing the seas we would travel. When I said we would not be able to pay for all the good things we were getting, the craftsman replied with a laugh that the government would pay for any supplies we needed. Never had anyone treated us so well.

Back at the halfway house I spread out the nautical chart on the dining-room table. The three of us hovered over the table for a good look. Jules and Ludo found it hard to believe we would have a road map, as it were, in our hands as we sailed. Before leaving for England, Cluseau had told me what he knew about nautical charts, and so I was able to read this one with few problems. He also taught me dead reckoning and how to mark it on the chart. I was certainly a novice when it came to navigation, and yet I felt confident in the little I knew.

"We can make it to the United States," I said to Jules and Ludo, "if we sail through the Caribbean to Miami."

With a pencil I pointed to islands on the chart. "Tobago is fifty-two miles north of Trinidad. Grenada is a hundred miles farther. Then we come to Saint Vincent, Saint Lucia, and Saint Kitts. Those are friendly islands. We'll have to be careful to avoid Martinique and Guadeloupe. If by some misfortune we should land on a French island, we'd be sent back to Devil's Island in a hurry."

"What about that island right there?" Jules asked, placing his finger on the chart. "It's much bigger than the others. Will we run into trouble if we happen to land there?"

"That's Puerto Rico. It's under American jurisdiction," I explained. "We shouldn't have a problem if we landed there. Haiti, I'm reasonably certain, would be safe too. But Cuba ... well, I think we'd better keep our distance from that island and go on toward Key West. It's a village only ninety miles from Cuba and the southernmost tip of the United States. Friendly people there. All we need to get there is lots of luck."

"Call it Freedom Street!" Ludo exclaimed with a bellow of laughter. "We'll soon be on Freedom Street! Our odyssey of suffering will be over! You know it,

Maurice. You did what most men only dream of doing, and you will live a free man again with dignity!"

"And you, Ludo. Will you soar like a silver bird above sunlit clouds? Will you find your freedom too and a good life?"

"I'm ready to have some fun on this island," said Jules before Ludo could answer. "It's a lively place and them mulatto girls are pretty. Why don't we see the sights and have some good food and a beer or two in a good bar before we even think about going to sea again?"

Ten minutes later we had put away the chart and were in the street. We needed to be close to people, to jostle them on the sidewalk, and become part of them. Isolation for years in prison demanded it. We went into a bar and ordered three beers. A smiling East Indian girl in a low-cut dress, her black hair tumbling to her shoulders, served them to us. We guzzled the cold beer in minutes and ordered three more. Doomed associates of the living dead were living again, really living as free men! The beer was tart, slightly bitter, but deliciously cold. The East Indian girl was warm and inviting. We were strangers to her, possibly exotic in her eyes, and she uttered a warm thanks as we left a generous tip.

We walked down the main street that runs from one end of the city to the other. Outside a café on a bed of crushed ice were oysters, sea urchins, shrimp, clams, mussels, and several varieties of fish. It was an amazing display to tempt passersby, and we couldn't resist. I got some francs exchanged for Antilles dollars, and we treated ourselves to an orgy of seafood, the best I ever tasted. We washed it all down with a fine white wine. Then back to our lodgings we went, a little drunk when the drinking got out of hand but full and happy. Once more we looked at the chart we believed would be our trusty roadmap through the Caribbean. My companions lost interest and fell into bed. I looked at it longer.

Three days later our boat was ready for launching. The bow had been decked over to give us a cuddy in which to sleep. The gunwales had been raised to keep the sea out. The standing rigging (stays and shrouds) had been expertly replaced with new cables. The running rigging (ropes or lines for adjusting the sails) was new and strong, and to my delight we had a sturdy new jib and mainsail. We were given an amazing assortment of supplies: pots and pans for the galley, two lamps for night travel, a compass for steering even at night, and three nautical charts depicting the entire region. Also we had an alcohol stove with extra fuel for cooking our food, and enough food and drink to take us all the way to Key West.

I wanted a document stating the boat officially belonged to me as the skipper. I explained we might run into naval authorities who would ask probing questions and suspect us of stealing the seaworthy vessel. With apology I was told it was not available. Venezuela and Colombia had complained, and so Trinidad stopped issuing documents of any kind to fugitives. We would have to take our chances. We crossed our fingers, a custom dating back to the Middle Ages in Europe and possibly Asia, and hoped no ship of any government would see our craft and stop us.

Early in the morning a powerboat towed us out of the harbor into the open sea. The day was balmy, clear, and becoming hot. A moderate breeze swept across the water from the southeast and filled our sails as soon as hoisted. On his way to becoming perhaps a citizen of England, Cluseau was not on hand to navigate or help with the steering. He had sided with me in times of stress, and I missed him. I was glad to have learned the basics from him and felt I would have no trouble navigating by stars at night and sun by day. He had mentioned celestial navigation, taking a noon sight with a sextant for latitude, but that I had never learned. I knew only the positions of the sun as a day wore on. I had my charts and a rudimentary knowledge of dead reckoning. Sailing among the islands of the Caribbean, as I thought about it, seemed to pose no troublesome navigational problems. We would eyeball each island as we came to it, find it on the chart, and mark it with a pencil.

"Stay east of the Lesser Antilles and north of the Greater Antilles," a seasoned sailor told us. "If you keep to the north of Puerto Rico, Haiti, and Cuba, you'll be on your way to Key West. Stop and rest at islands owned by the British and Americans. Avoid the Dutch and French."

When I checked the chart, I could see Tobago only a few miles from Trinidad. We would sail a northeasterly course toward that island and later northward to Grenada. "Northeast," I said to Jules at the tiller.

"Aye, aye skipper!" he responded. "Woohoo! We're on our way! And this time in a real boat that can handle anything that comes our way!"

"Wind from the southwest and rising," Ludo cautioned. "Keep an eye on the mainsail, Jules, and don't let that boom knock you over."

"I can handle this baby, old fellow! No need to give ol' Jules any of your schoolmarm instruction. Go below and get a good rest!"

"Listen up!" I yelled above the wind. "There will be no quarreling, no backbiting, on this leg of our voyage. If you accept me as your skipper and each other as mates, you will survive to greet the morning of many days. Go against me or go against each other and you won't."

"Aye, aye, skipper!" Jules replied after some hesitation.

"I'm your man, skipper," Ludo added. "Count on me. I signed on to attain freedom, to do it or die trying. So with me as with you it's freedom or death. No in between, I'm with you to the end."

He spoke with deep feeling and meant every word. I felt a lump in my throat but calmly replied, "Thank you, Ludo. And thanks to you too, Jules. You are both good sailors, fearless and capable. I know you can do the job we must all do. I depend on you."

Chapter Twenty-Five

Lost at Sea

Jules was in his early twenties and Ludo was in his late fifties. The age difference made them wary of each other and likely to generate conflict. Jules with the exuberance of youth had been in the habit of teasing the older man, and that had to stop. Ludo had suffered fifteen long years in a place that prided itself on robbing men of their dignity. Now on his way to freedom, he was not about to suffer insolence from Jules or anyone else, young or old. I could understand but couldn't be sure young and cocky Jules understood. So when Ludo went below before taking his turn at the helm, I decided to have a talk with the younger man.

"I want to make one thing very clear to you, Jules," I said to him in a calm and low voice, "if the three of us on this boat don't work together in harmony, we will likely die."

"I can understand as much," the young man said with a nod. "I know the old guy hates me because I've teased him, made him feel unworthy. I didn't really mean to hurt him, just wanted to see his reaction."

"Ludo doesn't hate you, Jules. But unless the two of you learn to get along in this small space surrounded by water, he might. You know he was sent to prison for killing a man. Though I doubt it, he might be able to kill again. I want you to keep that in mind."

"I'm not afraid of Ludo, and I think you know it. I think I might even learn to like the old guy if he would stop trying to tell me what I have to do just like a schoolmaster instructing a kid."

"At one time in his life he was a schoolmaster, and I agree with you; he still acts like one. I'll have a word with him."

"I know we have to sail this boat as comrades, Maurice. So I won't be baiting you or Ludo any more. I have trouble obeying orders, always been that way, but I will obey you as my skipper."

As a convict Jules had suffered grievously in prison. It caused him to resist authority wherever he found it, even from a comrade on a small sailboat. But obeying my orders meant safety at sea, and so he would act accordingly. Also he would do his dead-level best not to rub Ludo the wrong way. The man had his faults but a good heart too.

As I thanked him for wanting to do right, he began to talk about how well the good people of Trinidad had treated us, how they had accepted us as their friends. I said I would fondly remember those extraordinary people for the rest of my life and the happy days we spent with them. He nodded and smiled and said something that surprised me.

"One of these days I will return to that island and perhaps live there until I die. I really liked being there."

He was young enough to dream, a gift Ludo and I had probably lost. Hoping my remark would not sound like advice, I said he should hold on to that dream and realize it when he could.

I looked over my shoulder at the island that had given refuge to four desperate men. It was slowly disappearing in the mist. Our sturdy lifeboat converted into a sailboat was in harmony with the wind and waves and moving fast. Our provisions were stowed below, and we had no worries about losing food or drink or finding heavy weather. The sun was less hot than on shore and breezes were steady under balmy skies. We were passing Tobago on our way to Grenada. There as planned, the Salvation Army would replenish our supplies. When the sun fell below the horizon in a gorgeous display of orange, red, blue, green, and purple, we made ready for the night.

The nocturnal sailing we divided into three watches of three hours each. Our chronometer, which allowed us to measure the hours, was an ancient alarm clock a woman in Trinidad had given us. I wanted to ask the government official for a genuine chronometer but didn't because we already had so much. If the alarm clock stopped, we could have a problem. I regretted not having the real thing. Ludo would take the first watch, I the second, and Jules would greet the morning as he took the helm. Not one of us had known anything about how to sail a boat before our escape. Now Necessity had made us seasoned and hopefully intrepid sailors. We respected the wide ocean but knew it to be unpredictable in its behavior. We would take care.

"Keep an eye on the compass and steer northwesterly," I said to Ludo before finding my place to sleep. "You won't see much and neither will I on my watch, but after we've put behind us maybe seventy-five miles on my watch, Jules in the morning will see the Grenada Light."

I slept better on that sailboat than ever in my life. It must have been the motion that induced deep sleep. I would have slept till morning but was awakened after Ludo's stint. He had done a good job of keeping us on course, even when the wind shifted almost directly behind us. Now it was off our starboard quarter, and our sailboat was plunging along with a jerky motion that wasn't very comfortable. I was almost dozing and bending over to read the compass when a hand holding a mug of coffee in the semidarkness appeared before my face. Ludo had thought I would need it and made it before preparing to sleep. I thanked him heartily. A man who had suffered blatant inhumanity was showing kindness to another person. It was a good sign for all concerned. Slowly the stars had disappeared. The sea around us was black with jagged streaks of phosphorescence, green and violet. A small lantern supplied light for the compass. I was glad we had more than just a star to guide us.

Half way through my watch the sea wind from

the south shifted in speed and direction and ceased altogether. I tried as best I could to fill the sails with a breeze, but they fluttered and luffed lamely in no wind at all. Waves of one to two feet earlier were confused for a time but soon settled into calm. In heavy silence our sailboat sat still in the water. Our crisp mainsail was drooping, and the jib hung limp and silent. I heard nothing but a gentle lapping of water against the hull. The sound was comforting and almost musical. Then bleary-eyed Jules appeared in the companionway to ask what was going on.

"No wind," I answered. "We're marooned with no wind. Aggravating but better than too much I guess. Go on back to sleep, Jules. I'll wake you when it's time for your stint at the helm."

"I'm not sure I can sleep," he muttered, climbing into the cockpit. "I'm beginning to think we've bitten off more than we can chew. I ain't afraid, mind you, but do you really believe we can make Miami?"

"I do believe we can if we work together as a team and help each other. The boat is small but seaworthy. Professionals modified her for the open sea, for any kind of weather. So this vessel is a far cry from the rowboat that almost killed us, yet carried us many miles to Trinidad."

"Well, I hope we don't lose our way and head for Africa or wherever without knowing it. I can't see a damn thing even though on the eastern horizon is a flicker of gray. Is that a sign of a good day in the making."

"Yes, absolutely. A good day is coming. Now try to get some sleep. It's important for us to get as much rest as we can when not at work."

Two hours passed and he was up again for his watch. I gave him coffee as Ludo had given me a mug. He thanked me but complained of no sleep. I went below to crawl under a light blanket but couldn't sleep either. The silence was almost painful, and the boat became a seesaw in the swells. Then Jules loudly cried out he was certain a gigantic shark was bumping the boat. He couldn't see the shark but knew it was trying to get us. I tried to comfort him, saying sharks in warm waters don't prowl at night, but he was certain he felt a bump. I could see that fear of the unknown was rubbing against his reason and causing him distress. Not knowing where we were and what lay ahead weighed heavily on him, and there was very little we could do about it. After tossing in the narrow bunk for about an hour, I finally drifted into slumber. It seemed only a few minutes before an urgent voice jostled me awake.

"Wake up, skipper! Your turn at the helm. Time to move it!"

I expected to see land in the distance, but when the sun quickly rose above the horizon, we could see no land whatever. In still air Jules had given up trying to keep a course, but with the sun came a steady breeze and we began to move again. We now had the wind off our starboard beam as we resumed a northwesterly course. The boat picked up speed and began to heel with Ludo steering. I went below to prepare a quick breakfast. I didn't do a very good job of it. We had no gimbal for the stove, and the frying pan was unstable. Even so, I managed to cook up some bacon and eggs.

We ate our fill with bread dipped in bacon grease and afterwards felt stronger. However, no sight of land caused us to worry. At the end of the day, and the sailing was good, we had not seen land. All day long we had searched for it but found only sea and sky. No land brought on more worry. My companions thought we might have come close to Grenada at night and somehow missed it. That I couldn't believe. The chart showed Grenada as a large island. We couldn't have passed it in the dark without seeing it. The sky had no clouds, and the moon was almost full. The next day we saw not a sign of land. We had to admit we were lost.

"We should continue sailing on course anyway," I said, "because the chart tells me we can reach Haiti and Cuba that way. Or we may run into Puerto Rico toward the east. I want both of you to keep a close eye on the horizon at all times. Land could appear at any moment."

Both Ludo and Jules thought if we continued on our northwesterly course we could run into a French island and be arrested. They insisted we should forget the northerly course and head westerly toward land. I had no grounds on which to argue with them, and so I swung the helm over and began sailing for land. Heading westerly into the sun, the wind wasn't as favorable as on our previous course. But in time our little boat found her traces in a sunpath and galloped along.

The wind increased and we found ourselves in gale-force winds for several long hours. At the end of the day when the storm passed on, we were exhausted. Yet our boat had performed wonderfully well and was as perky as ever. That's when we realized the boat could take a lot more than we could. Early the next day we expected to spot land but saw only a cloudbank resembling land. Leaving Trinidad, we thought we could hop from one island to another all the way to Miami. We had sailed a week or more with no sign of land and no sight of land.

Another day we spent on the open ocean with nothing in sight but a circular horizon where the blue sky met the dark blue water. Then in late afternoon as I lay resting below I heard Ludo hoarsely shout, "A ship! I can't believe it, but I see a ship! I'm hallucinating! I'm crazy!"

I scrambled into the cockpit to see for myself, and sure enough on the eastern horizon we saw what appeared to be a cargo ship moving in our direction. We could see smoke from her stacks and the stacks a few minutes later. Then the black hull of the ship hove into view. At last the massive bow with white waves on either side approached us. The ship's crew had spotted our sail and had come to investigate.

"What boat is that?" came an accented inquiry in English.

At the stem of our boat, Jules shouted in French, "Help us, please! We need assistance! *M'aidez s'il vous plait, m'aidez!*"

"Can you come alongside? We'll drop a ladder."

"We can and we will, sir! Give us ten minutes!"

Because of her size the ship appeared to be much closer, and more than twenty minutes passed before we were able to drop our sail and nudge up against the steel hull. Skirting her stern, we saw that she was flying the German flag. A ladder with wooden steps had been lowered from the deck, and I climbed it. Jules and Ludo stayed in our sailboat to keep her from banging against the ship. We had two rubber fenders to protect the hull, but strong arms were needed also. On deck I spoke with a young officer who escorted me to the bridge of the ship. There I came face to face with the captain, Herbert Schultz. He was a handsome man with the stiff bearing of a German military officer. Though his face was young looking, his long hair was gray and his beard flecked with gray. He spoke to me in German, a language I didn't understand. Correcting his error, he spoke in English. When I told him I was a Frenchman, he spoke French with a Germanic thrust.

"How large is your vessel, M'sieur Bonheur? I'm astonished to find a vessel so small in these vast waters. And you hail from where?"

I hesitated before replying, but in a moment decided to tell all. The captain was our benefactor and deserved to hear the full story.

"We sailed from Trinidad, sir, after the kind people there extended heart-warming hospitality. They also gave us a sturdy boat with ample supplies for a long voyage. I won't deceive you, sir. We sailed to Trinidad in a makeshift boat from French Guiana. We had served our sentences there but were not allowed to leave. We escaped in a rowboat with a flimsy sail and made it all the way to Trinidad."

"Ah, yes! I've heard of your kind. You are desperate fugitives from Devil's Island! Worst prison on earth I hear. It has a bad reputation. Sad story, that. My country and your country have never been on the best of terms. I'm sure you know that. So I could say it's no business of mine what your country does, but that atrocious prison dishonors the French republic and its people."

I nodded my head in agreement, remaining silent. I had heard the same sentiment from others. In his chart room the captain drew from a large drawer a huge chart that covered the table. At a glance I could see it displayed most of the islands of the Caribbean. He pointed to an island well to the west of Grenada and close to the coast of Venezuela.

"That's the Dutch island of Curaçao," he said. "Sixty-five miles from, there is Aruba also owned by the Dutch. We found you more than one hundred miles north of those islands."

I stared at the chart in amazement. Our northwesterly course had taken us more than 500 miles from Trinidad to open water well to the north of the Dutch islands. If we had sailed more westerly, as my sailing companions suggested, we might have entered a hostile harbor. Dutch Guiana was known to arrest convicts trying to escape French Guiana. A Dutch island many miles distant probably had the same policy.

"I'm doubting you'll ever make it to Miami from here," the captain was saying. "With no engine the Gulf Stream would keep pushing you back. You would sail up to it and be pushed backward by the current. We can lift your boat on deck and take all three of you to Curaçao."

"I appreciate your kind and generous offer, sir, but must refuse it. My comrades and I believe we'd lose our freedom there and be sent back to Devil's Island. It's because Dutch Guiana arrests convicts from French Guiana, and it's probably a general policy among the Dutch."

"Oh, I see. Perhaps so," he said, "and you don't want to take risks that could be harmful. I admire your grit and wish you luck. The steward will give you a keg of water and some food supplies."

I thanked the good captain sincerely and returned to our sailboat with a large canvas bag of food, a big keg of water, some bottles of wine, and a generous supply of cigarettes. Sailors loaded the stuff on board, and turning to climb the ladder wished us well. We pushed off with no difficulty and hoisted sail. A new leg of the voyage had begun. This leg, we hoped, would take us to Panama. We would sail due west for several days and then southward. To keep track of the miles, I would mark our progress on the chart and hope for the best. Because I had studied the captain's professional chart, I knew our exact position.

Also he gave me a little booklet in English on dead reckoning and urged me to study it in my spare time. Necessity and the thin booklet taught me basic nautical navigation beyond what Cluseau had taught. I knew nothing of celestial navigation, only that the sun rose in the east and set in the west. Had I known more about navigating a boat when we left the isle of Trinidad, we wouldn't have missed Grenada. We wouldn't have sailed for many days without knowing where we happened to be in a vast desert of water. I felt I had to take all the blame for that colossal failure. If Ludo and Jules wanted a scapegoat to blame, they surely had one in me. However, because good luck had smiled upon us with the appearance of the German ship, there was no blame whatever extended to me. Ludo and Jules had come to believe in their skipper. How could they blame me when they knew I had experienced the same suffering as they and the same good feelings later? We had become a team, and for that I was truly thankful.

It was getting dark when I left the German ship. Ahead of us lay a new course to follow at night. We attached a lantern to the forestay and used the second lantern for reading the compass. Because the seas were mild under steady breezes, we decided to stand four-hour watches to give the two men off duty more sleep. Jules took the first watch running from eight to midnight, and I volunteered for the second. Ludo would take over in the early morning and be at the helm at first light. At that time he would scan the horizon for any sight of land. We were feeling better after talking with professional mariners, and chatted amicably as we sailed in fairly calm water. Our boat skipped across the surface as if knowing where she was going.

If we could make it to Panama, we believed American authorities wouldn't hinder our moving overland. We would go through Central America and Mexico to rest for a while in Texas. If immigration officials allowed us to enter Texas, and we thought they would, it would place us more than a thousand miles from Miami, our destination. We could put down stakes in Texas and make a life there, or go on to the east coast as planned. A thousand-mile trek across a country unknown to us would be just another obstacle to overcome.

Years later as I tried to catch up with my reading, I came across an obituary in the *New York Times* of one Herbert Schultz. The name was a common German name but also familiar. Was this the same man who had rescued us as we sailed lost in a big ocean? Was this the captain of the German ship who had set us on the right course with cigarettes and new provisions? Reading more of the obituary, I found that Herbert Schultz, our captain and savior, had served as a high-ranking officer in the German Bundeswehr during World War One and was decorated for bravery. My recollection of him was vivid. On meeting him I suspected he had been at one time a military man. He was indeed a brave man and a good man. He saved our lives.

Chapter Twenty-Six
Things Fall Apart

We struggled against strong currents that came and went, but the wind held all night and into the next day. It was a favorable wind blowing at moderate speed from the south. As we sailed due west, the wind on our portside beam heeled the boat well over but also gave her steady speed. Ludo wanted to know what I meant when I said the sailboat was heeling almost to thirty degrees. I explained it was a nautical term for how far the boat tipped from the horizontal plane. Thirty degrees meant the rail was almost in the water and too far. Yet the more we heeled the faster we went because it increased the length of the waterline. He thanked me for my lecture and wanted to know if I would like to hear about how Ulysses made his way home to Penelope after the Trojan War.

I politely declined for the moment but said I would certainly keep his offer in mind. My time at present had to be given to navigation. Each day I tried to plot our course to determine how far we had gone, and several times during the day I checked my chart. I had the presence of mind to ask for a knotmeter that measures speed when equipping the boat, and that instrument helped me a lot to determine our position. After a given number of miles we would have to tack and move in a different direction near the coast of Colombia to reach Panama. Three days and nights went by after we left the German ship. On the fourth day with feelings of great relief we sighted land to the south of us.

I thought it might surely be the Colombian coast and urged caution. We could sail along the coast but far out so as not to attract attention. Then we could veer off a bit and head toward Panama. My companions by now were exhausted from too much exposure and insisted we find a little cove, move into it, drop anchor, and try to find out exactly where we were. As before, they were sad victims of not knowing, and I couldn't convince them to stay with me on the water longer. Their state of mind interfered with sound thinking. It left them apprehensive and indecisive, but dominant when I tried to argue with them.

"We need to know our location," Ludo exclaimed. "I believe it's very important to know where we happen to be. When we know where we are, we can move again with confidence."

I tried to tell him my dead reckoning penciled on the chart gave us a good idea as to where we were, but he found that hard to believe. I had studied the booklet that Captain Schultz gave me and was reasonably certain I was doing the dead reckoning right. To him and Jules it was an esoteric thing, a mind-numbing mystery not to be trusted.

"That squiggly line on that chart don't tell me much,"

Ludo said. "I'm for moving to shore now that we're close enough. I know we'll be taking a colossal risk, but we've lived with danger for a long time."

"I'm with Ludo on this," said Jules. "We don't often agree on much of anything, but this time we do. With the shore so close, we'd be fools not to take advantage of it. We really need to be on dry land again."

"I'm wary of dropping anchor in a cove that could be hostile," I tried to argue, "and yet after all these days at sea it's hard to resist."

In front of us was a barren stretch of sandy beach. We sailed toward it, slowly at first and then faster. Our intention was to drop anchor in the calm water of a cove nearby and possibly swim ashore. But the breakers caught the boat, lifted it, and sped it forward. I was on the tiller but lost any power to steer the boat. All we could do at that moment was hang on. A rushing wave hit us broadside and capsized our sailboat, throwing the vessel on her side with the mast and boom digging into sand. All three of us tumbled into the surf and were carried head over heels to the beach. Minutes later we lay battered on hard sand.

Our sweet little boat lay half on her side under water a few yards from us. With frantic desperation giving us super strength, we struggled to right her. If she had been flat-bottomed like our rowboat, we could have done it. But the keel that had saved us from disaster in high winds and heavy seas wouldn't budge. Knowing our lives depended on it, we plunged into the sunken boat to rescue provisions and equipment. We placed the items away from the water and sprawled half conscious on the sand. By the time we were up again, the sun had dried our clothes.

Away from the beach we found plenty of dry wood to build a fire. I lit it with a match kept dry in a bottle and prepared a dinner of rice and beans. We had water to drink from a full keg we had rescued. As we were beginning to eat we looked over our shoulders to see a band of wild-looking Indians staring at us. I called to them in Spanish but got no response. They moved on down the beach, and we assumed they were leaving us alone, but they returned and boldly approached us. Again I spoke to them in the Spanish I had learned in Panama. They understood not a word, and they spoke a language we didn't understand.

For a few minutes none of us moved, neither they nor us. Then several painted men began to inspect the supplies we had struggled to rescue. When we tried to stop them, they threatened us with spears and helped themselves to our goods. They took possession of all we had: our clothing and personal effects, our food, drink, and lantern, even our compass. Then giggling among themselves in strong but high-pitched voices they danced off and disappeared.

"What brave men we are!" Jules squawked, slapping his forehead in disgust. "Why in holy hell didn't you shoot them slimy bastards with that revolver you threatened us with a while back?"

"Oh, that? I threw it into the sea as soon as we landed on the beach in Trinidad. It had become a burden, and I didn't think I'd have use for it any more. Also it wasn't a good idea to be armed when entering a new country. Now I'm thinking I should have kept it."

"Oh my God, Bonheur! What a dumbass thing to do! How dumb! Just plain dumb! You had a good weapon and you threw it into the ocean? Trinidad ain't French Guiana, you know. It's very doubtful a policeman would have searched you. Dumb, Bonheur, dumb! You're not my skipper any more, and so I can say what I feel like saying."

"Well, you've said enough, kid," Ludo cautioned. "Now put a cork in your piehole! We can't be fighting each other. It's them savages we need to worry about. I'll slit their throats when they come back again!"

"With what?" I asked. "You don't remember they put a spear to your chest, grabbed your knife, and ran off with it? I remember!"

I was about to apologize for my unseemly remark when Jules ran into the surf and swam out to our boat. It was battered and beaten and almost entirely under water. He dove down looking for something in the cuddy and came up with a machete. I didn't even know it was on the boat; he had hidden it in the bilge. He swam ashore waving the big blade triumphantly and shouting gleefully.

"Now let them bastard savages mess with us! This is the equalizer! I don't want to be killing, but if I have to I won't hesitate."

"That machete is better than nothing I guess," Ludo groused, "but it's too bad our skipper threw his stinking revolver away. I thought of getting a gun in Trinidad and keeping it on the boat. I thought I might get a rifle to shoot a big shark if it came near us. We could have hauled it aboard and made a feast of it. Well, we have a machete."

So the three of us had some protection, but what could it do when pitted against a bow and arrow or long spear? Even so, I was glad we had it, for we had almost nothing else. We moved away from the beach to a grove of trees, hoping to find a secure place to sleep. Hidden by the undergrowth, we slept hard but fitfully on empty bellies. When morning came, Jules killed a big lizard with his machete and struggled to skin it. We built a fire of dry sticks and lit it with the last match we had. We shared the slightly cooked lizard and agreed it didn't have much taste.

The tiny two bites of meat didn't satisfy our hunger. It only made us ravenous. Ludo remembered the bottles of wine we had stowed on the boat. Jules, a good swimmer, went in search of them and swam on his back to shore holding two bottles high. Then he returned for two more. The Indians had broken open the water keg, and so the wine imprisoned in corked bottles was all that we had to slake our thirst. Desperation will sometimes turn a man into a genius, and it happened with Ludo. He opened the bottles with the prong of his belt buckle. We drank our fill of good wine, reluctantly left the beach and our boat, and began walking inland. We didn't know what we were up against. We didn't know with certainty that we were in Colombia.

For an entire day we trudged along with no food and no water. We expected to find a river we might have trouble crossing but found no rivers. At last we came upon a stream of fresh water, drank and drank, and filled our wine bottles with water. Then we bathed in the stream to cool off and get clean again, but also to alleviate the pain of many insect bites. We were now some distance from the sand dunes and surrounded by jungle, yet close to the shore. At night we slept in the thickest thicket we could find with our one machete ready for whatever. Night roaming animals came near us but went on their way, causing no harm.

For several days we saw no other human being but had a nagging suspicion from time to time that someone was observing us. Ludo had read about stealthy American Indians who could creep up on a target so adeptly as to be invisible. He insisted that the natives of the Colombian jungle could do the same. So beware. Jules glared at him, and I defused the situation with a joke. I couldn't have the two in conflict again. They had gotten along rather well since my little talk with Jules.

We ate fish speared with a pointed bamboo stick, and we ate frogs we managed to spear. In a large seashell we carried coals to kindle a fire. Rubbing sticks together for half an hour was no longer necessary. All three of us had festering insect bites and bleeding feet. On the boat the soles of our feet had become tender, and we had lost our shoes in the surf. We wrapped our feet in leaves for walking, but they quickly gave way. Happily, we had not begun to quarrel again. We got along because we shared suffering and kept a sense of humor. Also we knew if we didn't stay together we could die.

Near sunset on the third day we came upon a grass hut in a circular clearing with jungle all around it. Some fishing nets were drying in the sun, and a sea turtle lay upside down in a tub nearby. With one blow of his machete Jules hacked off the shell. We boiled the turtle in the tub, and we ate thick hunks of tasty meat to our hearts' content. Full bellies improved our tolerance for each other. Ludo found an old calico dress inside the hut and on leaving wrapped chunks of meat in it. The meat we ate the next day was beginning to spoil, but it didn't make us sick.

Walking on the beach beside the jungle, we came to a native village with maybe twenty huts. We crept into the village at night but quickly exited when dogs began to bark. All night long we walked along the beach in cool air and cool water as it lapped on the beach. Soaking our damaged feet in the water got rid of the pain. We stopped only to relieve ourselves now and then but not to rest. When morning came with light filtering downward, we crawled under a jungle thicket and slept.

I thought I was having a bad dream when I heard an angry man speaking Spanish. "Don't you dare move, hombres, not a one of you! Who in hell are you and what are you doing here? Sleeping I can see but why here? Give me answers, hombres, and give them fast!"

A very brown young man in a soldier's uniform was confronting us. Another soldier stood behind him. He ordered us to walk. They had tied their horses to a tree on the edge of the jungle, and soon we were on the beach. We trudged behind their horses more than an hour and finally reached the Colombian coastal town of Santa Marta. They took us to the police station that served also as an army barracks. A crowd of noisy children, talkative adults, barking dogs, and braying donkeys followed us through the town. Three pale-skin strangers, obviously foreigners, bedraggled and sparely dressed made a festive occasion for them.

In a large and spare office behind a large mahogany desk, sat the soldiers' commanding officer. He was a little man, thin and wiry, but with a loud, authoritative voice. No ordinary soldier, he wore a military jacket with epaulets. On the jacket spread across its right side were medals he had earned. His rank and name I soon learned was Colonel Mateo Lopez. He wore his rank like a prized jewel.

"Your passports, please," he said in polite Spanish. "Passports."

But we had no legal passports, not even forged ones.

"Fugitivos de Cayenne!" he proclaimed with excitement. "Fugitivos!"

Ludo had been ailing for several days and was now shivering. I explained that my comrade was old and sick of the fever. The colonel had an assistant call a doctor who gave us all quinine. Native women brought us plenty of food and drink. Colonel Lopez picked up the phone and asked to be put through to another city some miles away.

"Tengo tres fugitivos de Cayenne. Notificar el Cónsul Francés."

Jules, feverish Ludo, and I stared blankly at one another. He was asking someone to notify the French Consul. After two fearful stints with the unpredictable sea, and after sailing hundreds of miles in the open ocean in a small boat, we were losing our bid for freedom. The misery we had suffered for many years had killed our ability to cry, and yet in disgust and sadness we felt like crying. It was my seventh attempt to escape the horror that was killing me, and I thought it would surely be the last. But like all the others it had ended in failure. I would not have the will or strength for another. I felt old and tired and disgusted.

"I'm finding no pleasure in this matter," Colonel Lopez explained. "But it's the law, and as a public figure I must obey it. You will be sent to Cartagena. There, if you can present your case forcefully, you may not be deported. I feel no pleasure detaining you, and yet I must."

The next day we found ourselves behind bars in the colorful old city of Cartagena, a key port in colonial days where pirates found refuge. Our mood was one of sad resignation until the warden paid us a visit with good news. If we had arrived only two days earlier, he told us with a glint in his eye, we would have gone back to Cayenne under guard on the French mail boat. So even though most of the time fate, nature, and human society were in line against us, we now relished an interval of good luck. There wouldn't be another mail boat headed to Cayenne for another month. That bit of good fortune gave us time to think about something that might help us squirm out of our predicament.

"You'll have to wait and bide your time here," warned the warden. "Don't try to escape. My men are the best sharpshooters in the business. You wouldn't live as long as a snowball in hell."

That afternoon, looking through the tiny window of my cell at the lush green jungle, I told myself I would indeed try to escape. I might be courting death, as the warden had warned, but every day I would make an effort to escape. I had tried it seven times and failed, but with each try, as I thought about it, I had come closer to succeeding. The latest attempt had taken me hundreds of miles from Devil's Island. The last leg of the journey would have brought me to Panama and onward to America. I would place my worn-out feet on the soil of America, or die trying. I wrestled with despair but had not given up.

The guards in my Colombian jail were crack shots, the warden had said. Just one false move and they would shoot me dead. But I reasoned after all I had been through it would be better to be dead in Colombia than alive in French Guiana. So I would try again, my eighth attempt to escape. Somehow I would escape my jail cell and not be shot dead. I would live free of degradation, oppression, pain, and human misery or find my peace in death. These thoughts flooded my heart and soul but with little comfort. They would have to supply warmth to the faculty I depended on for survival, plainly the mind, and my present predicament did not in the least allow it.

Chapter Twenty-Seven

Paragraphs Scribbled in French

Day after day I gazed fixedly at the green jungle. It seemed to beckon to my craving to escape and was becoming an obsession. Every morning in groggy imbalance, I stumbled to the small window and stood staring at the scene outside. I ate the breakfast the jailor gave me and went back to stare at the stretch of green. My companions in the somber cell refused to look through the bars at the outside world. They were despondent, defeated, cursing their fate, each other, and me. They seldom spoke, but when they did speak it was to complain bitterly of what lay in store for us. They were certain we would soon be on a mail boat headed to prison in French Guiana and a painful death after long suffering in solitary confinement. It was over, they said. Our lives were as good as ended.

Countless men had died or gone mad in those infamous solitary confinement cells, they told each other, and so would we. As the days passed, the two became more gloomy and quarrelsome. They found fault with each other, fault with me, fault with society and the entire world. Jules in a fit of rage triggered by something I had said, struck me with his fist between my shoulder blades when I turned away from him. I backed off, asserting in no uncertain terms that I was in no mood to fight him.

"Calm down bully boy. You must know I'm not afraid of you, not in the least afraid of you, but I won't brawl with you in a prison cell."

"Brawl, you say? Brawl? You'll be dead after three punches! Won't be no brawl, little man, just a killing. C'mon, lets have it! We wouldn't be in this place if you knew anything at all about navigation."

"Hold on now. Did I not identify the Colombian shore and try to tell you it would be dangerous to land there? Did you not insist that we sail toward the beach anyway? Calm down, Jules, and try to think."

"You swamped the boat in the surf, damn it, and we lost it all, our dream of gaining freedom lost with all we had. Now look at us!"

He glared at me with fists clenched and moved in closer, possibly to strike me again. I made ready for the blow and was ready to deliver one or more of my own. Ludo, siding with me, wrenched off a table leg to use as a cudgel and stood between the two of us.

"Now you listen to me, sonny boy, and you listen good! Try punching Maurice again, and I'll smash your skull to mush."

Jules got the message and calmed down. Eyes blazing, he lapsed into sullen silence and turned away. Ludo suddenly ready to defend me was a surprise. Earlier, as he and Jules talked just above whispers, I heard him finding fault with me. I knew he liked me better than young Jules, but as skipper I tried to treat both the same. But after we lost the boat I was no longer the skipper, as Jules made clear. We would soon be going our separate ways with little hope for the future.

The only slim hope I had was the possibility the Colombians would take pity on us and release us. They had come to hate over more than half a century the sprawling penal system in French Guiana. So on occasion, instead of arresting runaways and sending them back, they helped them on their way. Perhaps with good luck, I was thinking, it could happen to us. As it turned out, only I was the lucky one. A few days after our capture the editor of an influential newspaper in Cartagena asked the warden if he might interview me for a story. He had read a magazine article by Ellen Thornhurst in which she named me as a major source for supplying her with "hard facts instead of fiction."

The editor was careful to speak to me in private. He said he would pay me generously if I wrote for his paper a series of stories exposing the abuses of the French penal colony. He said in addition to payment he might be able to use his influence to get me released. Of course, I agreed to work with him, and a few days later he told me he had written to the French ambassador in Bogotá on my behalf. It was no surprise to learn that the ambassador adamantly refused to grant me even a semblance of freedom. Vehemently he insisted I be returned to French Guiana.

However, events did not unfold that way. The captain of the guards placed me in a cell of my own with pen and paper and a table. All day long and well into the night I scribbled paragraphs in French, thanking fate and the gods for making me literate. In record time I produced six articles of required length. The editor had them translated, read four of them, and handed me a roll of bills the size of my fist. Dumfounded, I stood amazed but not unwilling to receive the money.

Later I discovered among the bills something very curious and a bit troubling. Stuffed in with them was a note informing me it had been "arranged" for my cell door to be unlocked after midnight. Was it a ruse to get me into deeper trouble? I had heard of prisoners in Guiana egged on to escape only to be shot. The note was brief. I read it more than once. Then slowly I began to see it as authentic. The newspaper editor was influential in the old city; his newspaper in sixty years had become a powerful voice of the people there. As a bonus to me he had persuaded sympathetic prison officials to let me leave their institution. The note was astounding but believable. I was to be a free man again.

I decided to bide my time, not become overly excited, and be guided by reason. I ate the generous supper they gave me, and feeling warm and content lay down to rest but fell asleep. Near midnight I was jolted awake by sounds I took care to identify. I heard a key turn in the lock, shuffling footsteps retreating, and silence. I went to the door, turned the latch, and pushed. When the heavy door swung open, I looked into the corridor. Even though I saw not a single person in the hallway, I did see an iron gate in the prison wall that was slightly ajar. My heart raced with excitement. All I saw confirmed it was not a scheme to kill me.

The warden was permitting me to leave unnoticed by any person who might report me. I took a deep breath and ran for the iron gate. A few minutes later I was rapidly walking through the narrow streets of Cartagena. In the distance a dog was barking, but most of the people in the city were asleep. The streets had lamps that cast more shadow than light. I tried to imagine what I would do should a police car round the corner with siren blaring. On the road leading to the seacoast I broke into a slow jog that quickly turned into a run. When I stopped to rest and sleep for an hour or two, I couldn't help but think of Jules and Ludo. Hidden behind some wooden crates behind a drapery store, I wondered whether they too would be allowed to escape. I never found out.

I had but one plan: to reach the Canal Zone in Panama where the Americans were in charge. I knew they staunchly opposed the prison system in French Guiana and wouldn't deport me. But how would I get there? And how would I defend myself against primitive Indians who lived between Cartagena and Panama? I had heard of human traffickers working out of Cartagena getting rich by taking people to Panama. It crossed my mind to use their services, but knowing they couldn't be trusted I decided to make the journey on foot. It would require walking along the coast hundreds of miles and finding a place to sleep at night.

I wasn't sure I had the physical strength or stamina to accomplish so gargantuan a task, but how would I know if I didn't try? At a roadside store I bought a backpack and stuffed it with necessities. On the counter lay the owner's pistol, a small revolver. I asked if he would sell it to me. He quoted an outrageous price, saying he needed the weapon to protect his place. After haggling half an hour I bought the pistol and a box of shells for a figure I couldn't really afford. I loaded the revolver with six bullets and stuffed it in my backpack. It would serve me better, should I encounter hostile Indians, than a knife or machete. It was the second revolver I had bought for protection. I hoped it would be the last.

As I was leaving, the shopkeeper called me back, speaking Spanish spiced with a thick Mandarin accent and exerting excessive politeness. "You gonna need machete walking through tough jungle, mister. You gonna need sharp machete to cut through jungle growth. I sell you very nice machete, good price, sharp you betcha, never used much."

What he was saying made sense. I needed that instrument to clear a path through swampy areas and fend off killer snakes. I bought it at three times its worth and left the owner satisfied. An hour later I was using it to make headway in a Colombian shore jungle. For several days I struggled through thick undergrowth and a number of swamps. Then one afternoon I blundered into a clearing with thatched huts. Indians clad in loincloths grabbed their spears and ran toward me. One of them understood Spanish and calmed the others when I spoke to him. They took me to their chief, a much older man in a faded yellow tee shirt with "USA" on it in red letters. Around his neck he wore a necklace of boars' teeth. He questioned me through his interpreter. I responded to his questions as politely as possible.

"I will be entirely honest with you, good sir. Months ago I escaped the prison compound in French Guiana known as Devil's Island. It is a very bad place; you may have heard about it. Recently I was allowed to leave a Colombian jail in Cartagena, and now I go to Colon in Panama."

He listened patiently as I spoke and paid careful attention to what his interpreter said. Then speaking through the man who knew Spanish, he said I would have to turn back. The land ahead was "closed country." No white man could enter it. "You die if you go near it," the interpreter translated. The old chief nodded in agreement.

A group of Indians had gathered around my backpack to examine its contents. A woman drew out my revolver and quickly handed it to the chief. Aware of its value, he giggled as it lay in his lap. He picked up the loaded gun and pointed it at me, smiling happily with a show of blackened teeth. To test the gun, he pointed it upward and pulled the trigger. The safety mechanism prevented the pistol from firing, and so nothing happened. The chief frowned and muttered *no bueno* in the little Spanish he knew. I released the safety latch and he fired the gun twice in the air. Then smiling broadly, he instructed the interpreter to tell me the pistol was no longer mine.

I didn't like to hear that but knew I was in no position to oppose the chief. So speaking humbly I said it would be my gift to him. "My revolver I give to you, good sir, in exchange for your hospitality."

His blinking old eyes lit up and he nodded with delight. In tones of high authority, he announced I could spend the night in his village and be on my way the following day.

He put aside a hut for me, and a young woman brought me the lean pork of a wild hog, a hunk of sourdough bread, and a bowl of fermented guava juice. Afterwards, my belly was pleasantly full, and the primitive bed I found was comfortable. I could have fallen into deep slumber to last all night, but that wasn't my plan. When night fell and the village slept, I made my way to the beach and stole a canoe. I selected one with an outrigger and a sail. The sail would propel the boat, and the outrigger would make it stable in rough conditions.

I put a couple of paddles in the craft and slid it off

the beach into the water. I knew nothing about how to paddle a canoe as one person and had to learn fast. In about an hour I was shifting the paddle from side to side to keep moving forward. For hours I paddled furiously along the coast not having to worry about navigation. I tried to raise the sail in the choppy sea but couldn't do it. The canoe was too tender to move about in or stand. It would likely capsize despite the outrigger and throw all my equipment overboard. So I paddled to shore and began examining the sail. It was gaff-rigged with a heavy yard that complicated hoisting the sail. But at last I got it properly hoisted and set out again. A short tiller was attached to a makeshift rudder, but it was all I could do to keep the slender craft upright in building waves. Then I learned how to manage the outrigger, and that made the going easier.

I put behind me maybe thirty miles during the night and put in to shore when the sun came up. I was hesitant to move by day, knowing the Indians from whom I had stolen the boat would be looking for me. I hid the canoe in the bush and ate coconuts thrown down by the wind. With my machete I whacked open a few and drank the milk. I whacked them again to get at the meat, and it took the edge off my hunger. All day I remained in hiding and took to the water again as soon as darkness came. Shoal water made it easier to get back out to sea, but in the deep water curious sharks began to flash their fins.

One mighty bump against the canoe was all they needed for a feast of human flesh. Within minutes I felt the bump I knew was coming and then another. Although alone in black darkness on a vast and silent sea, I didn't relish the sharks as my companions. If they capsized the canoe, I would never be able to right it before they got me. Then I remembered something I had read in my youth. Because of poor eyesight, sharks in tropical waters seldom scavenge for food at night. Perhaps these were merely curious. They circled the boat twice after bumping it, apparently lost interest, and abandoned me. As daylight began to break in the east, I beached the canoe and hid it in a thick tangle of vines and brush. I slept hidden in the brush and didn't awaken until noon.

In my knapsack I found two hard biscuits with pieces of dried pork and bolted them down for breakfast. Walking resolutely on the beach in the heat of a blazing sun, I saw in the distance three human figures. Rapidly they approached, and I could see they were Indians with no love for white men. Scowling, they danced around me and asked questions I couldn't understand. In a matter of minutes they were pushing me along to their village at the mouth of a creek. Scores of Indians emerged from huts to look me over, a strange white man almost never seen in their country. Naked children driven by curiosity prodded me with sticks and shrieked when I cried out. Two or three touched me with their hands and ran frightened to bare-breasted mothers..

In the chief's hut was a man who knew Spanish. He helped me tell the chief I was a runaway from a terrible prison and meant no harm to him or his people. Clad only in a loincloth and wearing painted tribal symbols on his arms and chest, the chief nodded but said not a word. With a flick of his hand a pretty young woman came forward. Except for a grass skirt, she was naked. At the chief's command, she went away and came back with a basket of delicious fruit. An older woman led me to a hut for the night. The chief had granted me rare hospitality.

Chapter Twenty-Eight
Panama Lights

Inside the Indian hut was a mattress stuffed with the feathers of tropical birds. When I nestled into it, a strange odor filled my nostrils. Yet I slept as one dead until midnight. Awake I found a wooden bowl of fruit and a pan of water near me. The woman who led me to the hut had apparently decided to give me those items. I put the fruit in my knapsack, splashed the water on my face to become alert, crept away from the hut, and ran toward the beach. When a dog began to bark, I stopped in my tracks and held my breath. I knew the barking could awaken the village and give me away. As I was about to hide in jungle brush I heard a yelp and a whimper. The animal ceased barking and all was quiet.

On the beach a sturdy rowboat lay near several canoes close to the water. It had a wide beam and strong oars but no sail. It demanded all my strength to lug it to the water. In waist-deep breakers I jumped into the boat and began to row. I followed the coastline, clear and silent in the moonlight, and rowed just about all night. Pieces of cloth torn from my ragged trousers saved my hands from severe blisters. Above me was a brilliant display of stars so close I thought I could reach up, find a switch, and turn them off. The sea was almost calm, and that made the rowing easier than having to fight waves coming from where I was going. Perhaps because of the calm, I detected a strange odor that I had never smelled in all my time on the ocean. It was more flower-like than fishy. I wondered what could be causing it but never found out. Within a few minutes it disappeared.

In early light I landed on a spit of land that extended eastward for miles. I couldn't row around it and thought I might get to the other side by portage. But the boat was too heavy to drag across dry land. I had to leave it, hoping the owners would eventually find it. I walked mile after mile along the beach and through the jungle. While the beach was easy except for the sun, the jungle trek was difficult. I had to cut myself free of vines wanting to entrap me and was glad I had bought the machete. Thorns dug into my ankles and scratched my legs. Leeches in stagnant water attached themselves below my knees. My trousers had become shorts. When night came, it brought with it a palpable darkness very different from the moonlit beach. Near a dark pool of stagnant water I wrapped myself in mud to fend off the mosquitoes. Tired and hungry, I lay down between the roots of a gigantic tree and slept.

The next day I saw big cats that looked like jaguars and also wild boars. I wanted desperately to kill a boar and roast the meat but didn't dare get in the way of one with nothing more than a blunt machete. The old chief had confiscated my pistol, but what I really needed was a good rifle or a rawhide whip and the ability to use it. A day later, weak from hunger and thirst, I killed a land turtle and ate its raw meat soaked in coconut milk. Never had I thought I would ever be reduced to eating raw meat, and yet it wasn't bad. My hunger and the coconut flavor made the meat sweet and digestible. It quickly restored my strength, and slowly I moved onward. After three days of cutting through the jungle, I heard the roar of a pounding surf.

Trudging toward the sound, I soon found myself on a sunny beach approaching several men. Offshore in the blue-green water were several islands. Later I learned they belonged to Panama, were called the San Blas Islands, and were peopled by Kuna Indians. In the past, because brutish white men had stolen their possessions, raped their women, and enslaved their men, they had learned to hate with a passion any person who spoke Spanish. Brandishing long spears and yelling, the men ran fiercely forward as if to harm or kill. I stood waiting to defend myself, thinking I could die within minutes but clutching my machete. Yet when they encircled me they let me know with sign language that they wanted to talk. Communication was difficult, but slowly with admirable patience they learned I was not a greedy prospector seeking to wrest gold from them. Neither was I a slave hunter with shackles ready to enslave them, nor a rapist wanting to hurt their women. With elaborate sign language, I managed to tell them I was a poor runaway from a vile, detestable, and unforgiving prison. Hearing that, their behavior changed. They believed me and treated me kindly.

Not one of them knew a word of Spanish. It was the language of brutal men who had tormented them in the past, and they had decreed it would never be spoken in their village. So I would have to try another language. Before my fourth escape attempt failed, my loving Leywa had taught me much of her language. I tried talking to the Kuna in Leywa's language, but the dialect spoken by them differed from all other tribal languages. That difference caused sign language to be common among them, and it seemed to work all right. I went with them to their island stronghold and remained there several days.

They fed me their native food and drink to make me stronger. I rested there with good people, watched a lively ceremonial dance, and got drunk on fermented guava juice. When time came for me to leave, a shapely teenage girl kissed my cheek and bit my lips. A little girl of five or six gave me a bunch of delicate flowers. In the middle of them was a gorgeous orchid. The hospitality of those people was extraordinary. I was glad I didn't have to steal from them.

For several days — I lost track of the number — I worked my way northward with only one thought in mind: Colon on the Caribbean. I had visited the town during my year of freedom and knew it was Panama's second largest city. At last I reached that part of the Panamanian coast opposite the island of El Porvenir, *the future* in English. The Indians had told me a garrison of soldiers was quartered on that island, and I tried not to be seen by them. Since I could show no passport, I feared their commander would send me back to Colombia. I faded into the forest and walked all day under a thick canopy that shut out most of the sun. Near suppertime I came upon a crew of men cutting mahogany. A woodcutter who had killed a boar gave me a slab of roast pig and a mug of beer. He said Colon was seventy-five miles up the coast, and he warned me not to try getting there by canoe. A lone man in a little canoe would be in great danger trying to negotiate the strong currents and tides. Don't do it, he advised, don't even try. But I had to try.

I went along a trail he said would take me to an Indian village. It was a well-used trail with no obstacles and no need to hack anything with my machete. I came to the village faster than expected and lingered unseen on the outskirts. When night came with overcast and a moon behind it, I hustled to the beach hoping to find a boat. As expected, I found several canoes neatly lined in a row and selected one with a sail. I pushed it into the surf and after some struggle managed to get inside and get the sail up. I was glad to have heavy darkness and no moon, for in moonlight any person on the beach could have seen the white sail.

Once I got past the breakers, I made excellent speed with the wind behind me but quickly took on water. I had to bail constantly with a big gourd an Indian had left in the canoe. Several hours passed and then to my surprise and alarm a bright light flashed across the water. Instantly I thought a patrol boat had spotted me. As for my identity, a fugitive from a well-known prison, it was natural to think the worse, but then I saw the lighthouse on shore. That made for a moment of high excitement, particularly when I turned to my left to see a glowing sky. The glow, that marvelous glow, came from the lights of Panama.

As I moved in closer, the lights grew brighter and Colon began to rise up in full view. Steamers passed me several times, almost capsizing my clumsy boat in their wake. I had no light to warn them, and they wouldn't have seen me even with a light. In a breeze almost gone I moved in closer and closer to shore, aiming for a beach south of the town. It was important to avoid human contact. I couldn't be stopped or questioned, for that could lead to capture and misery. It was a needless worry. All the people on shore, except for a few authorities, were asleep. The night was late and dark, and the authorities were probably dozing.

The canoe moved slowly until it caught the surf. Then it picked up speed and began to dash toward the sloping beach. I held on tight to the boat's gunwales and held my breath. A few yards from the beach the craft seemed ready to capsize and dunk me in the water. When it didn't but shot to the sandy beach, I shouted syllables of joy. Knowing I would have to leave the canoe, I set about removing all that I owned as well as my knapsack from the water. Because it was made of canvas, some of the stuff inside was still dry. Concealed in bushes I made a pillow of the knapsack and slept as one dead within minutes.

How long I lay there, huddled under the brush and cuddling my knapsack, is anyone's guess. I woke in broad daylight groggy from too much sleep and tottered to the beach. I was looking out at the ocean, intensely blue and shimmering in the sun, when a young man in uniform approached and asked me if I was okay.

"You were very unsteady as you tried walking on the beach. I know the sand can be a problem for older people, but you appeared to be either sick or drunk. I thought I might help."

"Oh, I can assure you I'm neither sick nor drunk. I'm wobbly this morning because I slept too long and too hard in the open air. I'm sorry to cause you concern."

"That's okay, friend, No problem. Use the beach and have fun."

I think he had to be an American military policeman because of the way he spoke English. He smiled when I said in my schoolbook English that I was a stranger in town and didn't quite know my way around. I was speaking a white lie, of course, because I had lived briefly in Colon during my year of freedom. I think I must have told the policeman I was French because he mentioned the French quarter of Colon. Though time had passed, I remembered exactly how to get there.

It was the old historic part of the town near the waterfront. It was a colorful place and peopled with some of the most amazing outcasts one can imagine. I had been there earlier but now found an assortment of people I had never seen before. However, as soon as I uttered a few words in French they accepted me as one of their own and declared we were friends for life. A woman named Agatha with remnants of feminine beauty that must have turned heads when she was young offered me a change of clothes. Because the red shirt with white stripes and broad white pants reminded me too much of the south of France, I politely declined her offer. Her partner laid out for me a good pair of clean khaki pants, a well-made shirt, and linen underwear.

"You have no shoes," he said in disbelief. "What happened to your shoes? You can't walk these hot paved streets barefoot, man. I have a good pair of shoes you must have. Glad to be rid of them."

"I lost my shoes sometime ago coming up from the south. I was at sea in a canoe with a sail for maybe a week and didn't need shoes. I suffered pain when I had to walk through the jungle barefoot."

"You tell me you came up from the south? Maybe an island off the coast of South America? Maybe a place near the equator?"

The man was curious but affable. I told him the unvarnished truth, holding back no detail. From that day until he died we were the best of friends writing letters to each other. Another person in the Quarter fed me a delicious stew with tasty French bread and good wine. I wanted to reward her for her kindness, but she refused to accept anything more than heartfelt thanks. A gentleman who sold leather goods offered me his bathroom to shave and shower. I was glad to rake off a growth of beard that was beginning to itch. Being clean again brought a strange new feeling as if I had never been clean. Among those good people I felt at home. I could have spent a year with them, happily getting to know them, but had to be on my way. Time was beginning to tell on me, and I had to move on. The train for Panama City would be leaving soon.

Chapter Twenty-Nine
Golden Skulls and Butterflies

When I reached Panama City, I found myself in an urban area far more exciting than Colon. Situated on the Pacific side of the isthmus, the city was modern and progressive. In its streets I felt like a free human being at home. In Trinidad I had enjoyed feelings of freedom but nothing like the ones experienced in Panama. Recalling what I had done to get there, I couldn't believe it. I had walked more than 400 miles to get to Colon. I would have walked farther had I not remembered that the Canal Zone was government property and restricted. In the city I wasted no time going to the house of a man a French expatriate recommended. I learned he had written and published two books and worked as a well-known journalist. I felt certain he would allow me to live in his home until I could move northward again.

However, I discovered that he was away for a month on assignment and had left his house in the care of a good servant, Marietta Garcia. She was in her late forties with smooth, clear, olive skin and copper hair that had once been jet black. She spoke fluent Spanish, labored French, and some English. I, on the other hand, spoke fluent French, labored Spanish, and some English. So right away we hit it off well. Marietta was a good-looking woman, and we got along as friends as soon as we met. She was gregarious, talkative, easy to know, and glad to have my company in the empty house. She fed me well and I learned how to laugh again. It was a sound that surprised me. In the sitting room with a big and sturdy desk I scribbled page after page in my journal.

"Are you an author too?" She shyly asked.

"I wish I could answer that with a yes, Marietta, but in all honesty I can't really claim that identity."

"Oh, please call me Marie. I've been a grown woman for some years now. I'm no longer the little girl my parents loved. Marietta is Marie in little, a term of endearment, and suitable for little girls."

"I rather like the name Marietta but will certainly call you Marie. My first name is Arthur, but my parents always called me Maurice. That's my second name. If I ever become an author, I may use both."

"Oh, you will be an author, Maurice, if that is what you really want. You walked hundreds of miles to get here. If you can do that, I know you can write and publish not just one book but many."

"Well, I haven't done much with publishing so far, but an American journalist I met in Guiana published articles in a major magazine from notes of mine. Then not long ago an editor of a newspaper in Cartagena paid me well for six articles I wrote for him. I can't tell you whether the articles were ever published because I was able to leave the jail I wrote them in to make my way northward. I'm hoping the notes I place in my journal now will be raw material for a hefty book one of these days."

"I hope so too, Maurice, and I hope I may read the book as soon as you publish it. I just know it will be exciting and interesting."

Marie was a good woman, and she had a strong knowledge of current events. I assumed that interest derived from her employer, a freelance journalist. Although she had little formal education, her mind was sharp as any knife in her kitchen and she was also curious. She said political turmoil in the region would make it dangerous for me to continue my journey northward. Costa Rica and one other country appeared to be on the brink of revolution. The authorities, fearing an uprising at any hour, were particularly vigilant in regard to strangers who might be present to cause trouble. She advised me to wait until solutions could be found for current problems and until the tense political situation cooled down. I should go when the government was more stable and the country no longer in uproar. I asked her if she knew how long that would be, and she answered maybe six months, but no one could be certain.

"Oh, really?" I responded with alarm. "I don't believe I can stay in one place for half a year. I really can't."

I believed if I had to curtail my travels that long I might not travel again. I had to be on the move without suffering long intervals of no movement. Six months to my way of thinking was a long time.

"My boss," she said, observing my disappointment "owns a banana plantation not far from here. A boat will leave for the plantation tomorrow. Why don't you go there for a while? It'll do you good, and you can rest until it's safe to move northward again. I'll give you a letter of introduction, and the people there will treat you well."

I wanted to turn down her offer but had to accept the soundness of what she had said about unsafe conditions. So after a few days happily immersed in civilization, and with the good wishes of Marie, I was back in the jungle. The boat went into the Pacific, up the coast a few miles, and then up a river. It was more like a flat barge than a boat and carried supplies to the settlement and the villages along the way. It moved slowly up the river with a man at the bow signaling natives on shore with a loud horn. I asked why he was doing that and was told the barge would be collecting green bananas from Indian villages on its way back. The horn was to let them know the banana boat would be with them soon to do business, and they would have to be ready.

In the afternoon when the barge had gone as far as it could go, its supplies were put on boats with outboard motors to go even farther up the twisting river. In late afternoon the river was a beautiful sight with sparkling colors all over. But the farther we went, the more shallow its depth became. Also the steersman had to worry about weeds that were known to clog the propeller and bring the boat to a halt. When that happened, a swimmer had to dive into the snake-infested water to free the propeller. He wouldn't be able to see what he was doing. The muddy water didn't allow it, and the stringy weeds were often so tough even the sharpest of knives couldn't cut them. We missed the weeds, and near sunset we reached a long dock built along the riverbank. From there we walked into the jungle to find a large clearing with three buildings on stilts. In back of them were acres of Cavendish bananas.

At another time I might have liked the place very much. It was as far away from the prying eyes of authority figures as humanly possible and looked peaceful. However, it was a place of refuge when I needed no refuge, when I felt compelled to complete my journey. And as it turned out, the camp wasn't as pleasant as I thought on first arriving. At the end of the day dozens of fruit cutters, released for a few hours from hard labor, crammed into the houses and began drinking raw alcohol distilled from sugar cane. They gambled, quarreled, shared bawdy stories, broke into brawling and singing, yelled at one another, and set going a stream of vulgar noise in Spanish that lasted for hours.

I sat in a corner to listen and observe and couldn't help but think I had come a long way from Devil's Island only to find myself once more consorting with men no better than the ones there. The only difference between these rough workers and the convicts I had known for so many years was a firm belief that they were free. Of course, they were not. Their work didn't allow genuine freedom. They had to be on the job at an early hour each day to work all through the day. They were obligated to labor long and hard at low pay until they grew old or sick, and their physical strength was lost. Younger men would eagerly take place.

The Indians I met were freer. They came to the clearing painted and naked save for loincloths, but courteous and smiling. They spoke softly and listened when I spoke of catching butterflies for money. I showed them a giant morpho I had caught recently, and they claimed where they lived a person could find even bigger butterflies with blue wings even brighter. They found it hard to believe they might catch the butterflies and sell their wings for real money. Yet when they began to ask many questions, I knew they wanted to give it a try. So patiently I taught them how to do it, leaving out no detail. They were quick learners,

They were primitive people and their Spanish wasn't as good as mine, but of a sudden I decided I would rather spend time with them than with the boisterous banana cutters. As the Indians began walking to the dock, I walked with them. As their teacher I continued to explain how one catches the butterflies, how one prepares them for sale, and where to find buyers. When they got in their boats to leave, I asked if I might come along with them. Surprised by my request, they huddled to talk it over. It was not unanimous assent. Two or three didn't want a white man in their midst. White men brought trouble no one wanted. The majority listened but finally agreed to take me to their village.

So began a seven-month adventure that changed me as a man. For the first time in many years I began to feel every day an emotion related to peace and contentment. It was a feeling so foreign to me that initially I didn't recognize it or label it. Feelings of peace and self worth came first and through them came feelings of satisfaction and happiness. For the first time in my adult life I calmly accepted the reality surrounding me, a reality very different from Paris or Cayenne, and yet better than either. When the Indians learned they could acquire money and buy creature comforts by selling butterflies, I gained their respect.

They allowed me to move freely among their villages and among their people. I passed from one village to another deep inside Indian country where no white man went. Not a single person raised a hand against me. They had learned I was not looking to rob them of gold, and I was not a scout on the lookout for slave labor. I was merely an escaped convict who loved butterflies. "Crazy man," they all agreed. In time they escorted me to their most populous village where their chief lived.

In that village every man and many of the women wore ornaments of solid gold shaped like human skulls. A larger number than expected spoke colorful Spanish, but when talking to each other they often spoke a language I didn't understand. In his youth the old chief had been a splendid warrior, but in his golden years he seemed half infirm and not quite with it. He had lost all the vision in his left eye, and his right eye appeared to be losing it too. His potbelly effectively hid his loincloth, and his brown skin had the tone of fine leather. He glared at me with a firm hard eye when I offered to shake hands. It was the white man's custom, and he hated white men. The members of his tribe who brought me to him spoke on my behalf to soften his attitude toward me. In time he asked me to show him my collection of butterflies.

He gazed at them with a look of surprise and asked why I killed them. Why in the world would I kill a thing so beautiful? Shrugging his fat shoulders, he stared at me sternly with that one eye

"I can understand killing a mosquito" he announced through his interpreter. "It causes harm. The butterfly doesn't cause harm, doesn't bite or sting. It is merely a pretty thing, *a flower that flies*. We catch pretty things too but put them in cages to be admired. Why don't you do that? Why must you kill a gorgeous butterfly to display its wings?"

"I will try to explain, sir. Morpho butterflies have no commercial value alive. Their beautiful wings have to be dried to become coveted ornaments almost like pieces of jewelry. Then people will buy them. Women in particular see the dried wings almost as jewelry."

He shrugged to show his displeasure but said I could settle among his people as long as I followed certain rules. I couldn't penetrate the jungle on my own but would require a male companion when hunting butterflies. I couldn't have anything whatever to do with gold, couldn't dig for it, couldn't possess it, couldn't even touch it. Gold was strictly off limits. Also I was told that even the smallest theft could get me flogged and expelled in shame from the village. I couldn't bathe in the river with the villagers but had to do it alone and not in their sight. I couldn't look with a lustful eye at a native woman. That was strictly forbidden, but if I stayed longer than two moons I would have to take a wife.

"A man without a wife is liable to get in trouble with another man's wife," the chief intoned through his interpreter. "Without a wife, how you find time away from house and village chores to hunt butterflies? I say to you, White Man, you need a wife even now."

The warrior-chief was wiser and smarter than he looked. I needed a woman with growing desperation, but in the chief's plain and simple society any woman willing to lie with me would have to be my wife.

A girl in her teens emerged from the crowd. Wearing only a strip of cloth around her hips and smiling coyly, she looked me full in the face and nodded. Her black hair fell almost to the small of her back, and two ringlets provocatively covered her breasts. She moved her body with a fluid motion pleasing to watch. Without speaking she left and returned with a wooden bowl filled with sliced bananas and berries in coconut milk flavored with honey. She held the food at arm's length close to my face, causing the children to laugh. They understood what I did not.

The chief made them silent with a flick of his hand and said, "This woman would be a good wife for you. She works hard. Her offer of food is her way of giving herself to you as your wife. What do you say?"

I was in no position to quibble. Certainly I would need a partner to keep house and teach me their customs and their way of life. Moreover, I didn't want to make a mistake that might insult the old chief and bring about hard feelings or worse. So nodding my head I spoke in Spanish loud enough for all to hear: *Tendria a esta mujer. Ella es una persona buena.* "I would have this woman. She is good."

"Lowacki!" grunted the chief in his own language. And from his followers who knew some Spanish came *Bueno! Bueno! Lowacki!*

"Now eat the food this woman gives you," the chief commanded. "It signifies in our culture that you take her for your wife as she takes you for her husband. She will look after you, and you will care for her."

I dipped a wooden spoon into the berries and bananas and began to eat. The ripe fruit was delicious. Anyone who has never eaten a banana picked exactly when ripe doesn't know bananas. As I made the bowl empty and wiped the spiced coconut milk from my lips, the chief spoke softly to the girl, offering his warm regards. She listened politely, then turned and began to walk gracefully through the crowd.

"Follow her," enjoined the chief. "She will take you to the house I am giving you for a home. Be kind to her. You are right, White Man. The woman is good. She works hard and will make your life good."

I thanked the wise old man in the way I had seen others thank him. To show humility and respect, I stood at attention in front of him and bowed my head. He smiled in appreciation of my gesture and bade me catch up with the girl. I did and we walked to a dwelling raised eight feet off the ground. I tried speaking to her in Spanish. She understood not a word, nor could I understand any word she spoke.

But somehow all that didn't matter. We understood each other in body and spirit, and we got along well together. I lived with that gentle, healthy, good-looking girl for seven months, and I believe those months were as happy as any I've ever known. I was an errand boy in Paris, and I liked my work. Those fleeting days of carefree youth were exciting and happy. But I broke the law and was sent to a prison faraway. Later I maintained that fortune was not my friend. Any luck I had was bad luck. In that native village I had to revise my negative thinking. My tall glass had become half full, no longer half empty. Living with that engaging girl, I lost the misery that burned in my entrails from the moment my father disowned me. Certainly it was so when I stepped aboard a ship for my first sea voyage to find cages in the hold for human cargo. People who go to sea are seeking pleasure. As the old ship moved closer to the tropics, I found no pleasure at all.

Chapter Thirty
Tender Sleeping Flower

Hand in hand my gentle bride and I walked to the dwelling the chief had so generously given us. A heavy log with notches for steps led up to the flooring of the house. With no rail or banister on either side it required a fine sense of balance for anyone daring to mount it. The girl pointed to the open door eight feet above me and indicated I should enter first. I found the steps too small for my feet, and with nothing to hang onto I slipped and fell to the ground. My bride uttered a merry little laugh and helped me to my feet. On the second try with my shoes removed and almost crawling, I managed to ascend without falling.

The house was big but sparely furnished. It was maintained very well and clean. Away from the main room where people gathered were several small sleeping rooms with mats. In the middle of the large room was a stone hearth for cooking. Flat rocks covered with fiery embers formed a square of ample size. My new spouse fanned the embers to kindle a fire and began to cook our supper. She seemed to think the way to cook a meal was to toss all the raw food into a pot, pour water on it, and boil it. When I saw what she was doing, I decided to cook the supper myself. I had some experience from when I was young.

"Please get more wood," I said with gestures she could understand. "I'll do the cooking and soon we can eat! I don't have much experience when it comes to cooking, but I think I can do it better, maybe."

A look of deep puzzlement crossed her young and pretty face. Why would I want to do her work? Had not she become my woman to keep my house, look after me, and cook for me? Reluctantly she went into the forest for more wood, stopping to chat with a gaggle of native women and apparently telling them her new husband was cooking supper. Two or three women came to the house, shyly mounted the steps, looked at the man preparing the food and giggled. How strange! A man doing the cooking! No one in the tribe had ever heard of such a thing. Maybe it was scandalous? The chief would have to look into this. Already the white man appeared to be disobeying an important tribal rule.

Word spread through the village like wild fire. The crazy white man was doing woman's work! Several women young and old and many girls had to see it to believe it. They crept up the log steps, giggled, slipped easily to the ground, and ran off. The children picked up the excitement and wanted to see also. They came running in groups of five or six and had to be chased away by their elders. The hullabaloo reached the old chief who believed his sworn duty was to set me straight. He seemed disturbed, deeply puzzled by what he had heard.

"What is this I hear about you, Nikata? What are you doing in your new home to upset the women folk? Will not your woman work? They tell me you are doing her work. They say it's scandalous that you should do her work. It is not the way we run our households here."

"She's a good worker, my chieftain," I said humbly, "and a good wife too, but she doesn't know how to cook. She threw all the food we had for supper in one pot and boiled it. The mush it became had no taste."

"Solve your problem soon, Nikata. I cannot and will not tolerate any action in my village that sets the women folk in a frenzy and even the children. They find your behavior funny now but maybe not later."

A few days later I learned that my wife was celebrated as the best cook in the entire village. At all the great feasts when natives came from outlying villages, she and her mother always did the cooking. Several times each year she authored the ceremonial banquet and was revered for doing it with perfection. I made it known to her that I was very sorry for having usurped her honorable position. She did the cooking from then on, and slowly I learned to like her fare.

She was also good at other things, and she performed her duties as my wife skillfully and without hesitation. Her behavior on the floor mat stuffed with feathers was without parallel except for the kissing. Instead of pressing her lips against mine to show affection, she bit them hard as Leywa had done before her. And always she murmured, "Nikata fulewo Sawiki," *Nikata loves Sawiki*. I tried to tell her that in my culture when a wife speaks sweetly to her husband, she says *Sawiki loves Nikata*. It was the name the chief had given me the moment I accepted the young woman as my spouse. He had called me Nikata, "Monkey Man," because of my size and because I was pale and different. I didn't learn her name until I began to learn her language. It was Sawiki, *Sleeping Flower* in English. She was indeed a flower but seldom sleeping. Tender and gentle but strong of body and mind, she was dedicated to work and loved it.

In the world as I have come to know it, millions of people dream of living in opulence and hate their wretched existence. Primitive people have known for centuries that the key to a happy life is simplicity. In the village where I lived simplicity in all its forms was practiced daily as a cardinal rule. It wasn't what one owned that defined a man or woman but what he or she did with what they owned. That was the rule I soon learned to live by in Chief Catu's village. If a woman found she needed sweet potatoes to enhance her evening meal, she went to her neighbor and came home with an armful. She didn't borrow the potatoes; they were given to her simply because she needed them. The person doing the giving expected nothing in return, and yet was often rewarded. As I denied my French heritage and became a member of a native tribe in Central America, I understood for the first time in my life what it meant to have peace of mind. Having divested myself of material things the civilized world called essential, I found peace as a minimalist. Never had my days begun so well and ended so well.

The tropical heat could be endured if one sat in the shade, but like all the people of the village I wore few clothes. I passed my days much as they did. Not one person was wealthy, and no person suffered want. The river was full of fish. The jungle boasted an abundance of game and pure water. Clearings produced fruits and vegetables of every variety. Fertile fields on the edge of the jungle yielded cotton for clothing. Tobacco in thin sheets hung drying in the sun. Medicinal herbs healed one of aches and pains but were used with caution. Even though some of the adults got high gnawing on a plant that blackened their teeth, not a person in the village had heard of drug addiction, or drinking alcohol to get drunk. The people couldn't be called religious. Yet they were spiritual. Frequent ceremonial activity could be interpreted as food for the soul.

For the first time in my life I was truly free and living with good, intelligent, and caring people. I feared nothing and needed nothing. With a girl/woman at my side and supporting me in every way imaginable, I had it all. At last, after many years of hardship, I was tasting the simple pleasure of living. My work was rewarding, and I kept my mind keen by learning to speak my wife's language. She would point to an object and I would listen as she repeated its name. In little more than a month, we were able to sit in the shade and talk. Her language appeared simple and easy at first, but the more I learned, the more difficult it became.

I fished and hunted and spent many hours seeking butterflies. My collection of jewel-like wings grew larger each day. I soon placed a value on them of several hundred dollars. Since there was no market for them within easy range, they increased in value with each morpho caught. I attended tribal conferences and ceremonials and competed with young men to sit next to Chief Catu. Like them, I painted my face and chest but wore cut-off trousers instead of a loincloth. Natives who had never seen a white man asked many questions. A white man in their midst was an anomaly they found hard to accept.

They had been taught to hate white men, for didn't those men rape and burn their villages, steal their gold, and cast their young people into slavery? I made it known to them that men who occupied the region a long time ago were guilty of those vile offenses. They called themselves *conquistadores*, militaristic conquerors. Some years later men cut from the same cloth, scavengers and opportunists, swept through the region to oppress the natives. I made it clear I was not one of them.

I was a runaway and very different. I was running from pain and injustice to find peace and freedom. I had escaped oppression, privation, and death in a harsh prison to live with them, and I was not a plunderer. I chased butterflies and lived peacefully among them with my native wife. As the months passed every Indian I met became my friend. I wore a necklace of wild boars' teeth, and expertly fashioned silver ornaments. I couldn't touch their gold, but silver wasn't off limits.

In time, in spite of what seemed in every way an idyllic existence, I began to feel it necessary for me to complete my journey. I had come too far to replace my dream of freedom with a repeat of the life I had so thoroughly enjoyed with Leywa, my first native wife. And yet the more I thought about it the more indecisive I became. Was it not better to reject a world that had been very cruel to me for a simple world of peace and harmony? Could I find greater peace elsewhere? Certainly I couldn't find more freedom to live day by day with no fear of soldiers hauling me off to prison and solitary confinement again.

It was a conundrum demanding resolution. I worked on it for hours and was inclined to stay with Sawiki and the tribe that had become my tribe. However, on my thirty-ninth birthday I decided the primitive life though appealing was not what I wanted. I had survived fifteen years in an institution that had tried to destroy me. I felt at thirty-nine years I could live happily for another thirty-nine, especially if I could adjust and turn the larger world to my advantage. I believed the good people of the United States would help me achieve my dream of living in peace with no worry. Didn't they call their vast country the land of opportunity?

If I could get back to Panama City and take a plane to New York, I could be there in a day. But I would need money for air travel, which I didn't have. Also I had no passport. To travel thousands of miles in a good car, if I could afford it, would be expensive and take many days. To do the journey by foot, even if it were possible, would consume months. Maybe I was tilting at windmills. Yet somehow I felt I had to reach the end of my pilgrimage. So one evening as we sat outside to catch the cool breezes, I turned to Sawiki and told her I would soon be leaving.

"Do you go to catch more butterflies?" she asked. "Many butterflies are in the mountains, and they are big and beautiful. I will go with you and help you catch them. I will go wherever you go, sleep wherever you sleep, eat whatever you eat because I am your woman."

"I will not be catching butterflies after I leave our home," I replied after a long silence. "You've been very good to me, Sawiki, *and good for me*, but I belong in another country. I love you and your people, and yet we both know I'm not one of you. Also I must complete the odyssey I began many months ago. Something within me is driving me to do it. I may return and raise a family with you, and live out my days with you and our children, but that I can't promise."

Nothing more was said. She didn't ask more questions

and didn't seem unduly upset. Even so, she put her head between her knees and sighed deeply. That was the extent of it. Tribal custom had taught her not to show emotion. When morning came I consulted Chief Catu and asked if he would have some men take me down river to the trading station. His one eye squinting, he looked me full in the face and grunted but said the trip could be arranged.

He spoke not a word of regret, nor did anyone else. Not a person thought my leaving Sawiki was a betrayal. She told me she would wait eight moons for my return. If I had not returned by the ninth moon, she would take a new husband. She spoke softly and with feeling, but with no perceptible tears. It was the way her people embraced life and the hardships it brought. Stoicism was in their blood.

All the village gathered to see me off. Chattering children danced around me as if in celebration. The women called out to me in friendly voices, crying: "Goodbye, Monkey Man! Goodbye, White Man! Goodbye, beloved Nikata!" The men made a friendly fist and raised it to the sky in salute. Standing on a platform to be seen by all and gesticulating with movements they had taught me, I communicated my thanks to them. In a sleek canoe we moved away from the village fast. All day we paddled, often struggling against swift currents and bouncing through rapids. As night came we camped with a small fire under tremendous trees. The next day we reached the trading post and found the monthly banana boat at the dock, a stroke of good luck. A day later it was plying its way downstream loaded with green bananas for the Canal Zone. The captain, a stocky fellow with very short legs, was glad to have a passenger. We got along well and drank bitter beer together.

Arriving in Panama City, the first thing I did was go visit Marietta Garcia, the good woman who was responsible for sending me to the edge of paradise for so many months. I was sorry to find her no longer employed by the journalist as his servant. He told me she had gone to Argentina to live with relatives. I'm sure she must have wondered why I never came back to see her. My stay at the banana camp was to be only a few weeks. Then I would see Marietta and thank her and be on my way again. I asked if I might write to her, but no one knew her address. I sought out an American who owned a curio shop in the city. He bought my butterflies at a good price with very little haggling. With my wallet stuffed with money enough to travel, I spent two days in a good hotel to rest before continuing my journey.

I left the city as a hitchhiker in a truck that had seen better days. The affable driver was big and fat and jovial, but sweaty and smelly. He said his name was Carlos Gomez, and he spoke his brand of Spanish rapidly. Though I couldn't understand much of what he said, I listened politely. He spoke strings of words that seemed quite serious, but at the end of each sentence he'd roar with laughter. Every sentence he spoke, instead of having a period at the end, had a peal of laughter. Perhaps it was his way of saying he was enjoying life as he found it. I wanted to cross the border without attracting attention. Then I would be able to move toward Nicaragua. It didn't happen. The reality of life, as my old grandma was fond of saying, has a way of crushing the dream of life.

Chapter Thirty-One
Walking My Shoes Away

Carlos let me ride with him in his truck all the way to his destination. It was night when we arrived, and I had no place to go. He said if I didn't mind, I could sleep with the furniture. I lay on the hard boards within a foot of a comfortable sofa that was upside down. When morning came, stiff and groggy, I paid Carlos for the ride, shook his hand, and began to walk. In a town with a railway station I took a train to a border town called Palo Seco, getting off unobtrusively with other passengers. Dry Stick lived up to its name as a very dry and dusty little place. I must have stood out like a sore thumb among the brown residents.

They eyed me closely as they passed, probably thinking I was an American gringo, but said nothing. I was in Costa Rica, a new country I had never seen before and knew very little about. I was glad I could understand the only language in the place. Outside a restaurant I met a boy of fourteen or so who looked hungry. We had a lunch together of rice and black beans in an eating-place with too many flies. Pablo gladly agreed to guide me through the town and place me on the main road northward. He said rebels were trying to seize the capital.

After we started walking, two policemen stopped and searched us, insisting we might be smuggling drugs. They saw the pack on my back and politely asked if they might inspect it. I knew I couldn't refuse. One of them rifled through the pack, leaving my small belongings in a pile on the dusty road. He seemed disappointed when he found no drugs. Then the other asked to see my papers, my identification and passport. Those I didn't have and couldn't show them anything. So they hauled me off to jail, admonishing the boy to choose his company better in future.

They gave me water to drink in their jail but no beer nor food. In the morning they lost no time escorting me back across the border and turning me over to the Panamanian police. I was jailed in a place called Concepción for two nights before being taken to the Governor of the province. That really scared me. If the Governor sent me back to Panama City and the authorities turned me over to the French Consul, I would be immediately on my way to French Guiana. My eighth attempt to escape, so promising until that moment, would quickly become a failure. Just the thought of losing and being sent back again left me in shock. All I could do was hold on to the slim hope that it wouldn't happen.

The Governor belonged to the highest social class in the country and had the suave manners of a gentleman. Thin and angular, he was immaculately dressed in a blue and white seersucker suit that matched his white beard, white hair, and white shoes. He sat behind a huge desk twiddling a red fountain pen and looking at me over reading spectacles perched on his nose. In excellent Spanish he asked me to tell him about me, and I decided to be frank and honest. I told him without going into a lot of detail that I was French and a fugitive from Devil's Island. I had served my time but was not allowed to leave the penal colony. He had heard of that unjust law and felt deep sympathy for any man daring enough to break it. I spoke of my desire to reach the United States, and to my surprise without saying a word he signed a form releasing me of criminal intent and declaring me a privileged traveler.

"Carry this on your person, Señor Bonheur. Show it to any police officer who might accost you. Any person seeing the form will show you respect. I hope you achieve what you are seeking. I wish you well."

I thanked him sincerely and was about to leave when his assistant touched my elbow and ushered me into the hallway. He offered some friendly advice, saying I should go to a seaport on the Pacific coast and visit a restaurant on the main street. There in all likelihood I would find Costa Rican smugglers not unwilling to take me on one of their nightly trips up the coast. He cautioned me to pay them only a few dollars.

"They will state an enormous sum but will do it for less," he said. "Haggle with them in a friendly way. They may not understand every syllable of your accented Spanish but will react to tone. Let them know you are a traveler and not a tourist. They expect you to haggle, but don't lose your temper or patience."

A few hours later I found myself in a dingy café bargaining with swarthy bandits prepared to smuggle into Costa Rica a large collection of Japanese shirts. They had stolen the expensive shirts from a shipping container left unlocked on the dock beside an Asian ship. After haggling for almost an hour, they agreed to include me in their cargo for only ten dollars. I would go with them as cargo and would not have the amenities of a passenger. I could have water to drink and a beer if I bought it, but no food unless I paid dearly for it.

Soon afterwards we were at sea moving rapidly up the Costa Rican coast as far as a seaport called Jaco. A few miles south of the port their shallow-draft boat put into a sandy beach, and we jumped into the surf. Every man knew exactly what to do and did his job. Before daylight the merchandise was unloaded on the beach. Two associates waited in a parked truck. They came as soon as the boat was back at sea and picked up the wooden crates along with me. As we rode toward a town, I asked the men how I might cross the Nicaraguan border.

"Pay some money to rent a horse and guide," they said. "You got money to pay us smugglers, so pay a guide for help. Then you ride four days northward and cross the border at San Juan del Sur. Hire a guide. You'll get lost and run into a ton of trouble if you try to do it on your own. Bandits up that way don't like the looks of white men."

"Can I trust just any guide I might come across? You tell me to hire a guide but how? I'm guessing they don't advertise their services."

"Go to the restaurant and order a beer. Don't order food. Don't eat the food and don't drink the water. It's known to give tourists and even travelers the trots. Someone will see you as a traveler and will offer to guide you. They do it all the time."

"What's the difference between a tourist and a traveler? How will anyone know I'm a traveler?"

"Ah, that's a question we've heard many times but can't answer. We think it's the way you walk and talk, not looks or how dressed. And you will be alone. That's a big difference. Tourists travel in groups."

When daylight came I was indeed alone in a hot and dusty little town that sizzled in the sun. Wasting no time, I went to a restaurant called *La Cocina de la Abuela* (Grandma's Kitchen) and talked to the owner. He greeted me with a friendly smile and spoke as if someone had told him I would be there looking for him. In half an hour he arranged for his cousin to guide me for a few U.S. dollars. In all my life I had never been on a horse and was expected to ride one in wild terrain for four days. Fortunately I had a tame horse and a good saddle. Even so, at the end of each day my buttocks and thighs were so painful I could barely walk or sit, and my stomach hurt. It was comforting to lie down near a sputtering campfire on the hard ground. In the tropics the ground is often damp but never cold. So any song that speaks of the cold, cold ground in Central America is spreading misinformation. The stew my guide cooked on a campfire eased my stomach pain. It was good.

Morning came and I had to climb into the saddle again. I recalled an old family motto my grandma often muttered: *when you have to do it, child, you do it.* So I did it. I persevered, to use a big word. Certainly in the years behind me I had suffered worse abuse and was able to take the latest in stride. Then one day in a narrow canyon my guide asked for his eleven dollars. He had agreed to guide me for four days, and that he had done. I gave him an extra dollar as a tip. Four days of guiding for twelve dollars; it was a bargain but time to part ways. He told me I would have to travel alone and on foot to the other side of the mountain that was blocking our view. If I could somehow make it over or around the mountain, he said as he rode away with the horses, I would have no problem finding Nicaragua sleeping in the sun.

I wanted to ask him a few questions about what lay ahead, but he was gone before I could collect my thoughts. So I began walking along a hot and rocky trail. Soon to my relief I lost the saddle pain and began to feel normal again. All day I walked alone in dusty and barren country. Cacti and sagebrush were the main vegetation. Along the way I saw the bones of goats and donkeys at a watering hole that had long been dry. Near sunset I began to search for a place to bed down for the night.

I expected to get a few hours' sleep and resume my journey at first light. Too tired from all the walking to think clearly, I stumbled into a nest of swarthy banditos. They were sitting on rocks around a small campfire and numbered maybe a dozen. Every man, or so it seemed to me, was big and burly and held a long rifle pointed directly at my head. More confused than fearful, I raised both hands and stood still.

Their leader had a big wad of tobacco in his mouth and spit a dollop of brown juice at my feet. He came up close to question me, thrusting his ugly face close to mine. I could smell his foul breath above the tobacco odor. On his left cheek was a festering sore and his fat lips sagged at one corner. He was in dire need of a bath, and his clothes were very dirty. But in spite of his appearance, in that setting he was a figure of authority to be obeyed. I answered every one of his questions truthfully, and he softened his attitude visibly when I told him I was a runaway convict. He snorted and smiled and seemed almost friendly when I informed him I had run away from Devil's Island. Vigorously chomping on his juicy wad of tobacco, he turned away and made a gesture to henchmen to let me go. Then pausing as if thinking it over, he ordered one of them to frisk me. I stood at attention for the frisking. I knew with any sudden move I'd be shot. Waiting for it to end, I could hear myself breathing

The man's rough hands found a handkerchief, a pocketknife, and a pack of cigarettes. He missed my prison knife strapped to my leg. I had dropped my backpack to the ground in the gathering darkness and was hoping he would overlook it. He didn't. The henchman searched through my belongings and found my money, the cash I was using to finance my escape. When they were satisfied they had seized everything I had of worth, the gang indicated I could leave. I gathered from the dirt all that was left of my backpack and slowly moved away.

It alarmed me to lose my money, and I kept thinking how I might get it back. I was one man against many and unarmed. They were killers and could have murdered me on the spot with no one knowing. One move on my part just slightly aggressive meant certain death. I thought of an old saying in my confusion: *you don't enter a gunfight with a knife.* Instantly I saw the wisdom behind it. Though angry and astounded by what had happened, I was glad to go with my life.

I stumbled along the trail in darkness for maybe half an hour and decided it would be foolish to go farther. So I curled up behind some large rocks located well off the trail and got some sleep. In the middle of the night I awoke with a start, thinking the banditos had caught up with me to pummel my body with heavy clubs. Yet I felt no pain. All was very quiet. I was suffering a nightmare. I hid in a thicket so no one could find me in the morning and went back to sleep. I was up and walking again just as the sun was rising. I walked and walked all day, eating almost nothing. For three days I walked as briskly as I could and finally came to Managua, the capital city of Nicaragua. Poor people meeting me on the road shared their food with me and gave me water.

Managua was a pleasant place, a sleepy town at midday. I had no money even for a cheap hotel room but just enough in one of my boots to send a brief telegram to the American shop owner in Panama City. I explained that bandits had robbed me of all the money he had paid me for the butterflies. Could he send me a hundred dollars for morpho butterflies? I would collect them for him at a value of two hundred or more. I couldn't believe it, but within a few hours I had money in my pocket and was no longer a vagrant. I promised myself I wouldn't betray the trust that good man had shown me. Years later, learning he was still in business at the same address, I sent him $300 in American money. It pleased me to imagine his surprise.

Hanging outside a fish market was a net. I bought it and hoped I could use for butterflies it right away. Since I would be in the tropics for months, there would be ample time to catch and prepare the collection of brilliant wings that I hoped to send him. But of first importance was finding a way to move onward and northward. I discovered many little towns between the capital of the country and its border. I would have to get through them without causing suspicion. They were sleepy towns filled with peasants who would see me as a stranger right away.

A stranger in their midst could mean trouble. I solved the problem by taking a crowded train heading for Honduras. I lost myself among the many people on that overloaded train. I found a seat, slouched in it, and pulled the brim of my hat over my face. In the midst of noisy women and children, and old men transporting live hens in burlap bags, not a single person noticed me. So without a great deal of effort I reached Honduras, another place of violence and unrest. I heard the country was in political turmoil and also the victim of deadly gangs that roamed the streets. It was dangerous to be there, for the gangs were known to attack and rob and even kill foreigners. Different in appearance, I was a prime target. I wanted to hop another train going northward, but found nothing that was moving in that direction. Because the road had very little traffic, I couldn't hitchhike. So mile after mile I walked the empty road.

For more than two weeks I trudged northward. I walked until my sturdy boots began to fall apart, and I traded my prison knife for used boots. I went down paved roads and up steep mule roads of gravel and dirt. I climbed mountains, descended into ravines, and skirted banana plantations of many acres. At night when I had to find a place to sleep, poor people offered me space in an outlying building, a barn or shed. When morning came early, they shared a spare breakfast with me.

One evening a family of eighteen invited me to have

dinner with them. We sat outdoors around a rustic table loaded with food. Though some of the dishes seemed strange to me, I ate my fill and went away with food they insisted I take with me. It lasted longer than expected. Some days when I felt hungry I found bananas growing beside the road. I was able to move into El Salvador with no problems, but on more than one occasion well-meaning persons warned me not to try crossing into Guatemala. Civil unrest existed there. I recalled trying to keep a low profile in Honduras and heeded the warning.

A new regime in the country had tightened the borders. Policemen were on the lookout for strangers even in the cities. Special permits were needed to enter and leave the country. The mayor of a town where I spent a day drinking cheap cold beer advised me to go to La Libertad on the Pacific coast. He and his son were going there to visit relatives, and he offered me a ride there. It was a long ride through the mountains, but the back seat was comfortable and the scenery astounding. In late afternoon we came into the port city. I thanked him heartily and offered to pay for the ride. He shook his head, saying they had to make the trip anyway. Adamantly he refused to accept my money but allowed me to buy gasoline for his Buick. I filled the tank to overflowing.

El Puerto de la Libertad, one of the first ports in El Salvador, was a pretty town with beautiful tropical beaches, a long pier, and a harbor for nautical traffic. I hoped that by hanging around the waterfront I might be able to embark on a ship heading north. Somehow I had to get past Guatemala, and the best way to do that was by sea. It wouldn't be a long voyage because Guatemala's coastline was short compared to Mexico's. I had heard the Mexican authorities wouldn't be asking for identification, but harsh experience had taught me not to trust hearsay. Their bandit problem had placed the Mexican police on high alert, and that I had to consider. I dreaded trying to travel through Mexico. Like Honduras and Guatemala, banditos had made it a dangerous place. Murder of innocent people was common, and that included travelers. Also being arrested as an illegal person without papers was more likely in Mexico than in other countries. If I managed to evade the bandits, I might still end up in a Mexican jail for entering the country illegally. I had heard the jails were almost as bad as the prison in French Guiana, but that I doubted.

Chapter Thirty-Two

Stowaway and USA

On the waterfront I looked for smugglers but found none. A man in a bar told me they were lying low after a big operation. An hour later I found a freighter bound for Canada loading cargo. I didn't have enough money to buy passage on the big ship, but thought I might sneak aboard and stow away. So I went to a store nearby and bought two loaves of bread, a few cans of sardines, and candy bars. I put the stuff in my knapsack. I figured it could be days before I'd be eating another meal. So I went to a restaurant to fill my stomach with native food. The waitress, a shapely young woman with sensual lips, bronze skin, and yellow hair, noticed how much I was eating and came over to chat.

"I will top off your meal with a big slice of lemon pie," she said in good Spanish, "and it won't cost you one colon extra. It's on the house."

"That's awfully kind of you," I replied. I'm sure the pie is very tasty, but I've already eaten more than I can hold. Maybe some other time?

"I will give you a rain check. Come back tomorrow, and your pie will be waiting for you. I will be here too."

She was pleasant, simpatico, flirtatious, and alive.

At another time I would have gladly accepted her invitation, but on that day I planned to be on the ship. I thanked her cordially and went back to the docks.

As soon as it got dark I joined the men who were loading the ship and went on board. Then I slipped away from them, holding an empty box I had found on deck, and walked to the stern of the ship. If anyone accosted me, glibly I would say I had been ordered to take the box aft. No one stood in my way, and I went down a companionway to a lower deck and through a small trapdoor into the ship's shadowy hold. It had a flickering light at the time I entered, but an hour later a sailor quenched it. I found myself in darkness so thick I couldn't see my hand in front of my face. That's when I began to doubt the wisdom of stowing away. It had not occurred to me that I might have to spend many days in damp and darkness. Also I remembered rats occupy the holds of most ships. I shuddered at the thought of one gnawing on my face as I slept, but the thing couldn't be undone. I would have to make the most of it.

The ship's engines throbbed with a rhythmic thrum, and I knew we had moved away from the dock to enter the open sea. In the darkness I got undressed except for my underwear. The hold wasn't a clean place for a stowaway, and I knew if I didn't remove and protect my clothes they'd become filthy. I would have to get off the ship later, and to be seen in very dirty clothing would be a dead giveaway. Hour after hour I lay against the steel hull sleeping as much as possible to pass the time. Even in the tropics the steel hull was cool, even cold at times, and my sleep fitful at best. With nothing soft for me to lie on, no pillow and no covering, dreams good and bad assailed me.

In the black hold I couldn't know how much time was passing, but when my bread and sardines ran out and with only two candy bars left, I knew I would have to find something to eat soon. Also I needed water to quench a thirst that was burning my throat. Though salty, the sardines had supplied enough liquid to stave off rampant thirst. The candy bars could offer a bit of nutrition but no water. I decided if it were night I would sneak on deck and make a search. Slowly I climbed the ladder, opened the trapdoor, found it was night, and looked for food and water. To my surprise, only a few feet away, I saw a bowl of table scraps beside a pan of water. The food had been left in that place for a dog sleeping against the deckhouse. I dared not awaken the dog.

In silence I drank the water in one gulp, dumped the scraps in my underwear, and scurried back to the hold. It would have been easier to snatch the bowl and take it with me, but that I had to leave. Anyone feeding the dog later would wonder what happened to it, might even decide to feed the mutt in another place. Eight or ten times or more — I lost count — I was hungry and thirsty enough to sneak on deck and steal the dog's food and water. Its owner must have thought the animal was eating wonderfully well though sleeping too much. Fortune was my friend on that trip; I didn't get caught and I didn't starve or die of thirst. Also because the climate was in my favor, I didn't suffer from cold and remained fairly comfortable nearly nude.

Twice, however, I came close to being discovered by two sailors when they came into the hold with flashlights to check the security of the cargo. In rough seas they had to make certain the heavy cargo didn't break away and shift position. Ships had sunk when that happened, and so their frequent inspection was important and necessary. I hid behind some wooden crates and could hear them talking. They didn't like the ornery job they were ordered to do but knew it had to be done. Loose cargo in the hold could sink even a large ship in heavy weather. I held my breath when they checked the wooden crates where I was hiding. Flashing their light here and there, they passed without seeing me and exited. In the dark, my heart racing, I felt enormously relieved.

For several days, at least a week, I lay against the hull in darkness but managed to evade the inspectors. I knew they came according to a regular schedule, and that helped me know the days were passing. Then one day or one night, as I lay dozing with my backpack as a pillow, I heard a blast of the ship's horn. It meant we were moving into a harbor, but where? I began to put on my clothes. Slowly the ship came to a halt and stopped her engines. I heard water slapping against the hull and the sound of hawsers made fast to a dock. We were no longer moving.

I took my time to dress carefully and climbed the

ladder. I opened the trapdoor and faced a morning so bright it blinded me. The dazzling sunlight compelled me to sink downward on the ladder with the door slightly open to let my eyesight adjust. I feared someone might see what was going on, but again luck was on my side. When I could see again I peeked along the deck to see sailors busy at work. Not a one was nearby. I had double vision when I climbed to the deck, but it soon disappeared to give me confidence. With the wondrous eyes of a child, I stood at the rail and looked at the landscape, brown and green in the sun. I thought we had come to a Mexican port and was thinking I would have to walk many miles again. Later as I stood on shore, I learned to my amazement that in ten days we had come much farther than I ever expected. The ship had docked in San Pedro, California.

I had never heard of the place and asked about it. I was told it was once a separate city but had since become a community within the city of Los Angeles and served as its seaport. So again I received news that left me dumfounded but excited. I had come as a stowaway all the way from El Salvador to Los Angeles, California in record time. I had eaten dog food to stay alive, had drunk water the dog had lapped, and had endured total darkness in my underwear for more than ten days. Then dressed in presentable clothing I had emerged into dazzling sunshine. It was an indisputable highlight of my life. I was delighted but had trouble believing it. At last I was a free man in America!

Looking down from the deck, I saw a man in uniform at the foot of the gangplank. He appeared to be checking the pockets of sailors as they left the ship. I fell in behind an officer of rank and followed him down the gangplank. The man in uniform greeted the officer cordially and let him pass with no frisking. I stepped forward and opened my knapsack to indicate I was ready to be searched. The inspector ran his hands over my pockets, glanced at my scraggly beard, and motioned me to move on. At the end of the dock I saw a gate with another man performing the same task. He made a quick search, running his hands rapidly over my clothing, glanced at my looks, and nodded. I strolled nonchalantly into the streets, came to railway tracks, and walked along them.

A work crew was nearby, and I asked one of the men a question: "Can you tell me where these tracks go?"

I spoke halting English with an accent and he must have thought I was an immigrant, lost and confused. He looked at me for a full minute before answering, "To Los Angeles, you old fart, Los Angeles."

I was in America, in California, in the City of Angels. I wasn't quite an old man and I was free! I could forget the past, the long years of suffering in captivity, and plan a future.

Hesitantly, blinking in the bright sunlight, I asked the same man another question: "Can you tell me what day this happens to be?"

Stopping his work and looking me squarely in the face, he was clearly annoyed but gruffly replied. "It's a Wednesday, you moron! Now get lost! Can't you see I got work to do here? Where did you come from anyway? A booby hatch? Get back there and take a bath and shave."

He picked up his tools and walked away to join the rest of his crew. As he did so I noticed something on the ground that looked like a leather wallet. I picked it up and rifled through it. Neatly tucked inside were eighty American dollars, two weeks' wages. I needed that money to add to the little I had left. I needed it to make my way in my new country. I could pocket the money and move on. Who would know? The answer was obvious. I would know, and I couldn't live in America as a thief. The man had called me an old fart and a moron, but I returned his wallet.

"Hey! This is my wallet! How did you get it? Must of fell outta my pocket when I was picking up my tools. Damn pocket too shallow. Well, thanks, buddy. Good of you to return it."

Quickly he looked inside and fingered the money there. He smiled and chuckled and thanked me again. The fellow wasn't a bad sort. To this day he probably tells an amusing story of meeting a lunatic on the railroad tracks in San Pedro, asking crazy questions but returning his wallet with its money untouched.

I truly believe I was crazy to have attempted what I accomplished. For more than two years, fronting unbelievable obstacles as a fugitive, I had overcome them all to reach a nation of tolerance and opportunity. I remembered Lafayette helping the young country become a sovereign nation in its time of most need. I would help it too, though forty-one and toothless. I looked old with a sallow skin and no teeth, and yet I believed a man of forty-one was relatively young. Should I be lucky enough to settle down and live free, I would become a model citizen and live to a ripe old age. I would renounce my identity as a Frenchman and become entirely a brave American. Of necessity I had learned to speak and write Spanish. Now in this nation of free English speakers I would forget the language I grew up with and work on my English.

Author's Note: *Arthur Maurice Bonheur made his way eastward to settle in Florida. In Miami he worked as a gardener for two years and studied accounting in his spare time. In that city he met a comely Hispanic woman, married her, and soon afterwards moved to New York City. There he found a good dentist and a comfortable life as a stockbroker. His two children learned Spanish in school and from their mother. The two often spoke the language at home but seldom with their father, who spoke only English. Arthur Maurice never returned to France and never learned what happened to Gabrielle, the woman he hoped to marry before losing his youth in prison. Evenings after work he wrote three books in English and rarely spoke his native tongue. Though he never became a U.S. citizen, he lived thirty-four years as a free American. The prison colony in French Guiana, commonly known as Devil's Island and called Bagne de Cayenne by the French, was closed in 1953. It had operated one year more than an entire century. It later became a tourist attraction.*

Printed in the United States
by Baker & Taylor Publisher Services